THE POTLUCK PEOPLE

A NOVEL ABOUT QUIRKY CHURCH LIFE

RON SHEVELAND

Ron Sheveland/I-Training
33302 Golden Meadow Ct
Yucaipa, CA 92399
www.potluckpeople.com

Publisher's Note: This is a work of fiction. Names, characters,
places, and incidents are a product of the author's imagination.
Locales and public names are sometimes used for atmospheric
purposes. Any resemblance to actual people, living or dead, or
to businesses, companies, events, institutions, or locales is
completely coincidental.

Book Layout ©2013 BookDesignTemplates.com

Ordering Information:
Quantity sales. Special discounts are available on quantity pur-
chases by churches, associations, and others. For details, contact the "Special Sales Department" at the address above.

The Potluck People/ Ron Sheveland. -- 1st ed.
ISBN 978-0-9644674-1-5

"Our mouths were filled with laughter,
our tongues with songs of joy...
The Lord has done great things for us,
and we are filled with joy."

–Psalm 126:2-3

....

ONE

A STORMY SUNDAY IN MEANWHILE, MICHIGAN. 1980

It would become an infamous Sunday—providing a memory that the members of Meanwhile Baptist Church would never shake. Tensions in their midst had caused the atmosphere to become so charged with negative static that many expected a little lightning. But no one could have anticipated the pastor's behavioral thunderstorm or the debris that it would leave...

"Before we go any further in our service, I would like to invite Marvin DeBoer to come up and lead us in prayer."

Like a deer caught in headlights, Marvin's eyes took on a startled, frozen glare back at the pulpit. He and Pastor Sherman were locked in conflict, *a holy war,* and he didn't trust this present overture.

"Come on, Marvin. You're a prayer warrior. You've been meeting with others in your home to pray for me and now I would love for you to do it in church. Come up. Please."

Bruce Sherman smiled widely. Too widely. *A wolf's grin,* Marvin thought. And in the pastor's voice Marvin detected the edge of a challenge.

Esther DeBoer nudged her husband. "Go. He wants you to pray."

"I don't know about this," he mumbled back as he got to his feet. *But how could he refuse to pray?*

"As Brother Marvin makes his way up here from the back pew, let me share some candid thoughts. During the two and a half years I've served as your pastor, several saints have been concerned about my ministry. They've been kind enough to try to straighten me out with their suggestions, complaints, and objections. They've been so burdened that they have sacrificially given up their time to hold private little prayer meetings that haven't included me but have been about me. And there have been phone calls, again not to me but about me. I have, however, gotten letters, mostly anonymous, telling me to change or leave." His fingers fluttered on both sides of his pulpit.

"Up until now I've been just plain obstinate. I haven't listened. I've had a real problem with a lack of teachability." He thumped his head. "Just hard-headedness, I guess. Me and the Missus feel bad that we can't please some of you."

Marvin had reached the front but he hesitated at the bottom of the stairs.

"Please Marvin, come up." Pastor Sherman reached out his hand. "It's time to set things right." Marvin reluctantly took his hand and joined him on stage.

"Will you pray for me, Marvin?"

"Pastor Bruce," Marvin proclaimed loudly, "I've been praying for you and will be happy to pray for you again. I just want the best for you and our church." Then he started for the pulpit.

Pastor Sherman used his thick arm to encircle Marvin's back and redirect him toward the front left edge of the platform. "For something this important, would you mind kneeling? I need serious prayer."

"Oh, I don't think that's necessary. I think I'll just --"

"Brother Marvin," the pastor intoned as he placed his hands on DeBoer's shoulders, "kneeling seems to be a prayer posture that is treasured in Scripture. You're certainly not too proud to kneel?"

"No, but I, ah..." Inwardly Marvin seethed, but he allowed his body to be pushed downward.

"Here. Kneel right here and pray for me. You might also want to pray for yourself." Marvin found himself on his knees at the edge of the platform looking out at the empty front row. "You had better pray real good because I've got one more thing to say and do before your intercession. And that's this." His voice became shrill. "You and others have been kicking me around for way too long. Now it's my turn!"

Reverend Sherman booted Marvin DeBoer right off the platform. Before Marvin even hit the floor, the pastor shot both arms into the air and shouted, "Field goal!"

A collective gasp went up in the congregation. While Stan Glass and a few others quickly moved to Marvin's aid, Pastor Bruce marched down the platform stairs and toward the seldom-used side exit door.

"I'm outta here! You people can get yourself another pastor!"

Before the punter could leave, a bright red Marvin was back on his feet. "You better get out of here, you stupid, stinkin' doofus! You aren't no pastor, you're just an... an ornery old pig-headed..."

"Marv!" Esther's warning was loud enough to be heard from the back.

"If I getta hold of you, you'll learn what it's like to be kicked. I'll kick your backside down every street in Meanwhile. Do you hear me, you big, ugly, pig-brained doofus..." he struggled with the right words to sum up his disdain, "stupid person, you!"

"Marvin!" Esther said with increased volume.

The pastor's amused grin, now completely authentic, pushed his victim even further out of control.

"Sherman!" He shook a fist, "You want this upside your head?"

"*MARVIN ROBERT!*"

This time Esther's yell put the brakes on him. He stopped and surveyed the crowd. Everyone in the small auditorium was aghast. Their open mouths looked like donuts. He was filled with humiliation.

The pastor rubbed it in further. With a bobbing head and a satisfied smirk, Bruce Sherman said, "You just keep praying for my best, okay, *Marvin Robert?*" He ended his pastorate with a wave and walked out the door into the rain and wind to where his wife was waiting in a 24-foot yellow Ryder truck.

With the terse command, "Esther, let's go!" the DeBoer's hustled out of the sanctuary.

And then there was quiet. No one moved. It seemed like someone should stand up, take charge and say something appropriate. Some of the deacons thought about it. But what was there to say? Even Stan Glass was speechless – and that was rare. Two minutes went by – two long minutes that were stretched out of proportion by the awkwardness.

Finally, it was Margaret McElroy that stood. With the flair of someone who possessed seventy-two years of gumption, she bellowed, "WELL NOW, since we're getting out a little early, Old Margaret is going to try to catch the breakfast buffet at Big Boy's. Join me if you wanta." A deaf man could have felt her deep rumbling voice. Following her lead, others immediately stood, reached for Bibles and purses, and filed out.

It was time to get a new pastor.

TWO

....

THE INSTALLATION OF PASTOR MIKE

Mike Lewis was stretched out on a very experienced green couch in his new parsonage. Across from him in a matching chair was Dan Hall. They were both fighting the Sunday afternoon sleepies.

"Dan, thanks again for coming down and being the special speaker at my installation service."

"Wouldn't have missed it. But why do you think they call the dedication of a new pastor an installation service? It makes you sound like an appliance."

"Got me. I just hope I'm a Whirlpool. I want to keep running here at Meanwhile Baptist Church for a long time."

"I'm with you. Unlike most of your predecessors who have had short pastorates, I hope you are here for a long time, too."

There was an extended silence during which Mike shut his eyes. "After that lengthy morning service and the potluck, I can hardly stay awake. Could you believe all that great food? And then, of course, it was my pastoral responsibility to sample from each dish so as not to hurt anyone's feelings. Sacrificing for Jesus! That's my thing. I had to roll across the yard from the church to the parsonage."

"Your church has got a lot of good cooks."

"Phenomenal cooks. Stupendous cooks. World-class cooks. Sandy has already nicknamed the folks here the 'potluck people' because they are famous for their wonderful potluck meals."

"I have discovered a very interesting parallel. The churches with the best potlucks are also the churches with the roundest people."

"Hey, are you saying my congregation is fat?"

Dan laughed. "Well, pound for pound, I think they might come out ahead of most. But that's okay. Plump and jolly people are my favorite."

"They are a friendly crew, aren't they?" Mike turned on his side and looked over at Dan.

"Yes, they really are. I'm glad I got to meet them. From what I had heard... oh, never mind. That's a sentence I shouldn't have started."

"Come on, you can always be straight with me."

"Well, Mike, here's a little bit of advice... or maybe I should say, warning. I think your new church is going to require some exceptional patience and fortitude."

Mike used his index finger to push up his glasses from where they had slipped down on his nose. "Doesn't every church, Dan? People are people wherever you go. Coming to Christ puts them on a new journey but they still tend to carry a lot of baggage. We all wrestle with that."

"Let me put it like this." Dan spoke softly as he continued through a verbal minefield. Mike was so gung-ho about his new position, Dan knew that he had to cushion his words. "You know how some families are pretty healthy but others are dysfunctional?"

"Yes..."

"In the same way, although every church has a few odd ducks, there are some congregations that are just packed with them. For the four years that you served as my youth pastor, you were in a rather positive environment. But now you and Sandy have left a church that's heavily populated with exceptional members to take the pastorate of a congregation that's somewhat... ah, quirky. I'm not trying to be insulting, but frankly, that's the best way I can describe it. The church is rather quirky."

"Why would you say that?" Mike's voice had an edge that indicated he had already pledged his heart to his new church and wanted to protect them. "During my interviewing weekend I spent time getting acquainted and I think the people are very nice."

9

"Oh, they are that. Like I told you, I like them." Dan thought highly of Mike and was sad to lose him as his assistant. The young man was committed to the Lord, full of drive, gifted for ministry and a good people person. But, in his perpetual enthusiasm, he could be very naïve...

Mike moved through the world like a Labrador puppy. He had winning brown eyes, dusty brown hair and a few leftover, little-boy freckles. He had always been handsome enough, smart enough, and funny enough to draw attention but never so handsome, so smart, or so funny to be threatening. He was warm and comfortable and accustomed to people liking him. Dan was afraid of Mike being blindsided. Pastoring could be wonderful; but in some situations, it could also be hazardous.

"Mike," Dan continued. "I really did like everyone I met today and I'm sure that they're wonderful people. God loves them and so should you. But the church still has a colorful reputation. They're part of our association and for years I've heard stories about them. I'm simply suggesting that if you expect that church to think and operate like ours in Grand Rapids, you might end up disillusioned. I just don't want you to be caught unawares."

"Stories?"

Hall pulled his lanky legs off the footstool, placed them on the floor and leaned toward Mike. "I'm not going to repeat a bunch of old tales. But if you want an example, just reflect on the previous pastor's last Sunday. You've got to admit, that was really bizarre. Even if the pastor was the only one at fault—and I doubt that he was, that kind of episode leaves a big mess that will probably take years to clean up."

Mike released a thin smile of resignation. "Okay. I can't deny that whole thing was, using your word, pretty bizarre. Don't you wish we could see a videotape of that? Pastor Shermon kicking Marvin DeBoer—who left the church, by the way—off the platform like that? But I think that simply shows the pastor was screwy."

"Obviously, but there are usually two sides to a story."

"Frankly, I'm not too worried about it."

"Mike, if you do hit rough patches, I am only a phone call away."

Mike stood to his feet and stretched. "I appreciate it. I was hoping we could talk on the phone every couple of weeks anyway. You have been a great mentor and I would like to keep learning from you. But, as I said, I'm not too worried about the situation here..."

He should have been. After a "honeymoon" phase, Pastor Mike Lewis would discover the "twilight zone" of church life where people and situations are morphed into funny and whacky scenarios or... frustrating and threatening ordeals.

THREE

....

THE MALL ENCOUNTER

Lucille had just left Penneys. Now she was weaving her way through the Oakbridge Shopping Mall's chaotic crowd toward the exit by parking lot B. Since her twenty-minute search for her car in July, she always memorized the letter of her parking lot. "B" as in Bud, her husband. The modest mall only had two lots, but even so...

Suddenly, out of the generic noise, a distinct voice came directed specifically at her. "Ma'am...maaaam!"

She hesitated. Irritation jerked her into a dilemma. She had to leave if she was going to make it to the Christian Education committee on time. Promptness was a virtue she valued. *Those who aren't prompt are thieves of other people's time.* But now she was being hijacked by the voice.

She unwillingly turned toward its source.

The young man's eyes peered at her with intensity. "Ma'am," he said with the hushed confidential tone of an underwear salesman, "you dropped this." She was confronted with a small, mostly green banana.

She tossed out a short laugh that was meant to disguise her annoyance and denied that the fruit belonged to her. "But," he insisted, "I saw it drop from your pocket."

Her forced smile parted to let out an objection. "I don't think so." Lucille insisted that she had never seen the banana before.

"Well, perhaps your husband put it into your pocket."

"No, Bud wouldn't do that."

"Maybe it was one of your children?"

"The youngest is in college two hundred miles away."

"Oh, a college student. You must be so proud."

"Yes, yes, we are very pleased." She glanced anxiously at her Timex watch that she could wear, if necessary, two hundred feet underwater. Ten minutes before six. She gasped and said, "Now I must be going. I'm really in a hurry."

"Well," he rebounded softly, "don't forget your banana."

Lucille discarded her smile, raised her right eyebrow and her voice, and said, "Now listen. That is not my banana!"

"Please don't yell at me... I was only trying to help."

His tone quivered and she was immediately filled with regret. "I'm so sorry. I really am. I shouldn't have gotten short with you. It's just that I have to leave immediately for a meeting at our church. You see, our meeting has to begin right at six o'clock. We all need to be on time because we only have forty-five minutes to discuss a lot of important things. Then we have to quit so that we don't interfere with the evening service at seven."

She suddenly realized that she was volunteering more information than was necessary -- a tendency Bud often pointed out; yet the boy kept looking at her with such an empathetic interest. Why, he couldn't be much more than sixteen or seventeen. He really appeared to be such a nice teenager.

"What church do you go to, Mrs. Ahhh...?"

"Swensen. Lucille Swensen. We go to Meanwhile Baptist Church. It's only a couple of blocks from here but it's tucked in a neighborhood over on Tenth Street." And then, with caution she added, "We would love to have you visit."

For a moment his face seemed to cloud over but then with strained cheer he said, "Well, maybe. Really, I just might. Sometime. But, ah, until then, what do you want me to do with your banana?"

"Why don't you just throw *the* banana away?"

"I couldn't waste a perfectly good banana."

"Then why don't you eat it?"

"Because of some allergy, bananas make my throat itch."

"Well, then, give it away."

"Would you like it?"

"*No. No, thank you.*" Now that he knew she was a churchgoer, she didn't feel the freedom to yell, but she still formed every syllable with pronounced seriousness. Then she blatantly looked at her Timex and allowed frustration to flush her features. "Oh my goodness. It is six o'clock now! I'm going to be late, late, late. Sorry, but I've got to hustle!"

She spun away and dashed determinably toward parking lot B. Behind her, she heard the plaintive cry, "But, Mrs. Swensen..." This time, however, she refused to heed the plea. She charged through the mall door into the fading early evening sunshine. After a brief search she proudly located her brown Ford LTD and quickly grappled around her purse for the keys.

Her frenzied movements ceased when her hand rested on a foreign object. "Why, that's odd." With a shake of her head, she bent her puzzled face down to gaze at... an apple.

Back in the mall, Whit Carson stopped outside of *It's Your Move* – a store that specialized in games. He looked at himself in the reflection of the storefront glass and wondered what made himself tick. He was obsessed with games – mind games. He liked to playfully toy with people.

Lucille Swensen had been a soft touch. He had been walking by a sales counter in Penneys when he had noticed her purse hanging open on her arm while she was writing a check. Feeling the two pieces of fruit that he had packed in his pocket for a future snack, he followed the sudden urge to drop an apple into her bag. And then his game began.

She was so much fun that he missed her. Very naive and gullible but transparent and nice. A good person—the kind that used to hang around the house with his parents. He wished the game could go on.

Perhaps it could....

But at a church? He winced with a blend of remorse and anger. The thought of going to a church—any church—sent his mind back to the dark night that... *Ugh.* He shook his head as if to chuck away dark thoughts and then rubbed his temples. He hated being bullied by his memories.

Determination surged within him. He would continue the game... at Meanwhile Baptist Church.

FOUR

····································

THE C. E. MEETING

"I'm so, so, so, so sorry that I'm late," Lucille said as she rushed into the church library—the meeting room of the Christian Education meeting. "You know this isn't like me. I always try to be prompt. Really, I'm sorry."

"That's okay, Lucille. It's just good to have you join us." The others expressed their agreement to Pastor Mike Lewis' words.

"It's just that I should have been on time, but then I was detained at the mall by this very talkative teenager."

Betty Sweeting tried to soothe her. "Don't worry about it, Lucille. Things happen. We're all late sometimes."

"This is the first time I've ever been tardy for a C. E. meeting and I wouldn't have been late this time but this boy practically accosted me with a banana!"

"A banana?" Betty echoed.

"Accosted?" Sharon Rickard added.

"Well, he didn't really *accost* me. That sounds rather extreme, I suppose. But he came up to me with this banana and tried to give it to me. Because, you see, he thought it was mine. Which it wasn't, I don't think. No, of course it wasn't... well, it's a long story."

"Lucille, if you don't mind, we need to get back to our agenda." Stan Glass, in his role as the deacon board representative, felt a special responsibility to make sure that the meeting was productive.

"Yes, of course, I tried to explain to the boy that we only have so much time before the evening service for our meeting but he wouldn't listen. Talk, talk, talk. Some people just can't stop talking. And all about this silly banana. And then I found an apple..."

"Lucille," Stan tried again, "maybe we can talk about this later. Before you came in Betty had just begun describing a recruiting problem." He gave Betty a nod. "Betty?"

Taking her cue, Betty clicked on a complaining tone of voice to say, "Ah, yes. Well as I was saying, we can't find teachers for either our second-grade-girls' class or the four-year-olds' class. Right now we are limping along with substitutes but they won't last long."

Sharon asked Betty what had been done to recruit teachers.

"Well, I put a notice in the bulletin and gave a plea for teachers during the announcement time the Sunday before last."

Mike Lewis inwardly groaned when he remembered her "plea." Betty was a creative, energetic teacher when she was in front of kids. But in her role as the Sunday school superintendent, she was a poor recruiter. Her guilt-edged announcement had given the impression that the children's ministries were going to go down the tube if people did not immediately volunteer. *Who would want to participate in a program that appeared to be doing so poorly? No one wants to get on board a sinking ship.* In Mike's mind the kids ministry was pretty good. Some holes but good for a church of their size.

"What do you suggest we do?" Stan asked.

"Simple. We don't have class!" Betty shot back. "Let the kids run around for a couple weeks until people wake up around here and decide to pull their weight."

"Oh my," Lucille said, "how sad for those children."

"Yes," Sharon quickly added, "I'm not sure we can shut down Sunday school."

Stan knit his eyebrows together, pursed his lips and began to speak slowly. If spirituality could be detected by an intensely modulated voice, he was highly sanctified—Mike's wife, Sandy, had nicknamed Stan Glass, *Stainglass*. "Lucille, Sharon, I am confident all of us would concur that it would be sad to cancel classes but it is equally sad that the spiritual apathy resident in our church results in an insufficient number of Christian workers. Since there is so little commitment, perhaps we need to resort to shock therapy."

The pastor coughed into his hand. He had hoped that the conversation would take a positive turn, but like usual, Stan highlighted the bleak.

"Maybe we'll have to use the shock therapy eventually," Mike said, "but I think it might be better to explore other options before we go down that road. I'm afraid that such a step might demoralize people and even cause some to consider finding a different church that still has classes."

"What are these other options?" Betty asked.

"We start by asking the Lord of the harvest to send us workers. And then we consider implementing a variety of other practical steps. Some of you may already have suggestions that you could share. Anyone?"

There was silence. So Mike continued. "Well, let me throw out a few ideas to begin our brainstorming. First, I think we need to personally ask individuals to consider involvement. Public and printed announcements are seldom very effective in recruitment efforts. Second, I think we should provide job descriptions that spell out our expectations. People are reluctant to accept assignments that have no parameters. Third, it might be—"

"Excuse me for butting in, pastor," Stan intoned, "but I don't think these little gadget plays would be needed if our flock was more spiritually motivated. I was once part of a church where they had a waiting list for people who wanted to teach. Everyone wanted to serve the Lord."

Mike wondered what church that may have been. He knew Stan had left his last church due to dissatisfaction.

"Stan, that must have been some church. All the churches I've ever been associated with have often struggled to mobilize enough workers to man all their programs. That's why I think it's helpful to utilize the kind of methods that will ease people into the places of service that are right for them." Mike hoped for a constructive conversation where they could discuss a broader recruitment strategy. But it wasn't to be.

"I still think it would be better to consider how to spiritually motivate them." Stan crossed his arms. He appeared quite willing to turn this into a contest.

Declining the debate, Mike reluctantly chose to follow Stan's path. "How do you suggest that we spiritually motivate them?"

"Pastor, I believe that must come from the pulpit. Through the ministry of preaching, God can use you to light a fire under his people."

Betty used vigorous nods to cheer Stan on. "I wholeheartedly concur. If people were on fire, they would come to me. I shouldn't have to go person by person through the church with pleas and job descriptions. My goodness, I'm a Sunday school superintendent, not the director of an employment agency." Her voice quivered and she dabbed at her eye with a Kleenex.

Sharon just looked straight ahead, her face not betraying her feelings. But out of the side of her mouth she whispered her feelings to Lucille. "Here we go again. Stan is poking at the pastor and Betty is getting blubbery. I hate this."

"Me, too." Lucille responded, hand over mouth. "I hate it when the conflict starts. It's suffocating. I wish I were somewhere else. Maybe I should have stayed at the mall longer. By now I would have had a basket of fruit."

"What?"

"Well..., Oh, never mind."

They froze when Stan peered at them. "Sharon, Lucille, anything you would like to contribute?"

Sharon just shook her head but Lucille looked like a disobedient child caught by her teacher. "I'm sorry for whispering; we were, that is I was just referring to my mall encounter."

"Well, let's get back on track with the Lord's business. I believe that we were just coming to consensus on the need for Pastor Mike to address our recruitment problems through his pulpit ministry."

Mike had heard enough of Stan's talks to know where he was going. He knew that Stan preferred a forceful pulpit-pounding style of preaching that abounded with volume and finger pointing. And Mike simply couldn't measure up.

"I've preached on the importance of every Christian using his or her gifts to serve the Lord in the church," Mike said. He immediately knew he shouldn't have tried to defend himself.

"Young man, we all appreciate your ability to teach the Bible, but there is a difference between teaching and preaching. I'm praying that the Holy Spirit would anoint you with power so that your pulpit might rumble with thunder and flash with lightning!"

That's the way Stan would preach if he had the chance. Mike had heard the story many times before. Stan felt that he had the calling but not the opportunity. He had gone to Bible school for a year but had dropped out because he was unimpressed with his professors and didn't want to waste time with books when there was a lost world to be won. For income, he sold life insurance from a little brick office on Main Street. In that he liked shaking hands, it was a job that fit him well. When he would warn about the potential of unexpected death, he would soften his melodious voice and gently shake a hand with both of his. Since meeting prospects was always a possibility, he was careful with his appearance. He oiled his hair and wore a tie seven days a week – just the way he would if he were a pastor, which he still hoped he would someday be. Somewhere there must be a church that would want a pastor that had godly zeal rather than fancy degrees. Until then he would use his adult Sunday school class as his preaching platform.

"Speaking of preaching," Mike dodged, "I need to leave to get ready for tonight's service."

Stan put his hand on Mike's shoulder and said, "We will be praying for you."

Mike stood. "Well, thanks."

Thanks a lot. Suddenly there was a part of him that didn't feel up to preaching.

When Mike got to his office he knelt by his desk chair. "Lord," he silently prayed, "I need your strength and your help." As the pastor of Meanwhile Baptist Church he was experiencing frustrations that he had not expected. As a youth pastor he had felt very popular, but here... though many had quickly embraced him with their love, others withheld their trust. *That could have been caused by the last pastor who liked to kick people off the platform* (That was not the kind of speculation one dared to make publicly; many were still sensitive about the incident). Then there were some that tended to resist and resent his leadership. *Maybe it's my age?* At 26 he was younger than most of the adults in the church. *Or maybe it's just me?*

He cringed as he looked at his watch. 6:55. He had spent more time thinking than praying but now he needed to get into the auditorium.

Oh, no, he thought when he left his office and scanned the vestibule, *the Clingers!* If they caught him it would be difficult to get in the sanctuary on time. The Klings, privately called *the Clingers* by Sandy the nicknamer, were an incredibly sweet older couple. But they were close talkers that could endlessly monopolize your time – at what often seemed the *wrong* time.

Fortunately, they were preoccupied with Sharon Rickard (she wore the condescending look that one puts on when dealing with Kindergartners), so he sneaked behind them – and almost made it.

"Pastor!" It was Sharon. Did she really want to talk to him or was she using him to break free of the *Clingers?* Still moving, Mike tapped his watch and asked, "Can it wait?"

"I just want to tell you one thing." She rushed up and whispered into his ear, "Don't let Stan Glass get to you. I love your preaching!"

"Well, thanks, Sharon." Inwardly he prayed, "Thanks, Lord!"

"And pastor, there was something I wanted to talk to you about, too," said Mrs. Kling as she grabbed his sleeve.

FIVE

....

THE ALTAR CALL

Lucille entered the sanctuary at exactly seven o'clock. That was close. She didn't want to be late for two things on the same day. Fortunately, Bud had saved her a seat in the third pew from the rear—the place they sat every service.

On Sunday mornings the church averaged about a hundred and forty attendees—more on the holidays, less in the summers. Evening services ran seventy to eighty, quite a drop but a better percentage than most churches could boast. It was bolstered by a strong youth group that often met for an "afterglow" following the service, and a traditional congregation with many who believed most of the "Lord's Day" should be reserved for church.

The long, narrow sanctuary had a high, steep-pitched ceiling. Light green walls constructed of concrete blocks straddled burnt orange pews. The northern front corner had a steel door under a brightly-lighted red exit sign— the route Pastor Sherman had used for his get-away. A huge, handcrafted pulpit monopolized the platform. Behind it was a floor to ceiling stained glass window. Actually made of plastic, its blue, green and red color combination was reminiscent of an earlier era. When the sun shined just right, or to be more accurate, just wrong, the gleam coming through the glass caused the people in the center section to squint. For them, the preacher looked like a dark featureless silhouette. Since no one was going to speak ill of the sacred stained glass, this was a problem that would remain unresolved. It was just better to sit off to the sides.

Unlike the morning service that restricted itself to hymns, the evening gathering provided praise choruses displayed by an overhead projector on the wall to the right of the stained glass window. Even though most of the choruses were at least twenty years old, this was their "contemporary" service. It was conducted with caution. For the sake of unity, the leaders were careful not to let things get out of hand. They had hired a young pastor to attract a younger generation, but they weren't about to be "conformed to this world" by catering to the latest tastes and styles.

For tonight's service, song leader Fred, or "Red" due to his hair, Monkmeier had pieced together a "Holy Water Medley." "We start with 'Drinking at the Springs of Living Water.' This is a lively chorus, so let's raise our voices and lift the rafters. And, of course, we must stand!"

"Of course, of course," Bud whispered to Lucille, "Red thinks it's impossible to worship unless we are standing."

"Shhh."

"He always makes us stand for every song. In my opinion, people with tired legs can't concentrate on worship."

"Honey, please!" Lucille said. "People will hear you."

When the song was done, Red provided a transition. "While we are drinking at the springs of living water, let's also be refreshed by God's showers of blessings. And that is our next chorus, 'Showers of Blessings.'" Red used these transitional links to make the worship services flow.

"The women will sing the first verse and the men will sing the second. Let's make it a little contest to see who can sing the loudest. Ladies, join me now." He used a falsetto voice to get them going. "Very good, girls, now everyone on the chorus." Then after the men, the obvious losers, sang their verse, Red had everyone sing the third verse without the instruments. "On the last verse, let's really belt it out." He moved out from behind the pulpit and physically motivated them with waving arms and spirited bounces. His choreographed jumping jacks pulled out a shirttail. His wife, Dorothy, pounded on the organ keys. She, too, had red hair, as did their four children, Mathew, Mark. Luke and Bob. Sandy called them the Reds. In that they all sang and played a multitude of instruments, they called themselves the Musical Monkmeiers.

"God does, indeed, shower us with blessings. How many? Let's count them one by one. That is our next song, 'Count Your Many Blessings.'" On the next verse Red had them change the words from "count them one by one" to "count them ton by ton."

"And now for our water medley finale, we will sing, 'I've Got A River of Life Flowing Out of Me.' This is a new one, so we will sing it through twice to learn it."

Bud whispered, "All this singing about water makes me have to go to the bathroom."

"Shh."

When the congregation finally sat down after the chorus time, Lucille took the apple out of her bag, put it on Bud's lap and waited for his reaction.

Rubbing his sore leg with one hand, Bud picked up the fruit with the other. "What's this for?" he whispered too loudly.

"Shh!" she said, giving him a face. "Tell me, did you put this in my purse?"

"What?"

"I said," she spoke a little louder (she was frustrated that Bud was too stubborn to get a much-needed hearing aid), "did you put this in my purse?"

"No."

"Did you put a banana in my pocket?"

"Did I put a band aid on your socket?"

Lucille shook her head with consternation. Bud had to know that's not what she said. He thinks his little miscommunications are so funny.

"Did you put a BANANA in my POCKET?"

"No, did you want me to?"

"No. Never mind. We can talk about it when we get home."

"Thanks for the apple." He pretended he was going to take a bite out of it. She flushed, took it away, and plunked it back into her purse. Bud smiled.

After the announcements came "the tithes and offerings." The offertory was a solo by Red. He introduced it with these words, "When Pastor Mike told me earlier this week that he was speaking tonight about Naaman and his cleansing from leprosy that occurred when he was repeatedly dunked in the Jordan river, I felt inspired to write a new chorus based upon this text. I've named it The Dip. Hopefully it will help reinforce the message. With modesty I must admit that the tune is a little catchy. I suspect that it may become a favorite around here. Who knows, it may climb to the top of our church's Top Ten Hit List. Ha!" He gave a nod to Dorothy at the organ and, with a country twang, sang,

> Leprosy is awful but so is all your sin.
> Take a dip in the river and let the healing begin.
>
> Naaman, Naaman, Naaman, Naaman, Naaman, Naaman!
> Take a dip in the river and let the healing begin.
>
> Sure the water's muddy but so are you within.
> Take a dip in the river and let the healing begin.
>
> Amen, Amen, Amen, Amen, Amen, Amen!
> Take a dip in the river and let the healing begin!

Maxine Glass, sitting right in front of Lucille, made a public display of her opinion of Red's new song. Wrinkling her nose like she was smelling sour milk, she said loud enough to be heard to those in the vicinity, "We already have enough good music. We don't need any new songs—especially hillbilly stuff like that. It hurts my ears and grieves my spirit."

"Well said," Stan Glass added. "I may have to take this to the deacons."

When he finished, Red got the whole church—with the exception of Maxine and Stan—to sing the chorus a couple times so they would know it well enough to sing it all week long in their own times of personal worship.

Bud poked Lucille. "Look at Pastor Mike." Instead of singing the chorus Mike was writing on some papers on his Bible.

"Know what he's doing? Marking up his sermon notes. Due to the length of the Water Medley he is having to do immediate surgery on his sermon."

"You don't know that," Lucille protested.

"Betcha I'm right. Right now he is amputating one of his three points. Ouch! Look at the pain on his face."

"Hush. You should be singing along instead of talking."

"Look at the sermon title." He pointed at the bulletin. "Seven Ducks In A Muddy River." Bud chuckled. "That's a clever title. Want me to explain it to you?"

"No, I get it." She figured it must be a nature sermon. "Can't you stop talking? If you want to speak, go up to the pulpit."

"Okay." When Bud started to move, Lucille pulled him back. "For goodness sake," Lucille said, "behave!"

When Pastor Mike got up to preach Lucille settled into a relaxed posture, opened her Bible and proceeded to zone out. Mentally she went back to the mall. What was that all about?

At the conclusion of the sermon, Red picked the hymn, "Shall We Gather at the River?", to go along with the altar call. The service was almost over. Since it was unlikely that anyone would come forward, Lucille reached for her purse just as movement in the aisle caught her eye... and then her full attention.

"Bud!" she hissed into her husband's ear as she roughly grabbed his leg.

He looked at her with startled eyes. She had scared him and he was afraid that something was wrong with her... or him.

"Bud, it's the banana boy!"

Walking down the aisle toward the front was the teenager she had talked to at the mall. Carol Harmon rose to provide counseling, but Pastor Mike waved her down and huddled with the boy himself while the pianist repeated the chorus. After a few minutes he returned to his microphone.

"This is Whitfield Carson. He has come forward because he has some spiritual questions that he would like to discuss. But first, he just wants to say something to all of you."

The teenager scuffed the toe of his shoe into the floor. Did it again. Finally he found his voice. "I'm not a public speaker and I'm a little nervous so I hope you'll be patient with me..."

"THAT'S OKAY, SON," Margaret McElroy blurted out. She pointed at him with both her hands and said, "Old Margaret thinks you should just speak your piece."

His shy smile grew and so did his volume. "I'm here tonight because this afternoon at the mall, Mrs. Lucille Swensen was kind enough to invite me to church. Well, the sermon touched me and so here I am at the front. And Mrs. Swensen, I'd like to publicly thank you."

Lucille was flustered with emotions she couldn't even begin to sort. Everyone turned to look at her and clap. Bud proudly put his arm around her. All she could do was nod toward Whit and the pastor. Pastor Mike used her as an example for the "rest of us" and slipped out with Whit. Red closed the service in prayer and then there was a crowd around Lucille asking about the boy and how often she did "mall evangelism."

....

SIX

COUNSELOR CAROL

Though she had never heard an audible voice, Carol Harmon felt certain that God had called her to be a counselor. This was confirmed in her mind by what seemed to be her "special insights." With extreme ease she could spot the shortcomings of others and offer quick remedial advice. Modestly, she recognized her adroit discernment as a "gift from God."

In a purple, embroidered bag she carried a large print Bible (she wasn't far-sighted but she found it easier to point at the big font type while she was confronting her counselees), a box of Kleenex tissues, and a yellow volume with the words, *The Christian Counselor's Pocket Encyclopedia*, imprinted in red (she had reviewed a chapter during the sermon about the birds in the creek). It was her "ready for anything" bag.

Because no one ever sought her counsel—a fact that puzzled her—Carol solicited clients wherever she went. After the pastor led the teenage boy off to a counseling room (*she should be in there helping!*), Carol sensed that perhaps God was reserving her services for someone else. Perhaps another teenager? Perhaps... Beth Kurick.?

Beth had just come out of the sanctuary into the lobby. With her above average height accentuated by a thin frame, the high school sophomore tended to compensate with a mild stoop of her shoulders. In spite of beautiful hair and large chocolate kiss eyes, it was the stoop that drew Carol like a magnet. This girl needed her.

"Beth," she said as she guided the young woman into a corner of the vestibule, "I've noticed you seem to lack zest and I think I know what your problem is."

With the darting eyes of an ensnared rabbit, Beth protested, "Mrs. Harmon, I'm fine."

"Fine?" Carol faced her squarely, moved to within six inches, nodded her head knowingly and softly added, "Beth, your body language is saying something totally different. Do you have any idea what *it* is saying?"

In a corner physically and emotionally, Beth had no choice but to hesitantly respond, "No, what?"

"Your body is screaming that you are wrestling with low self-esteem."

"Oh, I don't think so—"

"Yes, it is," Carol interrupted, "and the worst thing you can do is practice denial. You wouldn't want to do that, would you, Beth?"

Beth pulled on a sleeve of her blue and gold letter jacket. "Well, no—"

"You wouldn't want to embrace the kind of intrapersonal lies that strangle discovery and suffocate happiness, would you, Beth?"

"Ahh, no—"

"No, no, absolutely no. Beth, I'm so happy for you. Your choosing to say 'no' to your blanket of denial is the first step to self-actualization and wellness. Congratulations!"

Beth's lips twitched. She didn't seem to know what to say. But since Carol patiently gave her time to process her thoughts, Beth finally said, "Thank you."

"You are welcome, Beth, but your progress is my real gratification. Now are you ready for step two?"

"I'm not sure..."

"You are, Beth. Trust me. Say 'O.K.'"

"O.K."

"O.K. Two little letters that are your passageway to a transformed mind set. Beth, you cannot grow unless you are a willing participant and Beth, your 'O.K.' is your will granting permission for the biblio-therapeutic treatment of your soul."

"Huh?"

Carol looked around as if she was offering insider information from E. F. Hutton himself. "Beth," she breathed out with a tone of intimacy, "listen carefully to what I am going to say..."

She waited for an acknowledgement.

"Okay."

"O.K.," Carol repeated. "Beth, I love your teachability! Please listen carefully to what I'm going to say. You don't have to be attractive or intelligent to be special. Beth, I think you are special just the way you are. Do you hear what I am saying? You are special! Repeat these words after me: 'I am special.'"

Beth looked anxiously toward the door. "Could I please be dismissed? My friend Brenda is waiting for me outside."

"Beth, let's stay on target. You are resisting therapy. Don't let your old man hold you back."

"What? My dad isn't holding me back."

"Beth, you are precious. I'm not referring to your father. I am telling you not to let your old man—your flesh, your carnal nature—hold you back. To help you bond a transformational concept to your thinking I want you to repeat the words: 'I am special.'"

"I'm special?"

"Say it again, Beth, louder this time and with authority."

"Do I have to? Mrs. Harmon, I really gotta go."

"Beth, do you want to grow? Do you want to be free?"

"Sure, but—"

"Say it. 'I am special!' Say it loud."

"I am special!"

From the coat rack Mr. and Mrs. Kling turned and looked at Beth. Her ears became red.

"Yes, you are. You most definitely are." And then, raising her voice further, Carol shrilly emphasized, "Beth, you are very, very special!"

Now everyone looked. Beth turned into the corner to hide her blush. "Mrs. Harmon, can I please go now?"

"Just one minute more. Now please turn around and look at me. And could you bend over a little? You are so tall. Here's some super-duper extra cool wonderful news." She intentionally used teen lingo to communicate on Beth's level. "Not only do I think you are special, God does, too! Think about it. God created both the flower and the weed, didn't He?"

"Yes..."

"Don't you think that He loves both of these creations? Don't you think that He feels that both of them are special?"

"Yes..."

"Or do you think that He believes that only the flower is special because of its beauty and fragrance?"

"No..."

"'No' is right. God thinks that weeds are special too. And God thinks that you are special. Yes, He does. Beth, you are special! Amen?"

"Amen," she said stiffly, but then she mumbled, "Weeds?"

"Now don't you feel better?"

"Ah, well...sure. Mrs. Harmon, now can I..."

"Now stop right there. You don't need to say 'thank you'. Counseling is my ministry and I get joy out of caring. Now I know that you want to get away and meditate on what you have just learned but before you leave I want you to take this."

Out of her bag came a business card that said:

Carol Harmon

COUNSELOR

If you are hurt and confused,

call 447-CARE for a caring helper.

Remuneration is appreciated but not required.

"Beth, feel free to call me at any time—even in the middle of the night when you are depressed and crying. Alright?"

"Yeah, okay, now I gotta—"

"Yes, you need to go pray and meditate. I am so glad that I could be here for you. Now, one more time before you leave, what are you?"

"I'm late. I—"

"No, you are special. Say it one more time."

"I'm special. Bye." And with that Beth dodged around Carol's left flank and rushed across the narthex and out into the night.

Carol Harmon leaned against the wall and smiled to herself. It felt so good to help others.

....

SEVEN

WHO IS THIS KID?

As Pastor Mike led the teenager out of the sanctuary he wondered, and then despised himself for wondering, if Stan Glass had taken special notice that someone had responded to his sermon.

"Nice office," Whit said as they entered Mike's study.

He was being gracious, Mike thought. Outside of numerous shelves of books, it was rather plain. A poster on the wall. Trampled shag carpeting. A tan metal desk up against the wall. A swivel chair that could either face the desk or be turned, for counseling or social situations, toward a fake leather love seat. By the only window were two chairs – straight backed, wooden ones that looked quite uncomfortable. On top of a military green file cabinet, that mainly consisted of piles of unsorted papers, was a picture of Sandy and a few plaques.

"Thanks, Whitfield, why don't you sit down?

"Okay," the boy said as he plopped down in the office chair – the one Mike always sat in. Was that a glint of mischief in his eye? "And please call me 'Whit.'"

Mike looked at the love seat, which suddenly seemed too low, and then pulled up a wooden chair. "Whit, it was neat that you accepted Mrs. Swensen's invitation to come to church. That shows self-confidence on your part. And I'm so glad you accepted my offer to chat about spiritual matters."

"Thank you for your time."

"Do you live around here?"

"Not far. Our house is two blocks on the other side of the mall."

"Really? Which street?"

Whit seemed to squirm. "Ah, well, can I hold off on revealing my address? Don't get me wrong. I'm not trying to be rude. It's just that I am a little nervous about all of this and would prefer to take things one step at a time."

"That's fine. Forgive me for prying. Why don't you set the agenda and tell me why you came forward tonight?"

A cloud floated over Whit's face. "Well, I'm not as self-confident as you earlier suggested. To be honest, I'm scared. Real scared. And I don't know who I can turn to."

"Hopefully we can be of help."

"We?" Whit repeated, looking around.

"Me. The church. God."

"Oh, yeah. That would be great."

"Tell me what's up. Why are you scared?"

Glancing toward the window and the door as if to assure himself of the room's security, Whit slowly said, "It all began two years ago."

A pastorly nod urged him on.

"I had recently moved to Meanwhile and was a lonely kid without any friends."

"Moving can be hard."

"It was for me. It seemed like all the cliques were filled..." He continued for a while about his feelings of isolation. "Anyway, I hoped that things would change when some guys invited me to join this secret club they called 'The Society.'"

"Sounds like a mysterious name."

"The whole thing was mysterious—mysterious and spooky. In order to become a member I went through an initiation with another kid who was also joining. We had to go out into the country to an old deserted house that was said to be haunted."

"Do *you* think it was haunted?"

Long silence. "I don't know. Maybe. All I know is that place has haunted me ever since." His body shuddered.

Mike leaned forward. "What happened there, Whit?"

Whit also leaned forward. "Something horrible," he said hoarsely. And then he told about walking around to the back of the house. He described the structure and the night in detail. Too much detail, Mike thought. And periodically it appeared that Whit was looking towards Mike's wrist. *He's trying to see the time on my watch.* All of this seemed very odd. And then, as though emerging from a fog, Whit's voice and posture seemed to regrasp a sense of clarity.

"At 8:30 that night, a loud, creepy voice from the upper story of the house shouted, 'You are both cursed! In exactly one year one of you is going to go insane and then in exactly two years the other will go crazy, too!'"

Whit sucked in his breath, held it, and shut his eyes.

"Whit, you don't really buy all that curse stuff, do you? Couldn't it have been a practical joke by the members of the Society?"

Whit exhaled a long hiss. "That's what I hoped." Then he opened his eyes and stared fiercely at Mike. "But then, exactly one year later at 8:30 in the evening, the guy who had been with me went nuts. They put him in a mental asylum and he hasn't spoke a coherent word since."

Mike felt like this was all rather farfetched but it was apparent that Whit believed it. The pastor was already considering the possibility that the teenager might need to be referred to a more experienced counselor.

"Pastor Lewis?" Whit said with an eerie whisper.

"Yes?"

The boy's voice had deserted any inflections. Like a mechanical toy it came out in a low toned staccato. "Today is exactly two years after the night at the haunted house and I'm afraid... I am afraid that I'm going to go *out of my mind.*"

Mike didn't say anything. He just waited for Whit to continue. He held his patience through an agonizingly long pause. Then, looking like a scared, helpless child, Whit rolled his chair closer to Mike.

"Pastor... What time is it?"

Mike looked down at his watch and said, "Well, it just happens to be 8:30—."

"*AAAHHHHHHH!!!*" Whit screamed, leaping out of his chair.

Startled, Mike flew backwards, knocking over his own chair. To avoid crashing to the floor he vaulted his body onto the love seat.

Whit's posture loosened and he slowly put on a half grin.

Mike read the boy's features. "None of your story really happened, did it?" He spoke slowly, timing his words to coincide with his heavy breathing.

Whit slowly shook his head.

"You were just pulling my leg?"

"A little gag."

"A little gag," Mike controlled his response. "Well, you got me." For a moment he felt a surge of anger. But then it was usurped by a deep-throated chuckle. The humor of the situation grabbed him, his chuckling escalated and his body began to convulse with laughter. When something tickled him, Mike tended to lose control. Finally, when he was capable of further speech, he said, "Whit Carson, you are a character."

Whit took the words as a compliment and looked pleased with himself.

The pastor repositioned himself and tried to refocus. "Now that we are through with your little joke -- at least, I hope we are through, tell me, do you have any spiritual questions?"

"Everyone who is honest has spiritual questions. Maybe we'll get to mine someday. But not tonight."

"Does that mean you're willing to get together in the future?"

"I think so but don't pull out your calendar. Let's just play it by ear."

"That's fine." Mike, with overt casualness, lay back on the love seat. Throwing his legs over one arm of the short couch, he went on to say, "Just don't be a stranger. Drop by anytime. I need a little more excitement in my life."

Nothing was said for a moment—which seemed natural for both of them. And then the pastor said with a gesture, "I'm curious about your name. Whitfield. Have you ever heard of George Whitfield?"

Whit stood and coolly said, "Yes, he was a famous preacher during the Great Awakening period of the 1700's. An evangelist. My dad named me after him..."

"Really? Look up there." Mike pointed at a book shelf. "Do you see that orange book? It's a Whitfield biography. I've always been a fan of George Whitfield's ministry. Your dad must have admired him, too?"

Whit looked down and scratched his head. "Yes, but that's another story. Listen, I've got to go. Take care and thanks for being a good sport. Some people get bent out of shape over my little spoofs but you've got class." He stood to his feet.

When they left the office, Mike and Whit found they were the only ones left in the church. Before leaving, Mike would have to walk through the building to turn off lights and lock all exterior doors. But first he accompanied Whit to the main exit door in the lobby to bid him a farewell, invite him back to church, and to again try to set up a time when they could get back together. Unfortunately, the teenager chose to be non-committal and evaded making an appointment.

As Whit walked into the night, Mike wondered who this mystery boy was. *Why would a high-schooler show up out-of-the-blue, walk the aisle, and then use the occasion to play a practical joke on a pastor he had never met? And would he be back?*

Mike hoped so. Even though the circumstances suggested that Whit was a whacko, Mike doubted that that was the case. He sensed Whit Carson was a bright person with a lot of conflicting issues. Yoked together was an odd blend of warm humor and cold pain. Also paired were a desire for friendship and a corresponding flight from it. Mike might be wrong but those were his hunches.

And then there was the George Whitfield connection. The boy apparently had a Christian heritage and yet there was now an obvious discomfort regarding spiritual matters. Was he running from God? If so, why did he come to church?

So many questions. Below the surface there was undoubtedly a spider web of issues that needed to be resolved. Whit—like everyone—needed help. And since the ultimate source of help is God, Mike felt compelled to return to the sanctuary. With the exit sign providing his only light, he walked to the front, knelt by the first step of the platform and prayed. He felt so insufficient as a pastor—but this only increased his yearning to constantly turn to the One on the throne.

....

EIGHT

BEWARE THE MOTHER BEAR

B y the time Mike reached the parsonage, he was sagging. He just wanted to plop down on the couch and debrief Sandy on the events of his day as they ate their typical Sunday night popcorn. But he found that it would all have to be delayed.

"I'm sorry, honey," Sandy said, "but Mrs. Kurick called and she insists you call her immediately about something that happened to Beth tonight."

"Is she hurt?"

"No, I specifically asked her that. But she said it was something else that she would only talk to you about."

"Can't it wait until tomorrow?"

"Fine with me," Sandy said as she hugged him, "but she said this was an emergency. I doubt that it is, but here's the number. It's your call." She flashed him a smile. "It's your call whether to make your call."

With a weak shrug of surrender, he took the slip of paper and dialed the number. Sandy sat cross-legged on the floor with her back to the couch and listened with amusement to Mike's end of the conversation.

"Mrs. Kurick, I don't think Carol Harmon would say that Beth is a homely giant --"

"Well, no, I'm not accusing Beth of lying, it's just that--"

"No, of course not. I don't want Beth to leave the church."

"She doesn't have to be afraid of Mrs. Harmon. I'm sure Carol was just trying to help."

"The best way to handle something like this is to talk it out. Call Carol and tell her how you feel."

"No, I think it would be better if you called her."

"Okay, I don't think this is the best approach but I will call her. I will do it first thing tomorrow."

"Tonight? But it's getting a little late and --"

"Okay, I'll call her tonight. I'll pass on your concerns."

"But if I can't use your name, how can I adequately describe what you are unhappy about?"

"Well, I'll try, but—"

"Okay, but..."

"Mrs. Kurick? Mrs. Kurick?"

Looking incredulously at Sandy, he said, "She didn't even say goodbye."

"I figured that out."

"And now I have to call Carol Harmon. According to Mrs. Kurick, and I quote, 'that hawk-faced Carol traumatized my young daughter.' This," he said, while rubbing his eyes, "is turning into a very long day."

"I know, my poor baby. But when you get off the phone with Counselor Carol, we will take the phone off the hook, pull the drapes, and hide."

"That sounds so good."

"But this time I want to hear both ends of the conversation. Counselor Carol cracks me up. I'm going to get on the extension phone."

"Sandy, I am not sure that would be proper."

As he spoke, Sandy jumped to her feet, plugged her ears with her fingers and shouted, "Da, da, da, da. I can't hear anything you are saying. Da, da, da, da."

"You are being juvenile," he shouted as she disappeared around the corner, still chanting, "Da, da, da."

"Carol, I'm sorry to bother you this late on a Sunday evening, but I promised someone that I'd give you a quick call."

"That's okay, pastor, each of the twenty-four hours of my day belong to God. If I am needed, I'll answer the call."

"I appreciate your spirit, Carol."

"Let me guess. You want me to provide counseling for the boy that came forward tonight, don't you?"

"No, but thanks so much for the offer. I'm a... I am afraid that this is an awkward call. Apparently there has been a little misunderstanding."

"That is often the result of inadequate listening skills. I would be happy to give a seminar on that topic sometime."

There was a muffled laugh in the earpiece coming from Sandy. Mike camouflaged it with a cough and said, "Yes, well, that's a thought. Carol, let me get right to the point. I just talked to someone tonight who wishes to remain anonymous..."

"People struggle with transparency, don't they?"

"Yes, they often do. Anyway, she wanted me to ask you to no longer counsel a member of her family."

This time there was no quick response—just a slow, "Who is it?"

"Well, like I say, she prefers I don't say."

"Pastor, how am I supposed to know which of my many clients I am not supposed to counsel."

"Your many clients?" He doubted she had any clients. "That's a good question, Carol. Her wanting to remain unknown puts us in a difficult situation, doesn't it?"

"Very difficult. But I understand that you may be needing to protect confidentiality so then, let's play twenty questions. When did I counsel this family member?"

"Recently, Carol. But I'm feeling somewhat uncomfortable about this. Rather than trying to pin down the party in question, let me just suggest that you try not to push your counseling on anyone who seems resistant."

"Pastor, Pastor, Pastor. I am *never* pushy and I know of no one who has been resistant. I want to know this. Did I counsel the person this week?"

"Well, yes. Now, please, let's not go down this path."

"You got on this roller coaster and I think you better stay on until the ride is over. Did I counsel the person tonight?"

"Carol, the when and who is immaterial. The point is this—"

"I thought so. It was tonight. Pastor, God worked through me to transform a young woman who was bound with the insecurities naturally associated with her unfortunate physical make up. Now if you are opposed to miracles like that, then I think you may have a problem we need to discuss."

Mike was about to get confrontational when he realized he lacked the energy for it. He would appease her and get off the phone. "Carol, I don't know enough about your conversation with the... ah, person in question, to make any judgment calls. Who knows? You may have done a wonderful job. But apparently the person isn't open to any further counseling at this time. In such a circumstance, I think that she... or he... whatever... should really be given a little space. Don't you agree?"

Ignoring his question, Carol threw out her own. "Pastor, could it be that you resent my counseling gift? Perhaps you are wrestling with insecurity? Or envy?"

"Carol, please. None of that is true. I'm thrilled that you want to serve God. I believe every Christian should have a ministry. And if yours is counseling I would be happy to help you find the right avenues for you to sharpen and use that passion. In fact, Sandy and I would be happy to meet with you to go over some basic counseling methods."

Sandy leaned around the corner, stretching the coiled phone cord as long as she could, made a face and threw a kernel of popcorn at him. He thought he had heard some munching on the phone.

"Do you also give baseball tips to Mickey Mantle?" Carol asked.

"What?"

"Let me say it this way. Have I ever offered to train you on how to give your little Bible expositions?"

"If you mean my sermons, then the answer is no."

"Then isn't it a little condescending for you to offer to mentor me in 'basic counseling methods?' I don't want to brag but I am a gifted, experienced, certified counselor. I'm surprised that you don't refer all your counseling to me."

Sandy snorted and Mike almost echoed her. Carol's "certification" consisted of a certificate she had gotten from a one-day seminar in lay counseling given at a Sunday school convention at the Cobo Hall in Detroit.

"What was that?" Carol demanded.

"It was nothing, Carol. Listen, I certainly don't want to pretend that I'm a great counselor and you don't know what you're doing. Maybe we could just get together occasionally to compare notes and learn from each other. How about that?"

"Let me think about it. My caseload is awfully busy right now." Then with a voice sprinkled with artificial sweetener, she asked, "Tell me, how did your counseling go tonight with the boy that went forward?"

"Well," Mike said, happy to change the subject, "I enjoyed my time with him. I hope that it's the beginning of a long-term relationship. I want to get to know him better and perhaps be of help."

"No decisions were made?"

"No, not yet."

"No hint of a transformational, life-changing experience?"

"Not that I could perceive."

"Hmmm. That's unfortunate... Maybe we should get together to compare notes. Well, good night, pastor. It's always a treasure talking to you. Feel free to call me whenever you need my help. And remember this, 'the person you are tomorrow doesn't have to be the one you are today.' That's just a little saying that I've been sharing with people recently. I hope you find it encouraging. Bye bye."

Sandy scrambled around the corner with a mouthful of popcorn and what looked like a mouthful of comments. But when Mike made a cease-and-desist gesture with his hand, she relented with a smile. "Okay, but you are going to miss some good Counselor Carol imitations."

With Sandy nestled in Mike's arms, they settled into the couch with a shared bowl of popcorn. Mike ate it without making the effort of to taste it. For all he knew, it was Styrofoam.

NINE

....

RAINY DAYS AND MONDAYS

Mike, like many pastors, was an adrenaline junky. The days of his week would escalate in energy and anticipation until Sundays arrived when he would peak physically and emotionally. On most Mondays he crashed. Totally spent, he would be vulnerable to depression and discouragement. Perhaps, as Sandy had suggested, this was made worse by a "little bit of a melancholy streak."

Although many pastors take Mondays off, Mike didn't want to give Sandy the worst day of the week. So he tried to use Mondays as "desk days." He would catch up on paperwork, plan his week, and begin work on his upcoming sermons. All of this was easier than handling relational responsibilities.

But on this particular morning, he felt so fried that he struggled with productivity. Teaching Sunday School, preaching two sermons, having dinner with the Canfields, attending the unpleasant Christian Education meeting, counseling Whit, the Carol Harmon and Beth Kurick problem, a poor night's sleep... all of this had taken its toll.

He tried to organize the papers on his desk but only ended up shuffling them like a deck of cards. He crumpled a few and shot them at his wastebasket. Office claustrophobia started squeezing him and he thought of taking a quick walk but the drizzle outside his window squashed that idea.

He wandered into the hallway that ran from his office to the lobby. There he took a few moments to study the pictures of previous pastors that hung on the wood-paneled wall. They reminded him of deer heads in a hunter's study. He noted that most of the men—over twenty of them—had served less than four years. But at least they had made it into the hallway museum. The picture of his predecessor, Bruce Sherman, was noticeably absent. It was a vain effort to try to forget a pastor that they would remember far more intensely than most of the others.

Mike wondered if he would last four years. Would he get his image on the wall? He closed his eyes to pray but his mind kept spinning with negative thoughts and self-doubts.

What if Stan Glass was right about his preaching?
What if Carol Harmon was right about his counseling?

What if he had blown it with Whit?
What if the church was stalled out because of him?
What if this wasn't the right church for him?
What if he wasn't the right pastor for this church?
What if he wasn't the right pastor for any church?

He shook his head. He knew his depressed mood was causing him to view life through dark glasses, but still, *what if...*

Maybe he should return to the youth pastorate. He had felt so successful there. But hadn't God called him to this new role? His memory backtracked a couple of years...

He had loved being a youth pastor so much that he had often wondered if it was a lifetime calling. "I don't view this job as a stepping stone to the senior pastorate," he had frequently said. But then he gradually experienced a blend of discontent and yearning. Though he still loved the kids, many of the inherent tasks -- planning retreats, coming up with new clever "crowd breakers," organizing socials, etc. -- had become painfully tedious. What energized him the most were his occasional opportunities to prepare and deliver sermons. He would also dream of leading a whole church.

His feelings had almost shamed him. Was he losing his passion for youth work? Was his creativity drying up? Burnout maybe? A spiritual problem? Or was God redirecting his steps? After years of giving seminars on "How To Find God's Will," Mike was now finding the process agonizingly muddy. He and Sandy spent hours in prayer and endless discussions. They also sought input from people they respected.

The lights came on one Sunday when the senior pastor was gone and Mike was preaching. The message that had encouraged his heart during his studies now seemed to be touching his audience with similar emotion. He even got to pray and counsel with several people afterwards.

When the church finally emptied and he found himself alone with Sandy, he turned to her with open arms. She returned his embrace with a tight squeeze. "Babe," he whispered in her ear, "I've got something to tell you."

"No need," she chuckled. "God already told me!"

"The way I look at it, I won't be leaving youth ministry, just adding adult ministry."

"Let's do it. Senior pastorate, here we come!" she said.

When Meanwhile Baptist Church opened up, it seemed like the right fit. The leaders were looking for a young pastor who could help them reach new generations of people. They also needed a caring, relational leader who could help them heal the wounds of their past.

They were convinced that Mike was that man. And Mike shared the conclusion. There had been no audible voice of the Lord but Sandy and Mike had clearly sensed God's leading.

But now he wondered.

For the last year he had tried to change this church with a combination of leadership, shepherding, and preaching. He had envisioned the flock being transformed into a team that was actively carrying out the Great Commission by bringing people to Christ, baptizing them and guiding them toward spiritual maturity. He had anticipated more and more people getting saved and experiencing vital relationships with Christ and others. But such blessings had been rare. Not much had changed at all.

His contemplative stroll led him from the hallway into the auditorium. The sight of his gigantic pulpit, nicknamed *Noah's Ark* by Sandy, only reinforced his bleak conclusions. Shattering the sanctuary's solitude, he blurted out, "I couldn't even bring about a change of pulpits."

One evening, after he had been at the church for about six months, he had led his deacons to this very spot and delivered a carefully prepared speech about the need for either a smaller pulpit or no pulpit. "Men, this is a beautiful piece of furniture but I believe that its bulk makes it an obstacle to communication. Due to its size, many of my gestures are hidden, limiting my non-verbal communication. I also think that it constructs an emotional barrier between my listeners and me. I've noticed that it is easier to hold attention when I step to one side or come to the front. And think about the music ministry. With this here no one can see the complete choir."

He patted the side of the pulpit and went on. "On top of all these reasons is personal preference. You know how woodworkers pick the tools that work best for them? Well, this is my workplace and this tool—this pulpit—doesn't work well for me."

All this he said and more. He even threw in a joke about taking it outside and transforming it into a jungle gym for the kids. Finally he stopped and waited for their reactions to what was, in his mind, a very logical sales pitch.

Stan didn't even allow a pause before he threw his hands up in the air in exasperation. "Well," he punctuated with a loud sigh, "here we go again."

Mike was blindsided. "What are you talking about?"

Stan waved his hands like he was washing a car, shook his head with a shudder and turned away.

So Mike looked at Harvey Arnson, the natural leader of the group, but even he was silent. Finally, Kenny Frasier gave voice.

"Ah, Pastor," his speech came out with a soft peace-making tone. "You should know that we have been through all of this before. Pastor Sherman gave us a sales pitch that was much like yours."

"And?" Mike fished for a conclusion.

"Well, we said we would think about it –"

"We should have just said 'no,'" Morris Ubody interrupted. "That's what we were all thinking."

"I know. I know." Kenny said, in a thin whiney tone, "But he was a hard man to say 'no' to. He was very intimidating. But yes, we should have just said 'no' because somehow he took our response as a 'maybe' and by that Sunday he had somehow moved it out of the auditorium and replaced it with a music stand."

"A music stand!" Stan echoed with a bellow. "That man removed our pulpit—a monument to the centrality of the preaching of God's Word—and replaced it with a music stand."

Morris scratched his head and said, "I still can't figure out how he moved it all by himself. He was a big moose of a guy, but even so... He probably got his wife to help but even then... I think there must have been other conspirators involved... I mean, this is a big pulpit. I wouldn't be surprised if it weighs a ton..."

Kenny broke in and continued his narrative. "During the worship service people kept whispering, 'Where's the pulpit?' You could feel the tension. But Pastor Sherman seemed oblivious to all that. He seemed to be in seventh heaven, prancing back and forth across the platform."

"It was something, all right," said Morris. "The platform was as barren as a desert and the pastor danced around like he had ants in his pants." Morris bounced around the stage in his bib overhauls and reenacted his memory.

"Yeah, well anyway," Kenny went on, 'that afternoon Stan and Marvin DeBoer—you know who Marvin is, don't you? He doesn't come anymore because Pastor Sherman kicked him off the platform—"

Stan grabbed the conversation. "This here was the scene of the crime." He spoke with a loud baritone as an arm gesture swept the stage. "I will never forget our dear brother being booted off this platform. As he flew through the air he windmilled his arms in a futile attempt to get his legs underneath him. But no, he went down face first. Kirsmack! Pitiful. Absolutely pitiful. It breaks my heart to remember." He went still for a moment and shook his head. "We all got hurt that day—not just Marvin. That brutal kick knocked the wind out of the whole church. I wouldn't want that kind of thing to ever happen again. No, sir, I won't let it happen again. Never again!"

"Men," Mike replied, "I've often heard the story about the kick. That was an awful thing to have happened and none of us want anything like that repeated. But I would like to hear the end of the story that Kenny started. Stan, what did you and Marvin do that afternoon after you discovered the missing pulpit?"

"We," Stan said, "took action. Somebody had to. We came down in the afternoon and found the pulpit hidden under a tarp behind the church. Can you believe that? We then called Kenny and Morris and together we moved it back on the platform where it belonged. And then we bolted it to the floor. Now we only remove it for our Christmas and Easter productions."

This brought Morris in again. "That night the pastor was really ticked off. Ticked off like a time bomb. Tick. Tick. Tick. Boom. He got up and said that if we worked as hard looking for lost souls as we did looking for this pulpit that the whole church would be filled with new converts."

Bud chuckled.

"Most of the people," Stan said, glaring at Bud, "did NOT think that was funny. It didn't go over very well at all."

"So, tell me," Stan said, pointing at Mike with his chin, "do you still think it's a good idea to replace the pulpit?"

It was a challenge and Mike backed down. "Maybe it's best to let sleeping dogs lie."

That was five months ago. Now Mike stood by himself studying Noah's Ark. "No," he said dramatically to the empty auditorium, "things haven't changed much at all. This church is still a sleeping dog."

TEN

....

LUCILLE THE EVANGELIST

When Mike left the auditorium he was surprised to see Lucille Swensen active at the tract rack. He'd thought he had the building to himself.

The rack was attached to a wall in the vestibule just outside the sanctuary. It was filled with materials that Christians could give away to acquaintances that didn't yet know the Lord. There were *Four Spiritual Laws* from Campus Crusade for Christ, *How to Find Peace With God* by the Billy Graham Association, some cartoon-filled Chick tracts for teenagers, a variety of brochures from RBC Ministries, and several folded, one-page handouts from the World Tract League.

"Hi, Lucille, are you getting some tracts?"

The normally bubbly woman didn't reward him with her trademark smile. Instead, she stiffly said, "No, I'm putting them back."

"Oh?"

"Pastor, this has been a hard day." Lucille slowly turned to face Mike. "Last night after the evening service I grabbed a bunch of tracts and this morning I took them to the mall to do evangelism. But I was a flop."

"Tell me about it."

"There's not much to tell. You remember what happened yesterday. I struck up a conversation with that teenager—Whit Carson—with the result that he came to church and ended up walking the aisle. Afterwards some people suggested that maybe I had a gift in mall evangelism. Since I've always done a bad job sharing my faith, I wondered if the mall might be an avenue where God would allow me to be more effective. So I went there and waited for people to come to me like Whit did yesterday. But of course, they didn't. Then I tried to be more assertive. But when people saw me walking towards them they would purposely avoid eye contact and dart away. After an hour, I finally gave a tract to a custodian emptying a trash bin. Instead of reading it, he handed it back and told me that I wasn't allowed to do solicitation in the mall. At that point I gave up. Since there is no use wasting these tracts I am putting them back. Maybe someone else will be able to pass them out."

Lucille looked so defeated that Mike wrapped his arm around her shoulder and gave her a big sideways hug. In so doing, it was as though he squeezed out some extra emotions. She teared up and said, "Pastor, I don't know what is wrong with me. I love Jesus with all my heart. There is not a day that goes by that I don't thank him for coming into my life. I would love to help other people find him, too; I really would. It makes me feel terrible to know that so many are missing out. But then when it comes to the simple act of telling them about God, I freeze up. I am so ashamed of myself."

"Hmm. Lucille, most of us would freeze up attempting the kind of cold turkey evangelism that you tried today. And frankly, I sometimes question whether that is the best form of faith sharing. God sometimes does engineer spontaneous opportunities – like he did with you and Whit. And when he does, we need to be ready to take advantage of them. But I think the more normative track is to build friendship bridges to people and then cross those bridges with the good news of Jesus. At that point some people will be responsive and others won't be. That's up to them. As a friend, you will want to respect their choice. Don't be pushy, just be ready to share God's great gift to those who are open. Make sense?"

She nodded so he added, "You keep those tracts in your purse and I will pray with you that God will give you the right moments to share them."

She gave him a weak grin and began to place some tracts back into her bag. That simple act brightened his day.

Lucille was lifting one of her grocery bags out of the trunk of her LTD when Bud crossed the street in order to help her.

"Where you been?"

"What?" Bud cupped his hand behind his ear.

"I asked where you have been? Why do I have to always repeat myself?"

"Which question do you want answered?"

"Where have you been?"

"What?"

"Bud!"

"I was over at the neighbor's house fixing her screen door. I noticed that it was flopping around all crooked-like so I gave it a little alignment." He gestured toward his back pocket, out of which stuck a few tools.

"How is Gloria?" Gloria Mead was a single mother whose youngest child had just left home for the military. Bud and Lucille had befriended the family some years before.

"Sick."

"Sick?"

"Sick. Says she's hurtin' for certain. Got a cold."

"Poor thing. I'm going to bring her some supper."

Later, after Lucille had brought some chicken noodle soup and muffins to Gloria, they had a long talk. Gloria wasn't just suffering from her illness, she was struggling with loneliness. "Maybe my cold has just sapped my energies, but this week it's been really hard with the last of my kids now gone. Having an empty nest is difficult for an old hen like me."

"Gloria, don't talk that way. You're not an old hen."

"I feel like one. Oh, Lucille, I'm sorry. I know I shouldn't be indulging in a pity party but I've just hit bottom."

Lucille thought she should say something profound, but the only thing that came out was, "Gloria, can I pray for you?" As soon as she said it, Lucille was afraid that Gloria, not being a Christ follower, might be offended.

But instead, Gloria seemed appreciative. "I think I would really like that."

....

HE'S BACK

B y Sunday Mike felt like he was back in the saddle. In hindsight he was surprised that he had let a little turbulence get him so discouraged. Anticipating the Lord's blessing, he now looked forward to getting together with his church family. But he was especially hopeful that Whit Carson would show up again. God had placed the young man on his heart and he'd prayed for him faithfully.

From this chair on the platform, the pastor used the song time to scan the audience but after his gaze traveled in a fruitless pursuit up and down every pew, he determined that the boy was a no-show. Then, after he finished his pre-sermon prayer, he opened his eyes to discover Whit sitting almost directly in front of him in the third row. He gave him a one-corner smile and then began to preach.

His message, *Out Of the Mire and Into the Choir*, was based on the first part of Psalm 40 where David said that

God rescued him from a pit and put a new song in his mouth. Because the passage, which showed the value of faith and patience during trials, had touched him personally, it was easy to speak with passion.

But then his mind was distracted by thoughts about Whit. What if the boy had just returned to pull more practical jokes? Would he again come forward at the invitation and want to speak to the congregation? Or worse, would he pull something during the message? Whit had positioned himself in a highly visible place up front.

Losing his train of thought, Mike paused and looked with apprehension at Whit. To his relief he saw nothing in the boy's countenance that suggested further mischief. Instead, the teen met his stare and gave him a small nod of encouragement. The rest of the sermon went well. The same could not be said of the altar call...

Mike asked Red to close the service with "Take My Life and Let It Be." But Red butchered the seriousness of the moment by telling a joke about a man who liked to sing, "Take My Wife and Let Me Be." No one came forward.

After services people filled the lobby and chatted for a while before leaving for home, restaurants or other activities. For many, the church was more than a spiritual assembly, it was also the social center of their lives. Each week was like a family reunion -- the fact that many were actually related certainly contributed to this atmosphere.

There was an unspoken expectation that Mike and Sandy would work the crowd, chatting with as many people as possible. This prevented him from making a beeline toward Whit. While talking with others, however, he kept the boy in view.

First Whit talked with Bud and Lucille. After "inviting" him to church, Lucille apparently felt responsible for him. Despite the banana encounter, she must have decided to give him the benefit of the doubt and reach out to him with love.

The Klings soon replaced them. They zoomed in like catfish after a kernel of corn. They so monopolized Whit that the Swensens walked away to talk with others. Whit was now double-teamed, with Arnie in his face and Marilyn holding onto his right sleeve.

Mike was about to swim through the crowd to save Whit when he noticed that the teen didn't appear bothered by the smothering attention. He matched their animation with his own and actually seemed to be having a good time.

When Marilyn went after another victim, Whit did something peculiar. Though he continued to be nose-to-nose with Arnie he started to turn his shoulders slightly to the left. Because Arnie liked to face people squarely, this forced him to respond by moving over a step. Since

Whit's movements were subtle, Arnie never realized that Whit was maneuvering him about. First, Whit moved Arnie in a complete circle all the way around him and then he started swinging him back and forth in an arc. The pastor now thought it might be Arnie who needed rescuing.

Mike finally got to Whit just as Arnie walked away. "You don't know how good it is to see you again. I sure am glad you came back."

"Well, thanks, I am too. Your sermon was good; I needed it. I have a hard time learning how to wait patiently on God."

"I do, too. But I've discovered, just like the psalm teaches, that God always comes through when I trust him."

"Why," Whit asked with hesitation, "do you think he sometimes puts us on hold before he does that?"

"What do you mean?"

"Well," Whit said, "King David apparently was in the pit for a while before the Lord pulled him out. Why did He make him wait? God is mighty enough that He could have helped him immediately. Instead He lets David suffer for a long time in a dark slime hole. That doesn't seem very nice. Do you see what I mean?"

"Yes, I think I do. It's hard to understand God's timing or even His willingness to allow suffering. Unfortunately, there's no one simple and quick answer. But that doesn't mean there aren't good answers. I would love to sit down with you and show you Biblical explanations. Is there some time this week that I could buy you a Coke and we could talk a bit?"

"I'm not sure." He pushed his fingers through his dark brown hair. "Let me think about it and maybe check my schedule. If things look good, I'll call you and we can set up a time and place."

"Let me save you some hassle. Give me your number and I'll call you in a couple of days."

"Hey, it's no trouble. But thanks anyway."

The pastor sensed Whit was becoming resistant so he didn't push it. Instead he changed the subject. "Oh, by the way, I noticed your little dance with Mr. Kling." Mike almost slipped and called him Mr. Clinger.

Rather than giving a denial or even a bluffing "what dance?" question, Whit just smiled and said, "I hope we didn't break any rules. I've heard that Baptists can't dance."

"Well, it's true that some don't. Maybe that's because we're not very coordinated. You've probably noticed that we don't clap with music very well, either. But don't worry, our rules committee was disbanded a long time ago."

"And I don't want you to worry. Rest assured I would never go to a dance due to a carnal desire to actually dance. No, my motives would be pure. I would just go so I could hold girls."

Mike returned Whit's mock-serious stare with a smile and a shake of his head. Then he played along. "Oh good, that calms all my anxieties and puts me at peace. As long as you're just squeezing and not skipping. It's good to know that you have self-control over your wayward feet."

*   *   *

Mike and Sandy had been invited to Old Margaret McElroy's home for Sunday dinner. As they stepped into her house, the comforting scent of fresh-baked bread rushed straight up their nostrils. The living room was soft and simple. Though the tables and shelves were overburdened with knick-knacks, a tan corduroy couch was clear for those who accepted its invitation to sink into its warmth. And there, facing her television, was a large brown recliner that had "Sunday nap" written all over it.

Old Margaret, seeing Mike stare at it with longing, said, "Preacher, I've been listening to you talk all morning. Now I want Sandy's company. So park yourself in that chair, turn on the football game, and stay out of our way until dinner's ready."

"Really? Because—"

"Hush now and sit. My husband, when he was on this side of heaven, used to love that recliner. My guess is he has a duplicate up there in his mansion."

When Mike sat, she covered his legs with a comforter and tucked him in. Then she put a newspaper on his lap and a remote control in his hand. "Are you taking notes?" she said to Sandy, "I'm showing you how to keep a man happy."

"All you're doing is spoiling him rotten."

"Not yet, girl. That will come when I fill his plate with roast beef, mashed potatoes, green beans from my garden, hot bread with homemade strawberry jelly and the best apple pie in town."

"Margaret," Mike said, "I think I'm already in heaven. After your great cooking, your husband probably complains about the food up there."

It was rare to hear Old Margaret speak softly, but when she responded it was with a whisper. "No, he ain't complaining. He's enjoying the Bread of Life. I am so happy for him."

The surprising tenderness from one who liked to act gruff caught Sandy off guard and brought tears to her eyes. She reached out and touched the older woman's arm.

"ENOUGH OF THIS," Margaret shouted with her usual volume, "let's leave lazy bones here and get into the kitchen. We got work to do before we pig out."

Mike clicked on a Chicago Bear's game but struggled to focus on it. He kept thinking about his conversation with Whit. The boy's questions hinted that he was going through a long trial. Mike wondered about what it could be.

TWELVE

....

THE PIT

Since Mike never expected Whit to call, he was surprised to answer the phone on Monday night and
discover the teenager on the line. They met late
Tuesday afternoon at the mall food court.

They each got an Orange Julius and sat down facing
each other over a blue and yellow plastic table. Mike
tried to begin with small talk but Whit cut him short.

"So, why the wait?"

"You are referring to my sermon on Psalm 40 on why
David had to wait in a pit before God delivered him?"

"Exactly." Whit's jaw was jutting outward as though
he was trying to hold in anger.

The pastor wasn't used to seeing the teen so intense.
"Whit," he asked, "is this a theoretical question or might
you be feeling like you are in a trial that seems to have
no end? Your pit, so to speak?"

Whit looked down, twisted the straw wrapping in
front of him. Without lifting his head, he murmured,

"Both, I suppose. But can we not stare into my pit right now? Perhaps we could just deal with the issue?"

"That would be fine. I do hope someday you will trust me enough to share more, but for now let's deal with what can be learned from the Scripture passage. It shows us that those who wait in faith upon the Lord will be delivered, but... not always immediately. The Lord is eager, but not always hasty. In the Hebrew, this first verse would say, 'Waiting, I waited.' So, why does a loving God delay his deliverance? Isn't that the question you are asking?"

A nod.

"This text doesn't spell that out but the Bible gives many possible reasons. Let me suggest just two: for our discipline and for our development."

Mike reached out and grabbed the salt and pepper shakers. Holding up the pepper shaker, he said, "As to discipline, sometimes we are in a pit as a consequence of our own sins. And in that case, God may be waiting for us to change our direction before he changes our circumstances."

"So" Whit said, "God keeps us in our pit until we learn our lesson."

"I think that's a good way to say it. So whenever we are in a tough time I think it's appropriate for us to do a self-audit and see if our hearts are right with God. In one Psalm David asks for divine help to do this. He prayed, 'Search me, O Lord and know my heart; try me and know my thoughts and see if there is any wicked way in me.'"

"Psalm 139."

"That's right. Whit, you constantly surprise me. You really know the Bible."

"I know quite a bit. I was raised in a Christian home and grew up getting a good biblical education at church. And there was a time when I gave my life to God and accepted Him as my Savior. And it was great. But now everything has been shaken. I still know lots of verses but not much is making sense anymore."

"What happened, Whit?"

"Oh, pastor, I hate going there. It just hurts too much. Can we please get back to our discussion? You are saying that one reason that we go through trials is to be disciplined. When I am a bad boy, God throws me in a pit for punishment."

"That's a negative spin. I think a better way to say it is that when we wonder off God's path and fall into pits, God sometimes leaves us there long enough to determine that next time we're going to walk close to Him where it's safe. Discipline is more than punishment; it is formation. Doesn't your father sometimes discipline you in a good way for a good purpose? Like, for example, grounding you for a time so that you will learn from your mistakes."

"No, my dad doesn't." Whit's face was stone. "He's not in my life anymore. But I get the analogy. So let's move on to the second reason: development."

Mike cocked his head and lifted his eyebrows. "Do you want to talk about your dad?"

"Sheesh." A shake of the head. "Will you never stop prying? Maybe we should hang this up for the day."

"I'm sorry. Okay, let's move on to development, shall we?"

"I'm sorry, too. I guess that is a touchy issue. But thank you for letting me not drag it out right now. So, yeah, let's hit your second 'D.' And why, by the way, do you preachers always alliterate every point? I knew, after your first point began with a 'D' that the second one would, too." Whit chuckled and with the laugh he seemed to soften.

"It's just a way to help me remember stuff better. But I suppose that's a rut. *Anyway,* the second "D" is for development." He tapped the salt shaker. "And no matter what word you use, the point is this: Sometimes our trials are allowed to be faith-stretchers. Maybe there's no sin at all. Maybe it's just one of those times in God's plan for you to strengthen your perseverance and deepen your maturity. God may choose to develop you in the pit before He delivers you from the pit."

"Like one of my coaches used to say, 'No pain; no gain.'"

"Yes, Whit, you got it. There is more to life than meets the eye when God gets involved. We view everything from the perspective of our immediate experience and our limited vision. But behind the scenes, God is working things out in His own timing for our best good."

"So," Whit asked, "how do we know which of these two 'D's are the reason for any particular trial? Am I salt or pepper?"

"Hold on there. I only said that these are two potential possibilities. There are many possible reasons why God may allow you to endure trials. Sometimes God shows you what answers pertains to you and other times He doesn't. He just says, 'trust me.' We're not deep enough or wise enough or spiritual enough to figure out all the reasons why trials linger and don't come to a more rapid end. And besides, we don't want to put our trust in a reason; we want to put our trust in the Lord. You see, it's not enough to wait for an answer; we need to wait for the Lord. *He* is the answer. If I find a satisfying answer, I have a temporary solution. If I find a quick end to my troubles, I have temporary relief. But if I trust God's wisdom, power and love, I have an eternal Help. That's why Psalm 40 tells us to 'wait patiently' for the Lord. We are to be constantly looking up to God with the confidence that He is looking out for us."

They discussed this further until Whit said, "I still have this problem. We are talking about trials in an individualistic way. Our trials affect those around us. Say, for example..." Whit paused and Mike knew by the expression on the boy's face that this question cloaked a sensitive issue. "Say that I am in a pit due to my own sin and that my action caused other people to be hurt, too. How does God juggle all of the lives involved?"

"Whit, God is all loving and all powerful. He can simultaneously take care of you and everyone else, too. Juggling is no problem for Him."

"Oh, really?" Whit reached over and knocked over the two shakers. "From my experience, God sometimes drops a few things."

And that was the end of any more meaningful discussion. Talking became forced and both knew that it was time for their meeting to end.

*   *   *

As Whit walked home, he thought about the discussion and, against his will, he remembered that night two years ago when his father had been killed and his life had been shattered. He broke into a run and tried to distance himself from the memory.

....

THIRTEEN

AN ILL WIND

The next Sunday morning Arnie Kling came to church alone. And unlike his usual practice of corralling the pastor in the hallway, he stood off by himself. Even more concerning was the fact that Arnie wasn't wearing his omnipresent smile.

Mike moved over to him. "Morning, Arnie. You doing okay?"

Arnie leaned over to brush some lint off his pants. Without looking up he said, "I don't figure I have any right to complain."

"I haven't seen Marilyn this morning. Is she here?"

"No, she stayed home today."

Pastor Mike said nothing. He just waited for a more complete answer. After a moment it came. "She was just feeling a little out of sorts. I expect she'll be here tonight."

"Well, good. Church just doesn't seem the same without your vibrant wife around."

That night Marilyn did attend but Arnie stayed home. And like her counterpart, she, too, seemed drained of her perpetual electricity.

"Marilyn, I don't mean to intrude but it seems like you and Arnie are a little down. Is there something wrong?"

Her eyes moistened but she said, "We're fine, thank you for asking."

But Marilyn Kling knew that they weren't fine. She and Arnie had marriage problems. Who would have believed it? She treasured their reputation as such a sweet couple – a description that she felt was well deserved. But now it had become "sweet and sour." Perhaps mostly sour.

Their present difficulties began when an ill wind blew.... A draft coming through the partially opened passenger door window had suddenly cooled their marital bliss.

It all began on an ordinary trip to Kmart. Due to Arnie's recent retirement, they now did these errands together. But on this excursion, Arnie had the audacity to proclaim that Marilyn's open window was irritating. Since her window was always open, she was puzzled. Why would he complain now, after all these years? Had it always bugged him?

"Pardon?"

"Marilyn, honey, please shut the window. It's noisy." Arnie often called her honey but this time it had a phony sound to it.

"Arnie, I'm not following you." He must be miscommunicating, she thought.

"The wind blowing through the window gets on my nerves. Could you please close it?"

She felt like she had just been slapped. When she spoke her voice came out with a high-pitched edge. "Arnie, I can't believe what you're asking. My window is always open. Due to my medical condition it has to be. And you know that. What are you thinking?"

At the age of eight, Marilyn had traveled with her parents on a vacation to the Wisconsin Dells. On the way there she experienced carsickness. In the back of their station wagon her stomach began to churn with nausea. Every turn of the car increased her discomfort, which then increased—due to her complaints—the discomfort of her parents.

When she predicted she was going to "throw up," her dad pulled over and let her walk around. But a return to the car also meant a return to her symptoms. Not relishing the possibility that Marilyn might actually vomit, her mother opened her window a little and traded seats. "Honey, the fresh air will make you feel better. And in the front seat you won't feel the swerves as much."

The remedy worked well and the open window became a constant source of preventative medicine. Her sacrificial mother took up permanent residency in the back seat and Marilyn never experienced carsickness again.

During her courting days with Arnie, he had teased her over her window practice but never challenged her. He thought it was cute. Yes, that was the word he used, *cute*. Marilyn remembered that distinctly. It was inconceivable that after all these years he would now want the window shut. *What was he thinking?*

"What are you thinking?"

"I'm not thinking nothing. I just don't think it's necessary for you to always have that window open. It's not hot in here. We're not going down curvy roads. You're not stopping carsickness; you're just creating an annoying whistle."

"You're right about one thing—you aren't thinking! If I roll up this window, the air will get stuffy, I will get claustrophobic, my stomach will spin, my breathing will become shallow and I will—pardon my bluntness—toss my cookies. Is that what you want? *Upchuck* all over our car?"

She spoke in a tone that normally ended further discussion, but this time Arnie returned the volley. "Marilyn, it's time you grow up. You've been held hostage by some notion you got in your head when you were a kid. And that's where the problem still is—all in your head!"

"Arnold Kling! You're talking nonsense. My problem is congenital in nature. Signals in my inner ear conflict with what I see visually and I get motion sickness. It's a lifetime curse I wish I didn't have. But sadly I do. I feel bad if the open window annoys you but I assure you that the draft of fresh air is better than a car full of stinky *you know what*. Then we'd both be sorry!"

"I'm willing to take the risk. Shut the window and let's find out what happens."

"Okay, if that's what you want, fine!" With that she grabbed the crank and wound it up.

This has to be about more than a window, she thought. The sensitive man that she married would never have been this cruel. It was plain to her—

he must not love her any more. How could he? He was purposely causing her to become ill.

She could feel it coming. The air was becoming heavy – very heavy. Like syrup. Breathing was difficult; not unlike what drowning must feel like. The temperature seemed to rise. She unbuttoned the top button of her blouse. Next would come the swirling stomach. Yes, there it was. She clutched her belly.

"Arnie, I'm sick. I'm definitely sick."

"Like I said before, it's all in your head..."

"It may be now but it's soon going to be all over the front seat!"

"Ha, that's good. Listen, Marilyn, if you throw up I'll clean it up and you can keep the window down. But if you don't, maybe you can get past the silliness that has plagued you for six decades."

"You're acting spiteful."

"I'm just practicing tough love."

She mumbled in disagreement and looked out the dreaded window. The trip to Kmart had become a disaster. Her sweet husband had degenerated into a maniacal ogre and now she was in a crisis. If she went into a seizure or a coma, would Arnie even take her to the hospital?

She fanned her face with her hand and rocked backwards and forwards. Arnie just started whistling.

Hyperventilating was causing dizziness. Another button was undone. Even though she wasn't throwing up, she felt like she should be. Maybe there was a blockage somewhere. That could be even more serious. Did people ever have internal implosions? She put her finger down her throat and coughed. "I'm gagging! I'm gagging!"

"Keep your hand out of your mouth and you'll be fine."

She could stand it no more... She wound down the window and thrust her head all the way out. Like she was surfacing from the depths of water, she sucked in the fresh air and felt immediate rejuvenation. After a minute she retracted her head, rolled the window up part way and declared, "The window stays open a crack."

"Fine." He turned on the wipers. They scraped back and forth on the dry window with a screech.

"Oh, real mature." Marilyn said.

He said nothing.

"Arnie, please. That sounds like fingernails on a chalk board."

"Marilyn, when I was a child I was traumatized by a storm. The wipers somehow soothe the anxieties caused by that experience."

"Take me home. I don't want to go to Kmart with you anymore. In fact, I don't want to go anywhere with you!"

And she hadn't. They started taking turns coming to church. She wouldn't ride with him if the wipers were on and he wouldn't turn off the wipers if she cracked the window.

Mike visited the Klings that week and they spilled the beans. They also agreed to meet with him for counseling. He didn't do a lot of marriage and family therapy. Because of his youth and lack of children, he didn't have the credibility for some to come to him. But he wasn't worried. The Klings were so nice he figured that a little listening and a few suggestions would settle the problem. Little did he know he would be forced into excessive listening on his part and no listening on theirs.

Their first session began with them rearranging the furniture. Arnie moved his chair directly in front of Mike's and scooted it close. Marilyn maneuvered her chair away from Arnie's and situated it next to Mike's left where she could use his sleeve as a leash.

Mike had a hard time getting the session started. Once they got going, however, he had a harder time getting it ended.

FOURTEEN

....

THE NEW ADDITION

"Can you break free from the office and go for a ride with me?"

Mike was used to these kinds of calls. Sandy viewed it as her responsibility to keep him from working too many hours. It was her theory that Mike's propensity for overtime wasn't the result of work-a-holism but rather a subconscious attempt to compensate for what he believed to be a lack of productivity. She persistently tried to help him by affirming ministry highlights and by leading him from work to play.

But today's call didn't seem to be an attempt to minister to her husband. She just had something she really wanted to do.

"I could probably do that," Mike responded. It was Saturday morning and he was reviewing his sermon notes. "What's up, Sandy?"

"It's a secret. Just come as quick as you can, okay?"

"Sure, babe, I'll be right there." As he put the phone down, he chuckled. His wife was a big kid. When she got excited about something, she had the bubbly personality of a sixth grader. He could imagine her right now dancing around the kitchen.

"So where are we going?" When Mike had gotten home he had found Sandy sitting in the driver's seat of their 1958 Volkswagen Beetle, a car Sandy called their Luv Bug. It had been in Mike's family for many years. As soon as he got in, she took off.

"Hang on. You'll see. Anticipation will only heighten the experience."

"I'll heighten your experience," Mike said as he poked her in the ribs.

"Careful, buster, I'm driving here." She turned right onto Main Street. There they passed a yard sale at Chester Miller's house.

"That man is always selling something. If only Baptist churches had fund-raising auctions, we could put him in charge."

Sandy laughed and then went north on Main Street until she turned onto Eight Avenue. Due to the winding Marcellus River that cut through town, Eighth, like many of the roads, had a lot of curves. Hugged by trees dressed bright in harvest colors, the street gently swerved back and forth. They rode with the windows down, filling the car with Indian summer warmth and the smell of burning leaves.

Leaving the town and entering farm country, Sandy made a few more turns before picking a gravel road that cut through a cluster of large oaks. She approached a white farmhouse, slowed down and said, "I think this is it." Glancing at a torn piece of newspaper, she confirmed, "Yup, this is it."

"Let me guess, you've decided that we're going to become farmers?"

"Oh, you've guessed and now the surprise is ruined."

As they got out of the car, they were greeted by the excited barking of a golden retriever. "Hi, momma-dog," Sandy said, "you want to tell Mike what the secret really is?"

Mike looked at the dog's maternal features and said, "I think I am about to experience puppy love."

"I hope so. I was just glancing through the Penny Shopper when I saw a little ad about a litter of puppies for sale. So I called right away. Since they are a mixture of Golden Retriever and Irish Setter and not purebreds, they are only twenty-five dollars. We can afford twenty-five dollars, don't you think?"

"Well, let's look at the puppies before we decide."

"We've been talking about getting a dog for such a long time but it seems like all we do is talk. And now we have a chance to act..."

"Slow down, Sandy, I didn't say no. Just give me a chance to look at the puppies and think about it before we decide."

A man in blue bib overhauls met them at the door. He had the usual white forehead and burnt cheeks of a farmer. When he led them into a breezeway filled with six squirming puppies, the decision was immediately made. "They're adorable," Sandy squealed. She scooped one up and kissed it on the nose, allowing it to nibble her own. Mike followed suit.

The hard part was picking which puppy to adopt. They sat on the floor for forty-five minutes, examining and playing with each little dog. Going back and forth between their favorites, they finally picked a little pup with a light blond face. Or, maybe he, with his aggressive friendliness, had chosen them.

Mike drove the return trip as Sandy snuggled their new family member on her lap. "Now," Sandy asked, "can we please take our new dog to the park?"

"Sure, that would be fun."

It was a Hallmark experience – the kind of day that insists on becoming a memory. The two of them lay in the grass, watching yellow and red leaves float down the river. Between them was a blue, plastic Tupperware container filled with freshly baked chocolate chip cookies.

"You know," Sandy said, "that you wouldn't have gotten any of these if you hadn't let us get a puppy!"

Mike saw the fleck of a tear on her cheek, luminous in the sun. He was touched because he knew it was a happy tear. He removed it with his finger and placed it on his lips.

Pure unrestrained indulgence. It was all so good, Mike thought -- a spectacular day, a beautiful setting, chocolate chip cookies (his favorite), a new dog that was crawling all over them, and an incredible wife. She was so attractive, so fun, so everything. Could it be any better than this?

He rolled over to her and kissed her. Her lips were soft and warm and only the interference of a pooch separated them. "Ah," he said, "the sweet smell of puppy breath." She laughed and then Mike said, "We really are blessed, aren't we?"

"Yes, we are," she agreed. Then, throwing back her head, she started singing, "Count your blessings, name them ton by ton; count your blessings, see what God hath done..."

"If only God had given you a better voice, things would be perfect."

"Hey!"

....

FIFTEEN

THE PITTER-PATTER OF LITTLE FEET

After three counseling sessions with the Klings, Mike was totally frustrated. They had no interest in looking at Scriptures, analyzing personality types, considering conflict patterns, learning about communication techniques or pursuing any other avenues of discovery. Nor did they do any of the homework Mike assigned. They just wanted to repeat and embellish the story of the cracked window and the irritating wiper.

Why was it that so much of his time seemed to be used up by people who had no point, no purpose? They weren't making progress or pursuing it and Mike was left behind with them.

He saw no end in sight. The Klings seemed to enjoy counseling. They liked having Mike's focused attention. Every week they would come early and then stall their departure. Often Marilyn would bring refreshments. But each session was a rerun of the one before. Even though

Mike tried to steer them toward positive themes, they chose to become more and more entrenched in their positions.

Only one small success had been achieved. Arnie had agreed to allow Marilyn to maintain the open window while they were in counseling. As a result, they were back in church together.

Respecting confidentiality, Mike shared none of this with anyone – except Sandy. She relieved the pressure by helping him see the humor in all of it. One day she jokingly said, "Maybe you ought to refer the *Clingers* to Counselor Carol?"

He laughed. But later at the office, the thought returned. *What would it hurt? Carol can't do any worse than I've been doing.* And maybe a referral would help get her off his back. She could listen to them talk for hours and everyone would be happy.

The Klings hesitated at first but finally agreed. For Mike, it seemed too good to be true. And, as he would eventually discover, it was. But for a while, there was a treasured period of peace.

Sandy predicted failure. "Let's get an egg timer," she said, "and see just how long this counseling relationship works."

"It was your idea!"

"Michael, I was just making a joke. I can't believe you actually did it." And then she clapped her hands and started to giggle. "Hee hee. You've created a sitcom. I can't wait until future episodes!"

SEVENTEEN

....

LEAVE THE SLEEVE

The next Sunday morning Marilyn Kling and Whit Carson became the center of attention. After the service Brenda Strickland and Beth Kurick hurried up to Mike and Sandy. Giggling, the teens told of an incident they just witnessed down the hall.

"You know Mrs. Kling?" Beth raised her eyebrows and waited for a nod. "Well, yeah, of course you do. Well, you know how she likes to grab people's sleeves when she talks to them? Yeah? Well, she was talking to Whit Carson and she—" Beth had a teenager's eager, nasal voice. She spoke so rapidly she had to pause to take a breath. Like a tag team wrestler, Brenda took over for her. "Mrs. Kling tugged on Whit's sleeve so hard that it tore right off. You should have seen it! It came loose at the shoulder and dropped down around his wrist."

It was Beth's turn again. "Mrs. Kling goes like, 'Oh my! Oh my!' and then she tries to reattach it—you know, back at the shoulder? Like if she pinches it up there it'll stay. Really, it was so cute. And Whit goes like, 'Don't worry, it's just an old shirt.' But Mrs. Kling's still doing her 'oh my' thing. It was great!"

Brenda said, "It was really funny. We don't want to make fun of Mrs. Kling, but she's always tugging sleeves and this time she pulled one right off. It was hilarious! I'm telling you, you should've seen it!"

By this time, Kim, Kristy, Matthew and Kerry had also gathered around them. The children were laughing and pulling on each other's sleeves. Kristy said, "We all saw it. It was awesome."

Mike thought it was unlikely that the sleeve had torn loose. He assumed Whit had set up Mrs. *Clinger*.

His weekend had a happy finale that night when he shared a part in the "sleeve sequel." In the lobby, prior to the evening service, he watched Marilyn run up to Whit with a package in her arms.

"Whitfield, dear, I felt so bad about what happened this morning that I went out with Mr. Kling this afternoon and bought you a replacement."

"You didn't have to do that. The shirt was really old. I was thinking about throwing it away anyway."

"I wanted to, honey, and I think you're just going to love the little outfit we picked out."

"No, please return it and get your money back. I've got more shirts than I know what to do with."

"But, Whitfield, I've never seen you in a tie. And this little outfit has a tie. Now here, look at it."

By now, Mike and several others had all gathered around to see Whit's new "little outfit." When it came out of the bag, Mike stifled a laugh and some turned away to hide their reactions. The red and green striped shirt had long collars that had gone out of style years before. It must have come from a clearance table at the dollar store. A thin tie completed the ensemble.

"It's a large," Arnie said. "I'll bet it will fit you perfectly."

"I'll try it on when I get home."

"Whit, we've got a couple of minutes before church," Mike interjected. "Why don't you go into the restroom and put it on now?"

"Oh, would you, Whitfield? Please?" Marilyn had him by the arm and was looking at him with imploring eyes. Mike gave him an encouraging nod.

"Ah, well..." Whit hesitated, then finally relented. "Sure. I can do that. This is some shirt."

Mike regretted that he had to move into the auditorium and miss the modeling. But from the front he noticed Whit enter during the song service, dressed in Marilyn's gift. Rather than sitting in his regular seat, Whit found a place in the rear.

When the offering time came, the pastor noticed they were short one usher. Unable to resist temptation, Mike went to the microphone and said, "It looks like we could use another person to help pass the plates. Whit Carson, would you mind helping us out tonight?" Obviously embarrassed by his outfit, Whit's face wrinkled in chagrin as he shot the pastor an *I'm-going-to-get-you-for-this* look.

EIGHTEEN

....

SPECIAL MUSIC BY A
SPECIAL GUY

Solomon Blink provided the special music after the offering. At least monthly he would do a solo by request – his own. He neither played an instrument nor sang. He would either whistle or do hand-cooing. The whistling wasn't bad; when he added a warble to the hymns he chose, his Adam's apple would keep pace with rapid bobbing. But the hand-cooing was the crowd favorite. He would form a hollow chamber with both hands, blow into the gap between his thumbs, and create variations in pitch by squeezing his palms hither and thither.

Some argued that his version of "special music" wasn't appropriate for church; a whole deacon meeting had once been devoted to the topic. But the congregation loved Solomon's sweet spirit so he always received polite applause. The consequence of this clapping was further volunteering.

Another thing that brought Solomon fans were the sweets he would often pass out to the kids. On the Sundays he came, children would run to him—and out would come the candy.

Mike remembered a Sunday a month before when Sandy whisked down the hallway past him. He shouted after her, "Where are you going in such a hurry?" Without looking back she yelled, "I just heard Solomon's handing out Ho-Ho's. I've got to get to him before they're all gone."

Solomon was over six feet tall and only weighed about a hundred and thirty pounds. His long, stringy arms dangled like empty panty hose. Their length was amplified by the white shirt cuffs that hung far below the sleeves of his blue, pinstriped suit. And the generous collars made his neck look like the pole on a ventriloquist's dummy.

In his early childhood people thought Solomon was mentally slow. But then it was discovered he suffered from some visual and auditory disabilities. His intelligence was actually quite remarkable – in its own way. His thick glasses and hearing aids made him a target for teasing at school, and he had been ostracized and isolated. This difficult beginning contributed to his awkward social skills. But nothing could hinder his active mind. Like fly paper, everything stuck to it – historical facts, science, trivia, and whatever else sparked his interest.

Solomon worked at the library. He had been hired as a custodian and he still fulfilled those duties and wore a janitor's uniform—gray with his name embroidered on the breast pocket. But now he mostly filed books, did research and answered to the nickname, "Mr. Answer Man."

His main mental collection box was reserved for scripture. Solomon had been saved twenty years before through a bus program. Even after the program was abandoned and the church bus was sold, he continued to go to church. He won every memorization contest the children's department offered. Learning verses became an obsession and he knew passages from all over the Bible. His favorites came from those books penned by his namesake, King Solomon, and he quoted them at every opportunity. Unfortunately, any kind of connective link would cause him to recite a text even if it wasn't relevant or appropriate.

Mike would never forget some of Solomon's bloopers. Once, Solomon overheard Dorothy Monkmeier arguing with her husband Red. With his rapid-paced staccato voice, Solomon began spitting out proverbs. Sandwiched throughout was an odd little humming noise he liked to make.

"Better to live in a desert than with a quarrelsome and ill-tempered wife... Hmmm. Proverbs 21:19. Better to live on a corner of the roof than share a house with a quarrelsome wife... Hmmm. Proverbs 25:24. A quarrelsome wife is like a constant dripping on a rainy day; restraining her is like restraining the wind or grasping oil with the hand. Hmmm. Proverbs 27:15-16."

Enjoying Solomon's words, Red winked at him and said, "Let her have it!" But this just made Red the target.

"He who winks maliciously causes grief, and a chattering fool comes to ruin. Hmmm. Proverbs 10:10."

Now Dorothy was enjoying herself. "You tell him, Solomon. And also talk to him about his laziness. He was supposed to clean the garage yesterday, but he just laid around listening to records."

"Go to the ant, you sluggard; consider its ways and be wise! Hmmm. Proverbs 6:6. The sluggard says, 'There is a lion in the road, a fierce lion roaming the streets!' As a door turns on its hinges, so a sluggard turns on his bed. Hmmm. Proverbs 26:13-14."

"Now, Solomon," Red responded, "if I didn't know you better, I'd swear you were insulting me."

"A fool shows his annoyance at once, but a prudent man overlooks an insult. Hmmm. Proverbs 12:16."

Dorothy clapped her hands and started laughing. "Solomon, you are so funny!"

"A merry heart does good like good medicine. Hmmm. Proverbs 17:22"

"Solomon," Red said, "you better stop. You're giving Dorothy an overdose."

Solomon provided a good deal of entertainment for the entire church. Those who knew him took no offense at his clumsy verbal missteps. When it came to judgment calls, he continually misdialed but never intended to hurt anyone. He had an evident love for God and His people. Mike figured that when the rewards were handed out in heaven, Solomon Blink would get a large pile—but none for whistling. Hand-cooing maybe.

···

NINETEEN

WHIT UNLEASHED

After Solomon's hand-cooing special and the standard applause, Mike stepped forward to preach. Simultaneously, Morris Ubody came down the aisle and up on to the platform with a note. It read, "Please announce that Al Merfud should call home immediately. There is an emergency that requires his attention."

Mike was puzzled. He didn't know an Al Merfud and hadn't noticed any visitors at the service. But if this was an emergency, he knew he had better make the announcement just in case this man was out there somewhere.

"I have a note for Al Merfud. Is there an Al Merfud here? Al Merfud?"

A burst of laughter came from a group of teenagers and picked up in volume as it rippled across the audience. Mike couldn't figure out what was funny until he mentally replayed what he had said. The name read "Al Merfud" but it came out sounding like "Elmer Fudd."

He looked at Whit and saw his look of chagrin had been replaced by one of happy self-satisfaction. Retaliation had been swift.

"If Elmer Fudd is here," Mike adlibbed, "you need to call home immediately. Your friend Bugs Bunny is having a bad hare day and needs your help."

After the service, Mike looked for Whit. He wanted to tell him what a well-dressed usher he was. But not seeing him, he assumed the teen had quickly gone home to shed his outfit.

While looking around, he was approached by Solomon. "Hi pastor, I heard that you got a dog."

"That's right, Solomon, I'm sorry you weren't here last Sunday night to see her. It's too bad that your job keeps you from coming some Sundays. But I'm glad you could be here this evening. Your whistling was really something. Will you be back to church soon?"

"Yes, I get next Sunday off, too. Are you going to bring your dog again?"

"No, I'm afraid our foolish little pup is a back-slider. She won't be coming to any more services. But you can drop by and play with her any time."

"Hmmm. Foolish little pup. 'As a dog returns to its vomit, so a fool repeats his folly.' Hmmm. Proverbs 26:11."

"Ugh, that's a yucky thought—"

A frightening sight suddenly diverted his attention. Coming out of the library were Counselor Carol and Whit. *Oh no.* Mike had been hoping to keep them separated. The combination of two unstable elements sometimes caused explosions.

While pretending to be listening to Solomon ("Like one who seizes a dog by the ears is a passer-by who meddles in a quarrel not his own... Hmmmm."), he watched Whit walk across the vestibule and out the door. Spotting Mike, Carol beckoned him with her finger. Excusing himself from Solomon, Mike followed her into the library and took a chair that she was patting.

"Pastor Mike, I normally don't betray any confidences, but since you are also counseling Whitfield, I think you should know what I just discovered in a short session that I had with him during the second half of the evening service."

Mike lifted his eyebrows.

"Whitfield has multiple personalities."

"What?"

"That's right. That's why you probably couldn't make any progress with him. Without properly diagnosing him, you were working in the dark. In a blind haphazard way, you were probably just throwing verses at him. That approach certainly wouldn't—"

"Carol—"

"Pastor, just listen to me—"

"No, Carol. You listen to me. Whit does not have multiple personalities. He's simply a practical joker. He was teasing you. He's done the same thing with me and others."

Carol smiled and patted him on the arm. Mike hated it when she did that.

"Pastor, pastor. I can understand how the boy might have toyed with you a bit. But I am a trained professional. Do you honestly think he could pull one over on me? No, I am telling you that he has multiple personalities. Though more will probably continue to manifest themselves, a few actually came out tonight... a man named George Jetson and a girl from Kansas named Dorothy."

Mike suppressed a chuckle. *Did she never watch television or was she just incredibly naive?* "Carol, did you know that George Jetson is a cartoon character?"

"Yes, George is a comical character – he's really quite funny. He didn't seem to need much of our help – he's happily married with a good family and a dog named Astro. But the poor little girl was deeply depressed. Fortunately, with just a little bit of counsel, I was able to help her see the bright side of things. You should have seen Whit in there. Before I merged his personalities back together again, He was twirling around, singing a song about a yellow brick road."

"Yes, she is in the *Wizard of* Oz. Carol, wake up and smell the coffee. Whit is just pulling your strings. For your own sake, I'm asking you not to have any more *counseling sessions* with him."

With another condescending smile, she again patted Mike's arm. "Pastor, I have a little learning exercise that might help you with your blockage."

"Blockage?"

"Oh, pastor, pastor. Are you really blind to your personality impasse? Even after my amazing progress with the Klings, you don't trust me. Don't you see that your insecurities are keeping you from relying on me and utilizing my skills in a greater way?"

"Carol, I—"

"Now, stop right there. I sense an objection coming. Am I right?"

"Well, yes, as a matter of fact, I—"

"Please pastor, I implore you to rein in your incessant reservations. Each new objection increases your armor of denial."

"But—"

"But, but, but, but, but... Pastor, your 'but' is the seat of your problem. But don't fret. I have a role play exercise that will help you."

Mike crossed his arms. "Let me be candid. I'm not interested in your exercise. I'm—"

"Pastor—"

"Carol, please! Please let me finish. Maybe you should spend a little more time dealing with your issues and a little less focusing on my problems. As Jesus said, take the plank out of your own eye before trying to take a sliver out of someone else's. Do you hear what I am saying?"

"I hear more than you think. I hear your words give voice to your psychological defense mechanism. But between the lines I also hear the voice of a child. It is a quiet whisper... a plaintive murmur. And it says, 'I hurt. Will someone help me? Carol, will you please help me?' And do you know something, little one? I will. I will help you if you will work with me. We are going to do a little role-play. You will be me and I will be you."

"I'm sorry but I'm not interested."

"Please, pastor. Just give this a try. If it doesn't work, we can quit any time you want."

"Any time?"

"Any time."

"Okay, let's do it."

"Excellent. This is how this works. You will be me and I will be you. Do you get that? You are Carol. And you have come to the office—pretend this library is your office—to talk to me, the pastor. Here, let's switch chairs and get started."

They repositioned themselves and Mike immediately got into his part. "Pastor Mike," he said, "I just stopped in to tell you how special you are." He reached out and patted her arm. "Pastor, pastor, I know you have many other things you'd rather be doing, and since you don't really have any problems, I'm going to leave now. Bye."

While she sputtered, he raced out the door.

TWENTY

··

THE EXIT LINE

Another week slid by and it was Sunday morning once again. Mike preached a message on Christian citizenship. With the presidential election coming up, he was hoping that everyone would pray for the country and vote. Without endorsing a candidate, he talked about those political issues that corresponded with biblical teachings and where the two candidates stood. Although he praised Jimmy Carter's faith, it was obvious that he preferred Ronald Reagan. In that the church was primarily filled with Republicans, which was just fine with most.

After most church services Mike and Sandy stood outside the auditorium in the vestibule and shook people's hands as they left. Today, Kim and Kristy, two sisters in grade school, were the first ones through. Since they had inducted Mike into their "hug club" they gave him a weekly squeeze. He loved kids (to his and Sandy's disappointment, God hadn't granted them any of their own yet) and appreciated the joy that the church children brought him. He would often hold the little ones and give the bigger children high-fives. After the siblings came Clarence and Eunice Johansen. On Pastor Mike's first Sunday, Clarence had come through the line, looked deeply into Mike's eyes, and simply whispered, "Thank you. Thank you." The somber sincerity of his words and visage had moved Mike. But now, after a year of "Thank you. Thank you," each Sunday, Mike was a little less moved.

Next up were Mr. and Mrs. Broadmoor. She was a thin, wiry woman who had once been of average height but now was bowing to gravity and osteoporosis. Mike didn't expect her to speak and she didn't. He did expect a smile and she rewarded him generously with a flashbulb grin that lit up the room. Her thick glasses amplified gentle, sparkly eyes that gazed intently into his. Mike put his arms around her fragile, slumped shoulders and gave her a gentle hug.

Her husband, Harold T. Broadmoor, handled all of their public discourse. As though he was trying to draw water, Harold gave Mike's hand a couple big pumps. Then he said, "Preacher I was thinking about last week's sermon. It was a dandy but how come you didn't mention Joseph's coat of many colors? That would've made your sermon even more colorful. Colorful? Get it?"

"Got it, Harold. The only problem is that it was a sermon about Joseph the father of baby Jesus, not about the Old Testament Joseph who had the colorful coat."

"Well, don't get down on yourself. Maybe next time you'll get the right Joseph. Anyhow, it was still some sermon. Full of energy. I like that. You know something, young man? In a few more years, you're going to turn into a good preacher. Seriously, I'm not just buttering your toast; I mean it. You keep practicing and you're going to be a grade A preacher. Maybe then we'll put TV cameras in here and put you on a cable channel."

Mike pretended he didn't notice that Harold's compliment sounded like an insult. "Harold, speaking about clothes, I don't remember the brown suit that you're wearing. Is that double-knit?"

"Sure is. Look at this." He hitched up his pants from their accustomed place below his paunch, did a squat and added, "Now I don't have to worry about splitting my pants again. And get this, I bought it for twenty dollars at the Salvation Army. Also got a white one I will wear on a special occasion. Do you know how much a suit like this would've cost at Penneys? Let me tell you. Plenty. And they don't even carry any sizes over 52. They must specialize in petite people. Mother," Harold nodded toward his wife who was now sitting smiling over on a bench, "shortened the legs and arms and alakazam, a new suit for one Jackson."

"That sure sounds like a good deal."

"Just one damp Jackson – it's his picture on the twenty dollar bill you know. Jackson. Andrew Jackson. Not Jesse; Andrew. That's right; just twenty Washingtons. Those are ones. And the suit isn't even hardly worn. It's just a little shiny. My guess is the guy who had it probably died. No way someone would give away a new suit like this. No, he probably died and his family donated it. One man's loss; another man's gain. Must have died unexpectedly, otherwise he wouldn't have bought a suit this nice. That wouldn't make any sense. If you thought you were going to die soon, you wouldn't want to waste your money like that. I'm just surprised they didn't bury him in this suit. It would make a great burial suit. Look at me."

He shut his eyes and stood stiffly with his hands at his side. "Wouldn't you agree that this would make a great burial suit? I plan on using it. When you see Harold T. Broadmoor relaxing in his casket, you are going to see one classy corpse."

"That's something we can all look forward to."

"Huh?" Harold feathered the fingers of one hand through his white beard while his other rubbed his bald head. "Preacher, you got me... yup, you got me. Hey, what's that on your tie?" Harold touched Mike's tie with his pudgy finger. As Mike looked down, the finger shot up and flipped his nose. "Ha!" Harold shouted with a triumphant laugh, "now I got you!"

"Hey, Harold," Bud barked from behind them, "can you move along? We're all waiting our turn."

"Hold on. I've got an important question for our pastor. Tell me, have you heard about the three preachers out fishing in a rowboat?"

Bud said, "Harold, we have all heard about them. Get a new joke. Now move along – it's our turn."

"You haven't heard one tenth of my humor collection. Right now I am writing a joke book that will be a best seller and it is going to make me a million smackeroonies. But I can see you want your turn with the preacher so I'll just go tell my joke to Arnie. He appreciates my comedy."

Grateful for being rescued, Mike patted Harold on the shoulder and turned to Bud and Lucille. "How are the Swensens today?"

"Finer than frog's hair."

"Oh, Bud," Lucille said, giving her husband a pat. "Pastor, he can never give a straight answer. I live with this twenty-four hours a day. You need to pray for me."

"Changing Bud would take endless periods of prayer by someone far more spiritual than myself so I guess you're stuck with him just the way he is."

"Well, he's a pest but I think I will keep him."

"What was that?" Bud said loudly. "You say that I'm your pet?"

"PEST. Not pet. PEST. Like in PESTILENCE!"

"Lucille, you don't have to yell."

"Yes, I do. Bud, you need to get a hearing aid. Pastor, tell Bud to get a hearing aid."

"I don't need a hearing aid. People just need to learn not to mumble. And speaking about mumbling, pastor, they need to turn up the P.A. system; I could only hear half of your message. The part that I heard was so good I would've liked to have heard the rest of it."

Lucille patted Mike on the arm and said, "The whole sermon was excellent. And I need to take issue with what Harold told you. You're not *going* to be a good preacher; you are already a good preacher—a very good preacher."

"Well, thank you, Lucille. You're very kind."

"I mean it. I think you're better than Chuck Swindoll."

"Now you're exaggerating. He's awesome."

"I don't mean Swindoll on the radio where they cut out all of the bad parts before they air him. I mean Swindoll in person. Bud and I heard him in person and I didn't think he was that good."

"We've never seen Charles Swindoll in person," Bud challenged.

"Oh, yes, we did. It was at the conference in Chicago." Lucille clasped her hands together in front of her and continued. "Pastor, we were visiting my cousins in Chicago and they took us to a conference where Chuck Swindoll preached. After about five minutes, he totally stopped talking and put his head on the pulpit. I thought he had forgotten what he was going to say, but then he said that he was sick and quickly walked off the stage. Poor man. "Bud, surely you remember that?"

"I remember the event. But that wasn't Charles Swindoll."

"Well, then, who was it?"

"I'm not sure. It was a long time ago. Maybe it was Oral Roberts."

"Bud Swensen, don't be silly. If it was Oral Roberts, he would have immediately healed himself and kept preaching."

"Well, it wasn't Charles Swindoll. Maybe it was Charles Stanley."

"It wasn't Stanley. Stanley's not bald."

"Neither is Swindoll."

"Oh, okay then... Come to think of it, it may not have been Swindoll. But whoever it was wasn't as good as our own preacher." Lucille leaned into Mike with a smile, "Pastor, you're much better than that guy was. Bud and I just love listening to you."

"I only wish I could listen to you better," Bud said. "But with that P.A. turned off, I can only hear half of your sermon."

Next up was Betty Sweeting. "Pastor, just checking. Have you ordered the Sunday School curriculum for the next quarter yet?"

"No, Betty, I haven't. Do you think that, since you are the Sunday school superintendent, you could handle that?"

"Pastor, I live a busy life. It'd be better if you'd handle it. Now please don't put it off. It should have already been ordered."

"Alright. I'll do it this week." Just saying he would do it made Mike nervous. He was a weak administrator and had a terrible memory.

Eavesdropping, Stan Glass put his hand on Mike's shoulder. "A thing worth doing is worth doing well."

The stream of people that followed offered predictable comments that he heard every week. "Good sermon," many people would say. Some would remark, "That's just what I needed." Occasionally, someone would want to argue about a theological point or a matter of interpretation. The comments Mike appreciated the most weren't related to his preaching style; they dealt with the text. They came from people who seriously wanted to understand it or apply it in their lives.

There was one couple Mike missed—some visitors he had seen in the back. He hoped someone had gotten to them....

TWENTY-ONE

....

THE VISITOR RECEPTION

Carol squinted at the man. He sure looked familiar.

In that Meanwhile Baptist Church didn't get a lot of visitors, those who did come got considerable attention. But the couple sitting in the rear of the sanctuary would have grabbed the spotlight in any setting. The man was tall and distinguished. A charcoal, pinstriped suit and a patterned silver tie accessorized his gray-flecked dark hair. His wife was even more striking. She wore a dark red dress, a scarf, and some eye-catching jewelry.

But it was the man who had snagged Carol Harmon's scrutiny. As she kept glancing at him out of the corner of her eye, she became even more convinced that she recognized him.

Where do I know him from? Suddenly it came to her. *That is my doctor.*

Carol had only met him once, during a routine physical two years ago. But since she was a perceptive student of people, she now recalled him perfectly.

She was thrilled. Since she wasn't a proud person, she was content to associate with the common, blue-collar people of Meanwhile Baptist Church. But it would be wonderful—*so very wonderful*, if she could have the company of another professional like herself.

In her mind she could see the two of them huddled together in a hallway, conferring on cases. Out of respect, people would stand back and give them space as they dealt with critical situations. Though there wouldn't be a hint of snobbery on their part, the physician and the counselor would still be an informal fraternity.

It was important that they talk as soon as possible. Otherwise the doctor may feel like he wouldn't fit in around here and choose not to return. But when he found out that Carol, a crossing guard when they had met previously, was now a counselor, he would feel the affinity that a peer provides.

So when the service was over, she bee-lined toward the visitors. Because they quickly exited, her task wasn't easy. She also had to beat her competition. Seeing that the Klings were also closing in on them, Carol broke into a sprint and beat them to their target.

Out of breath, her first sentence came out with a gasp. "Hi there, good to see you again." Putting her hand on her chest, she paused to catch her breath.

He looked at her blankly, so Carol continued. "Surely you remember me?"

"You will have to forgive me, but I can't place you."

She felt a letdown but still continued. Thinking back to her physical, she said, "Well, maybe you just don't recognize me with my clothes on."

"What?" The man looked at Carol and then at his wife with a shocked expression. But instead of flashing back a hint of support, Mrs. Red Dress just crossed her arms in front of her and gave Carol a sharp stare.

"Lady, you are confused," he said. "We have never met."

Carol cocked her head and looked at him closely. Her study made her acknowledge that he was right. Though the man looked like her doctor, she now realized with disappointment that he was obviously an imposter. *The nerve of him.*

"It's now clear," Carol said, "that you're not the man I thought you were." With that, she spun and sped away. Her heals clicked loudly across the linoleum floor.

The tall man used his silver tie to pat down his forehead as he asked his wife, "Heavens, what was that crazy lady blabbering about?" She had no time to answer before the Klings engulfed them with enthusiastic congeniality. In typical Clinger tradition, they talked with animation as they moved in close, patted shoulders, tugged on sleeves and felt the texture of the woman's scarf. The lady, feeling like a swimmer entangled in weeds at the bottom of a lake, kept stepping backwards in an attempt to break free.

When they finally got away, the guests hurried toward the door. But they were snagged again – this time by Solomon Blink. He looked at them sideways and said, "It sure was good to have you folks join us on this Lord's Day. Did you have a blessed time?"

Having lost all patience, the woman retorted, "Do you want an honest answer?"

"Certainly," Solomon responded, leaning toward her. "An honest answer is like a kiss on the lips. Hmmm."

"What?" the couple said in stereo. They pushed past Solomon and exited the door. They were followed by his shout, "Proverbs 24:26."

When Edward Snowden got in his car, he was told by his wife, "Just go! You can put on your seat belt later."

*   *   *

On Monday night, Mike and Sandy traveled to 1243 West Lincoln Lane to call on the Snowdens. Though neither of them felt comfortable doing "visitation," they both recognized its importance. Sometimes Mike went with a deacon but because of their reluctance, Sandy was often his calling partner.

Usually it went well. Not tonight. On this occasion, the entire conversation felt forced.

Mrs. Snowden's face was dour and pinched, foreshadowing the tendency of her mouth to curl downward into an expression that said, "no." She carried herself with an air of impatient self-importance. After she made some tea, she sat down next to her husband on the loveseat. She perched at the edge, back straight, legs crossed at the ankles, hands in lap. Stiff and defensively genteel, she tightened her lips and steeled herself for their conversation.

When asked if they would return to the church, Edward said, "We will have to see. We intend to visit more churches before we choose which one to join."

When Mike wasn't able to hide his disappointment, Edward continued. "I'm sure that your little church is fine. We really liked your preaching. It's just that...well, ah..."

"Tell him," his wife said.

"Rochelle, please."

When they both withdrew into silence, Mike turned to Rochelle and said, "Mrs. Snowden, if you have any helpful criticism, we'd appreciate hearing it."

"How can I say this delicately? We found some of your people rather... peculiar. There, it's out. You have peculiar people at your church. And that is all I am going to say about it. Please don't ask me to amplify."

Edward gave her a look that communicated that she had said too much already. Her return glare said, *Oh, shut up!*

On Mike and Sandy's ride home, Mike asked the question they had both been contemplating. "Do you think our church is filled with *peculiar* people?"

"I think we have our share. I suppose every church does."

"Yes," he agreed. "We have a few."

"A few?" Sandy laughed. "We have scads. Like Sheriff Andy Taylor in Mayberry, you are surrounded by Gomers, Gubers and Barneys."

He smiled. "Well, at least your analogy makes me the normal one."

"Did I say that? Andy only looked normal because he was surrounded by oddballs. If he would've lived anywhere but Mayberry, Andy would've been the peculiar one."

"Well, thanks, honey. Since the book of First Peter calls Christians God's 'peculiar people,' I'll take that as a compliment."

"Mike, That's one of the things I love about you. You are so easy to please."

"Seriously though. They say 'like attracts like.' If that's so, and if we have a lot of people that are a little... different, that could make church growth hard."

"Not if we target offbeat people." Sandy snapped her fingers with a flourish. "We could market ourselves as the perfect church for misfits. We could soon become the wackiest mega-church in America."

"That's your serious answer?"

"No, Mike, my serious answer is this. I don't know much about 'like attracting like.' But I do know that I like our people. And I also know that God loves them. And in my opinion, that's what counts most."

"Amen, Amen. Sandy, I think it's time you start writing my sermons."

"Besides," Sandy said. "I prefer our people to high brows like Mrs. Snodgrass back there."

"That's 'Snowden.' And because of that remark, you've just been removed as my sermon writer."

....

TWENTY-TWO

THE HARVESTWEEN FESTIVAL

Harvestween. The Social Committee collectively agreed this idea was golden.

The year before Harold Broadmoor had intruded into one of their committee meetings to challenge them to do something special for the next Halloween. "The 'Costal Church," his designation for the Assembly of God church next to his home, "is eating our lunch every Halloween. They've got this big deal in their parking lot with a blow-up bounce house, carnival game booths, spotlights shooting up into the sky and tons of free candy. It is a kid magnet. Parents all over Meanwhile bring their children."

Harold stopped, looked condescendingly at each person in the room, and said, "Now that's what we ought to be doing! But... what do we have? A Harvest Festival with a Pumpkin Pie Potluck. Now, I'm not saying that's a bad thing; heaven knows Harold T. Broadmoor loves pumpkin pie. It's just that we're the only ones enjoying it. We've got to go big and plan something that will draw in the masses." Broadmoor stood quickly to his feet and said, "Well, that's my two cents worth. Other than being a marketing guru, I'm no expert. But think about it." Then he was out the door.

*　*　*

To their credit, the Social Committee had thought about it for about a year. Each month the topic was on their agenda. It wasn't easy; this was a controversial issue with some of the same comments resurfacing each month:

"Halloween began with druid devil worship. It is associated with witchcraft. Churches shouldn't have anything to do with it..."

"Aww shucks, there ain't nothing wrong with it. We grew up trick-or-treating and the only harm done was tummy aches caused by too much candy..."

"But there will be an uproar if we drop our traditional Pumpkin Pie Potluck Harvest Festival..."

Finally, it was decided to merge the best of Halloween and the Harvest Festival into a special new event. "Like," someone said, "the guy who first put peanut butter and jelly together in a sandwich. That was genius."

"Or," another added, "Like the Hershey's company. They combined peanut butter and chocolate together into those little cups. Now that's even more genius!"

"Have you ever put peanut butter on ice cream? That's pure genius."

"That's stupid. That would ruin a good bowl of ice cream. And then there are those idiots that put peanut butter on celery. That would even make George Washington Carver sick."

They couldn't agree on peanut butter but they all liked the idea of the Harvestween Festival.

Starting at the beginning of October they did a publicity blitz that included announcements from the platform, blurbs in the bulletin, posters in the local *Wishy Washy Laundromat* and paid advertisements in the *Penny Saver*, a popular sales booklet that was distributed all over the county.

They announced that there would be a costume contest with the winner getting a free Bible. Pastor Mike and Sandy wanted to show their support so Sandy bought some fun costumes; he would be Spider-Man and she would be Supergirl. This proved to be a poor investment when it was later determined, that due to the possibility of people wearing inappropriate outfits, everyone should only come as Bible characters.

Of course there would still be the Pumpkin Pie Potluck but this year there would be an extra special dish:

"Harvestweenies." Hot dogs would come with wieners inside of orange buns. There would be two huge bowls of treats -- one filled with candy corn and the other, a nod to those with nutritional sensibilities, containing carrot sticks hand-carved to look just like the candy corn. The special feature would be Gerald Roberts, a ventriloquist from Northern Indiana.

And then, anticipating the throngs of unchurched neighbors that would be bustling in, the Social Committee created a large bowl filled with treats for all the trick-or-treaters. But instead of using candy, they decided to use heavenly treats. They took *tootsie rolls* out of their wrappings, replaced them with rolled-up evangelistic tracts, and called them *truthie rolls*. This would spread the gospel without causing cavities.

When October 31 came, they were ready. Betty Swenson, in the role of Lot's wife, came dressed as a giant saltshaker. She won the contest and was given a New Testament. Most everyone else just wore bathrobes and towels on their heads. Samson's companion, Delilah, was unfortunately required to go home and change.

Other than the fact that no one from the community came, it was a pleasant night. The pies were phenomenal, the Harvestweenies were a hit and the bowl of candy corn was emptied quickly. The *truthie rolls* could be easily saved for the following year and the bowl of carrots would be happily consumed by the Smith's horses.

Though a few families with children left early to head to the Assembly of God church, many stayed for the whole evening and remarked that the *Harvestween Festival* should be an annual event.

The star attraction, a ventriloquist, was quite late. Fortunately he finally arrived...

....

TWENTY-THREE

WHO'S THE DUMMY NOW?

"I'm sorry I'm late." Gerald Roberts came bustling into the church carrying a suitcase. "My car over-heated and I had to add some water from a creek."

"That's okay," Red Monkmeier replied. As the evening's Master of Ceremonies, he had been waiting nervously at the door for Gerald to arrive. "We're just glad you made it." He looked the teenager over and was impressed. Gerald was thin framed, close to six feet tall and had dark hair that swooped over his forehead. On his nose were black glasses. But it was his presence that was most noticeable. He had a confidence, a charisma, which flowed from him.

Looking at the suitcase, Red said, "I'll bet your puppet is in there."

"No," said a muffled voice that appeared to come from the suitcase, "I'm his dirty laundry."

Caught off guard, Red cocked his puzzled face to one side and said, "What?"

"Oh, never mind him," Gerald said, "He's just a wise guy. Now where would you like me to set up?"

"Come with me. We have a microphone set up in the fellowship hall. Everyone is ready so we will start right away."

When they walked in, everyone was already seated. They began clapping and Harold put his fingers into his mouth and gave a shrill whistle. Gerald gave them a smile and said, "Wow, you folks know how to give a friendly welcome."

Harold shouted, "It's good to have you here. Did your ventriloquist come, too?" As others gave him the "You are being inappropriate" look, he laughed loudly and elbowed Arnie in the side. Arnie said, "Ouch," and budged his chair further away.

Red pulled out a piece of paper and read, "I would like to introduce Gerald Roberts to our Harvestween Festival. He is a senior at Concord High School in Elkhart, Indiana and he goes to First Baptist Church there. This Fall he will be going to a Christian college to prepare for the ministry. He is a teen preacher and a ventriloquist." He then looked up at Gerald and said, "Don't pay any attention to Harold. We know you are the ventriloquist. Harold thinks that he's a comedian." Harold T. Broadmoor stood and blew kisses to the crowd.

Looking back at his notes, Red continued, "Gerald is active on the speech and debate teams at his high school and travels quite a bit doing skits for churches and youth groups. So, with no further ado, here is Gerald Roberts and his little friend."

Gerald's hand went into the open suitcase on the floor and out came a dummy wearing bright blue pants, a bow tie and a gaudy yellow jacket. It was obvious this was no department store sales item. Gerald soon had him winking, moving his eyes back and forth and curling his upper lip back into a smile. Instead of cracks on both sides of his mouth, the face had been formed with soft leather making it look more lifelike.

"Ladies and gentlemen, I would like to introduce Herkimer Heathcliff Vanderbilt the Third. But we'll just call him 'Herkie'."

"That's because he can't say 'Herkimer Heathcliff Vanderbilt the Third without moving his lips," the dummy said.

"So true," Gerald said, "and Herkie, these are the good people of Meanwhile Baptist Church."

"Are they the harvestweenies you were talking about?"

"Of course not, those are hotdogs over on the table," protested Gerald.

"Well, then," said Herkie, "who are these hotdogs in bathrobes? Is this a pajama party?"

"No," came some voices in unison, "we are dressed as Bible characters."

"You are characters, alright. Okay, let me guess who you are." Staring at a toddler next to her mother, he said, "I know who that little guy is. Nehemiah. Ha! Get it. 'Knee-high-Miah.'" Get it? Ha! And the baby over there has to be Bildad the Shuhite. 'Shoe-height?' Ha!"

As the people laughed, Gerald said, "Yes, we get it, Herkie. Real funny. Now let's move on to what we were going to talk about tonight. We were going to talk about your airplane ride."

"Not yet. I've got some more guesses to make. See that guy over there? The short, hairy guy?" He pointed his head at Ted Hansen. "I know what character he is. That's Potifer -- because he looks just like a pot-of-fur. Ha! Get it? Pot-of-fur!"

Since Ted was laughing, the people felt like it was okay to laugh along.

"That's enough, Herkie, you are going to offend someone," Gerald said.

"No, let me do one more. Hey, Harold!" The dummy stared at the man who had made the loud jokes during the introduction.

"Yes?" Harold said with a big smile. He liked being the center of attention.

Herkie said, "I know who you are!"
"Who?"

"You are Elisha. I can tell that because he was bald, too!"

Everyone roared but Gerald got a stern look on his face and said, "Now that's enough. It's not polite to make fun of a person who's thin on top."

"That's the only place he is thin," Herkie shot back. The people seemed to like the dummy teasing Harold so they laughed heartily.

But Gerald shouted, "Please, folks, don't encourage him. I don't want him being rude to people." He twisted the dummy's face in his direction and said, "Now Herkie, I want you to apologize to Harold." The ventriloquist turned to Harold and said, "Harold, would you mind coming up here so that Herkie can apologize real proper like."

"Aw shucks, Gerald, I know the little fellow was just funnin'. He don't need to apologize."

"Please, Harold, come up. This will be a learning experience for Herkie. I don't want him acting like a Jerkie."

In that he loved being front and center, Harold ambled to the front of the room.

"Thanks, Harold, now please take his hand and shake it until he apologizes. And Herkie, I want you to say 'I'm sorry.'"

"Gerald is sorry."

"Herkie!"

"Oh, okay," The dummy softened his voice and said, "Mr. Harold, I'm sorry..." He wiggled his ears and then added, "that you are so bald!"

"Herkie. Apologize."

"Ahhh, Mr. Harold, I am sorry..." Then he spun his head all the way around and shouted, "...that you are so fat! Grow some hair and you would look just like Santa Claus."

The audience was roaring and Harold was laughing right along with them. But Gerald held up his free hand to silence them and said, "Herkimer Heathclift Vanderbilt the Third, this is your last chance. Just say that you are sorry and nothing else. Got it?"

"Yes, sir. Mr. Harold, I am truly sorry."

Everyone expected another retort but none came so Harold said, "That's okay, you're forgiven."

Gerald said, "Thank you, Harold, for helping us during this moment of character formation. But I do have a question? Did you feel a little silly shaking hands with a dummy?"

Before Harold could answer, Herkie shouted, "I sure did!"

Harold said, "Huh?" while most of the crowd hooted and clapped. Carol Harmon was one exception. She suddenly stepped to her feet and said, "Excuse me." Since she was ignored, she shouted louder, "Excuse me!" When an awkward silence ensued, she went on to say,

"Men, women, children, we are not helping here. Young Mr. Roberts is trying to use a teaching moment to correct the inappropriate behavior of the little man on his knee but many of you are hindering that process. With your inane laughter you are reinforcing Herkimer's ill treatment of others. I love each of you dearly; you are all so special. But I have been rather disappointed in you tonight." She sat down and folded her arms across her chest.

Gerald shrugged his shoulders. "I'm sorry if my humor was a little cutting."

"It's not your fault." Carol responded. "It's that little guy on your lap."

"Ahem." Stan Glass got to his feet. "Let's not blame the doll. Gerald, you may continue but please don't use any more demeaning humor. That is the kind of humor the world uses to tear down others." Then he turned to Harold Broadmoor and said, "Harold, are you okay? If you feel wounded, we sympathize."

Harold guffawed and shouted, "You two need to lighten up. This is a ventriloquist skit, for Pete's sake. It's meant to be full of funny jokes and it has been. So stop interrupting." He pointed at the stage and said, "On with the show."

Pastor Mike let out a sigh of relief. He and Sandy were sitting towards the back of the room. They had no specific responsibilities in the program and had hoped to keep a low profile. But when Carol and Stan had interrupted the ventriloquist skit, Mike was afraid he was going to have to resolve things. He whispered to Sandy, "Thank goodness for Harold. I was afraid I was going to have to get up and get the train back on its tracks."

Gerald looked shell-shocked. "I'm sorry for making any of you uncomfortable. I will try to be more careful."

Herkie looked up at the ceiling and said, "You think you make them feel uncomfortable? You have your hand under the back of my shirt. I'm afraid that you are going to give me a wedgy."

"Herkie, before you get me in more trouble, tell me about your recent airplane ride."

"What do you want to know?"

"Well, what kind of plane was it?"

"It was a little two-seater with an open cockpit."

"You mean that it had no roof? That's scary. You might have fallen out."

"I did," the dummy shouted.

"Oh, that's too bad."

"No, that's good. I had a parachute."

"Oh, that's good."

"No, that's bad. It didn't open."

Gerald gasped. "That's bad."

"No, that's good, I had an emergency chute."

"That's good."

"No, that's bad, it didn't open either."

"Oh my, Herkie, that's bad."

"No, that's good. There was a haystack below me."

"That's good."

"No that's bad. There was a pitchfork in the haystack."

"A pitchfork in the haystack?" Gerald repeated. "That is bad."

"No, that's good. I missed the pitchfork."

"Oh, that is good."

"No, that is bad." The dummy paused for effect and then shouted, "I missed the haystack, too! With that, he bent quickly towards the floor and said, "Thump!"

The effect let people know that the skit was over and they gave applause. Gerald went on to give a spiritual application. "You know something, everyone? Just like Herkie depended upon a lot of different things like the parachute and the haystack to save himself, all of those things failed him in the end. In real life, people try a lot of different things to save their souls -- things like doing good works or going to church or being baptized. Now all those things are good. But none of them save anyone. The Bible says, 'For it is by grace you are saved, not of works, lest any man should boast.' It is only by putting your trust in Jesus Christ that someone can be saved." He went on to explore this theme for a further five minutes and then wrapped things up and put the dummy back into the case.

Red Monkmeier stood and thanked Gerald and led another round of applause. He also thanked the many workers who had worked so hard to organize the evening and finally brought the night to an end with a word of prayer.

While people were leaving, Harold pulled Red aside into the library. "Red, I've got to be honest with you. This evening was pretty lame. Now, don't get me wrong. You did a good job as an M.C. and the kid with the dummy was great and of course the pie was wonderful, but everything else was dullsville. You know what I mean?" Without waiting for a response, he went on. "But the worst thing was the lack of any effective publicity. Did you see anyone new here tonight? Did you?" Red started to shake his head while Harold went on, "They call this an outreach night but no one is doing any reaching out. You hearing me, Red?"

"Ah yes, I, ah..."

"Of course you are. You are with me. And I am going to be with you. I am here to volunteer my services. I may be a dummy, ha ha, but I am also a marketing genius. So this is what I suggest. You know the annual Christmas production that you always put on?"

"Yes," Red said. "It's become a cherished tradition around here."

"Is it going to be evangelistic this year?"

"You mean, will it be designed to share the good news about Jesus? If that's what you mean, then yes. I've already talked it over with the pastor and the theme is going to be 'The Perfect Gift.' We are going to show how we can receive the gift of eternal life by putting our faith in Jesus Christ as our Savior."

"Perfecto! Well, I am volunteering to be your co-producer and your publicity chairman. How does that sound? You ready for Harold T. Broadmoor to bring in the crowds?"

"Well, I appreciate your offer..."

"Then," Harold said, cutting in. "Let's shake on it and put on the best Christmas production this church has ever seen." He stuck out his hand and, after a short hesitation, Red shook it.

....

TWENTY-FOUR

A HAIRLINE FRACTURE

After the Klings had met twice with Counselor Carol, they informed her that they had been cured. She was quite pleased with her success. They were back in church and all appeared well.

But it wasn't.

Arnie and Marilyn had merely worked out a compromise -- of sorts. He agreed that she could continue to open her car window a crack. She agreed that he wouldn't turn on his wipers when she did.

Arnie didn't view the solution as a win/win; but at least he didn't have to go back to the "nutty counselor lady." He shuddered as the sound of her voice returned to his mind. During their sessions he had felt like road kill pecked by a crow.

He knew he had his problems. Lots of them. In particular, he wondered why he was losing his patience with Marilyn. Since his retirement he had become a more critical person. For some reason he was becoming easily irritated at her. *Am I turning into a faultfinder?*

When he was still working at the grain mill he could endure her idiosyncrasies. But now that he lived with them day and night, they became heavier. It was all little stuff – the pitch of her voice, the cracked window, her always having to have her own way... but it was all so vexing. First he would get annoyed with her and then he would get annoyed with himself for getting annoyed. "Arnie," he would scold himself, "don't let things get under your skin, just grow thicker skin."

But despite his self-chastisements, once again he fixated on a little thing. A hair. Just one—no longer than an inch or two -- but he couldn't stop looking at it. Lots of women had a little facial hair, which, in his mind, was just fine, but this one was black, curly and grew out of a mole on her chin.

He should focus on her perfectly fine nose, her soft brown eyes, or her thick salt and pepper hair. Why, his own head just had random tufts of hair; who was he to be critical of the facial hair? But his attention kept going back to the unattractive chin ornament.

It was that dang Harold T. Broadmoor who had made the obsession worse. Last Sunday while Arnie and Marilyn had been listening to one of Harold's jokes, Arnie noticed Harold staring at Marilyn and it bugged him big time. What was he looking at?

He suspected Harold was looking at *the hair!* Though it'd long bothered Arnie, he'd told himself that he was being petty and critical and that nobody else even noticed it.

But Arnie thought Harold was staring at it. He wanted to know for sure. He surprised himself by assertively pulling Harold aside and asking, "Why were you staring at my wife?"

Harold, in his typical style, shocked Arnie with blunt honesty. "I was just wondering why Marilyn doesn't cut that big, burly mole hair off. One snip and it would be gone."

"Harold," Arnie hissed, "you're out of line. How would you like it if I pointed out the flaws in your wife and suggested changes?

"Frankly, I would love Mother to make changes. I can't budge the woman. Maybe if you talked to her that would help. Mother, come here. Arnie has some helpful suggestions."

Arnie turned white. "I don't have any suggestions for anybody. Harold's being silly. He's a joker...."

The embarrassing conversation planted seeds in the minds of both men—seeds that would later bear bad fruit.

But Harold T. Broadmoor was right. The hair could easily be cut off. *Snip. Gone.*

Knowing Marilyn's hypersensitivity and not wanting to repeat the window affair, Arnie spent days developing a diplomatic way to present his suggestion.

He took her out to a real nice restaurant—Denny's—and treated her to the Spaghetti Special. After a lot of small talk, he finally gained the courage to throw out his well-rehearsed spiel.

"Honey, I want you to know that I still believe you're a very beautiful woman."

"Oh, Arnie, that's sweet."

This is going well, he thought. "Well, I mean it. You're quite fetching!"

Marilyn, looking flattered, pulled a compact from her purse and checked her face before she returned her attention to her husband. The interlude of vanity gave Arnie a chance to observe her. For some reason, he focused on her eyebrows. They'd been plucked with a ferocity that was impossible to ignore. The remaining arc of hair was so narrow that it appeared to have been drawn into place with a fine-tipped pen. If only she would pluck her chin while she worked on her eyebrows.

She snapped the compact shut and asked, "Don't you wish I was a little younger?"

He realized later that his expected line was something like, "You look as young as when I first fell for you. But what he said was, "Oh no. Old people like us belong together." He could tell at once that his swing was a strike.

But she was gracious enough to pitch to him again. "Don't you wish I was thinner?"

He was determined to hit this one. He couldn't allow his carefully built ambience to dissipate. He took her hand and gently said, "Oh Marilyn dear, the way I look at it, you're so beautiful, the more of you the better!" He smiled broadly – partly because he was trying to win her over and partly because he was proud of his quick wit.

She flashed a tight-lipped smile and scratched her chin as her eyes looked up at a plastic plant hanging in a nearby pot.

Her hand movement drew his attention to the despised hair. He felt weak. He didn't know if he could complete his mission. But he also knew that he didn't want to put out the money for another expensive meal later.

He reached for the colorful laminated card next to the napkin container. "Care for some dessert?"

"I better not. If I put on any more beautiful pounds you may not be able to control yourself."

Sarcasm or humor? He couldn't tell. He stayed silent.

But Marilyn pushed on. "If you could change anything about me, what would it be?"

What an opening! This couldn't be going better. "Wow. Now that's a hard one. Let me think." He puckered his eyebrows and took a drink of water. *Well here it goes.*

"Honey, you're so beautiful I can only think of one it-ty-bitty change. But it's so teeny-weeny it's hardly worth mentioning."

She pursed her lips. "Go ahead. Mention it."

Retreat! Retreat! From her manner he had picked up an ominous signal. "No, it's nothing. Let me just say again how happy I am with your appearance."

"No, no. Mention it. Mention it."

Pause. "Well..." Longer pause. "I've raised this before so it's probably not worth bringing up again..."

She waited, pinning him to his chair with her stare. He no longer had any choices here. There was no emergency chute, no plan B, and no other direction than forward.

"Dear, I just wish that you would cut off that hair on your chin. Really, it's such a simple thing..."

"Arnie!"

"All it would take is a quick snip and..."

"Arnie!"

"Now I know what you're going to say..."

"Arnie! I've already explained this before..."

"Yes, that's what I was saying. I know what you're going to say..."

"As I've already explained, if you remove a facial hair, more hairs will take its place and they'll be thicker than the first. Is that what you want? Do you want a wife with a beard? Do you want a circus freak? I'm sorry you hate a little hair that's almost invisible—that is invisible to everyone excepting the most critical—but it stays. Besides you're no one to talk—you with the forest growing out of your nose. It looks like you have a paint brush sticking out of each nostril."

Arnie determined to ignore the topic of his own nasal hairs and stay on target. "But Marilyn, your reasoning about cut hair coming back thicker is just an old wives' tale. An article in *Reader's Digest* says that that is a common myth."

"Myth smith! The old wife you're talking about is my mother. She was my information source. And I won't have her attacked. She was a good and wise woman – and quite knowledgeable about hairs on the face. She suffered herself, as you know. And my dear father, God rest his soul, never tried to take lather and razor to her. No sir, he appreciated the way God made her."

"I'm sorry I brought it up."

"Me, too. A wonderful night has been spoiled." She pushed away her plate of spaghetti.

"I told you that I think you are beautiful. And I love you."

"Then why..." she began, then tossed her head in disgust.

"Like I said, I'm sorry. Now let's calm down and finish our meals. It's not every day that we can splurge on the Spaghetti Special."

The silence on the car ride back to their house was broken only by the sound of the wind whistling through the cracked window.

Arnie determined he would never again bring up the mole hair. She was right. What was wrong with him? He loved his wife and love means overlooking the negatives. Like the Bible says, "Love bears all things." He would, he determined, bear the hair.

But in those future moments when his carnality got the best of him, his mind would return to the hair. Satan himself, Arnie believed, was pulling him down. The cruel tempter. "Get thee behind me!"

In church the next Sunday he thought he caught Harold T. Broadmoor looking at the hair again. *Invisible? No way! If Harold can see it, everyone must be looking at it. They are probably whispering things like 'Poor Arnie. How can he stand being married to a woman with a giant black curly hair growing out of a mole?'*

The thought made him so mad he felt like telling Harold T. off again. So he pulled him aside and said, "What's wrong with you? Get your eyes off my wife's mole hair! You're the one needing work. You should go on a diet. You are fat and even though you have long hair on the sides, on top you're even balder than I am."

"I'm not fat, just rotund."

"What's the difference?"

"People that are fat are squishy and flabby. That's not me. Here, feel my gut."

"Harold T., don't be gross. I'm not touching your stomach."

"Come on. I dare you. You're going to find that I'm no fatso. I'm solid as a rock. Nope, not fat; just big. And I have to be."

"Why so?"

"Cause I've got a big personality. It's so big it wouldn't fit in a small container."

"That's ridiculous."

"No sirree. That's just the way it be. Now you wouldn't understand that because you've got a puny little personality. Why it's so small that it must roll around inside of you like a marble in a barrel. I'll bet that if I shook you I would hear a rattle. But enough of that, we shouldn't argue, we're in the same boat and we should empathize with each other."

"Same boat?"

"Why, sure. Your missus could improve her looks with one little snip, but she refuses. And Mother is a real looker but she could even be more of a doll if she would spruce herself up. But no, her parents drilled it into her not to draw attention to herself, so she goes around like a plain Jane. Pity. She's missing out on so much. And so am I. And you, too. Arnie, I wish there was something that could be done."

Arnie should have done nothing.

But he did do something—something stupid. He did something stupid that night.

He was watching TV in bed. Marilyn was sleeping. That was something he appreciated about her. Many wives would send their husbands to another room to watch the tube but she didn't mind it being on. *She was such a good wife. Why obsess over cracked windows and little hairs?* She said she could sleep through anything. Her exact words were "If I have said it once, I've said it a thousand times (Arnie believed that she probably had said it a thousand times), I could sleep through a tornado."

After getting up to use the bathroom, as he did a couple times a night, he returned to his bed. Before getting in, however, he was caught by a troubling sight. There in the blue light of the flickering television was Marilyn's sleeping profile. And yes, there was the hair.

He whispered the oft-repeated thought: "It could easily be cut off. *Snip. Gone.*"

The evil plan was immediately clear. She wouldn't know it was him. She wouldn't know it even happened. After all, *she could sleep through a tornado.* In the morning she would assume the hair just fell out in the night. That happens all the time. Hairs fall out.

She may not even miss it. If it was really so invisible, what was to miss?

A foolproof plan. Time to act. He scurried to the bathroom for a pair of scissors. He found them in one of Marilyn's drawers under a pile of brushes. As he reached for them he noticed some tweezers next to them. They would be even better! The scissors would leave a stub. He picked up the tweezers and headed for Marilyn...

The next morning Marilyn scheduled an emergency marriage counseling appointment with Counselor Carol.

....

TWENTY-FIVE

THE FINAL APPOINTMENT

"**B**ut all I did was pluck a little hair," Arnie said with a weary voice. For twenty minutes he had listened to Marilyn tell Counselor Carol how he'd physically abused her the night before.

"Arnie, you need a reality check." Carol looked at him hard. "If it was just a little hair, you would have never jerked it out of your dear wife's face. No, it was a big hair."

"It wasn't that big," Marilyn said.

"Marilyn, please, didn't you ever look in the mirror? It was the size of a redwood. But that's not what I'm talking about." She returned her gaze to Arnie.

"Arnie, it wasn't just a big hair, physically. It was a big hair, metaphorically. When you pulled it, you tore off a piece of your wife's personhood. You dismembered part of who she is. Do you understand what I'm saying?"

"No, I guess I don't." With a whine he repeated his earlier claim, "I just pulled a little hair."

"Arnie, Arnie, Arnie." Carol rolled her eyes." Quit the denial. Anyone could see that hair across the church!"

Marilyn put her hand to her breast and gasped.

"But -- and listen to me, Marilyn—that wasn't a bad thing. It showed your beauty. Listen to me, Arnie; it showed Marilyn's beauty. Are you with me?"

"It showed Marilyn's beauty?"

"That's absolutely right, Arnie. It showed Marilyn's beauty—her inner beauty. Most people would have removed such a long, curly hair, but not Marilyn. She refused to cater to society's tastes. She would not bow to our culture's definition of beauty. No, she defied all of that because she would not surrender her identity. She would not betray her sense of self. She would not allow her uniqueness to be crushed.

"Marilyn, I applaud you."

"Well, thank you," Marilyn said hesitantly. She crossed her legs.

"You are most welcome. But you deserve all of this tribute and more. Most people would have been ashamed to go out of the house with a thing like that sticking off their chins, but not you. You didn't let people's stares and giggles bother you. You determined that the hair was a quintessential part of your essence. It was what made Marilyn, Marilyn. You were the lady with the hair... the special lady with the special hair. Bravo, Marilyn!"

"Oh fiddle-faddle. I don't think there were stares and giggles," Marilyn said.

"How very precious! You are so secure in yourself that you were oblivious to everyone's derision. Yes, you are a special lady.

"And you, Arnie. Tssk, tssk. When you attacked that special hair, you attacked that special person. It was like taking a knife and cutting into the Mona Lisa. Look at your mate and think of what you have done."

Arnie turned to Marilyn. Though he hadn't seen a hint of blood, she wore gauze and a large bandage on her chin.

"I'm sorry," he muttered, "but I think you two are making a mountain out of a mole hill."

"Do you hear him?" Marilyn said shrilly, "not only is he unrepentant, but now he is ridiculing my mole. It is just a little thing. It is no mole hill."

"I wasn't referring to your mole, I was just..."

"You were just minimizing your hateful deed, that's what you were doing." Carol gave him a cold stare and then continued. "Arnie, you need to own up to your offense and give your wife a big apology."

Arnie squirmed. The way they looked at him made him feel like sludge. They were right, he suddenly determined, he was a bad man who had done a bad thing. Tears came to his eyes. With a quivering voice, he choked out an expression of regret.

"Marilyn, I am truly sorry. I beg your forgiveness. I have good intentions but I sin and fall short. My feet are made of clay, I confess it."

"Well, if you really mean it, I suppose I could forgive..."

"Not so fast!" Carol shouted, cutting off Marilyn. "Listen, mister, you're not getting off that easy. I said, 'a big apology.'"

"What do you want me to say? I'm genuinely sorry." In his nervousness, he picked at a scab on his scalp and examined the crust under his fingernails.

"It's not what," she said slowly, "it's where -- and to whom. I want you to make a public apology in front of the whole church."

Arnie gasped.

"Oh, that won't be necessary," Marilyn said quickly.

Arnie's appreciation for his wife surged.

"But it is necessary. There is a principle here: 'private offense, private apology; public offense, public apology.'"

"But he did it to me in the privacy of our bedroom. And look," she said, tearing off her bandage, "there's no real damage."

"He pulled out the special hair that made you, you. Since you belong to all of us, so did that hair. It was a public hair. In effect, he pulled out our 'hair.' Arnie has hurt all of us. When you show up for church on Sunday, people will notice. They will be thinking, 'where is the hair? Marilyn just isn't the same without it. Where is our special Marilyn?' No, this isn't up for debate. I'll arrange it with the pastor. Arnie is going to give a public apology."

Arnie felt horrified and the look that gripped Marilyn's face showed that she shared his terror. It was obvious to him that she'd never realized before today what a spectacle her hair had been. A public apology would draw even more attention to it, or, due to the circumstances, the lack of it.

Marilyn took Arnie's hand and said, "But, Carol..."

"No arguments. This case is settled. Arnie, work on the wording of your apology. I'll schedule it for Sunday morning. And now, Marilyn, I need to share some difficult news with you.

What could be more difficult than what she had already heard? Arnie thought.

"Your hair, despite its inherent specialness, could mean trouble."

"Trouble?"

"Giving sobering news isn't easy, but it's a necessary responsibility that goes along with being a caring professional. Since your phone call this morning, I checked my medical library and found that your hair might indicate serious medical problems."

"Oh, I don't think so. My mother had some facial hairs as well, and she lived a good long life."

"Is she dead now?"

"Well, yes..."

"Oh my, oh my. Arnie, I want you to move close to your wife and hold her. She may need your support as I lay out some of the dire medical possibilities."

He scooted over and put his arm around Marilyn but he could feel her tense under his touch. He didn't like any of this.

"Marilyn, female facial hair can be a family trait – an unconventional genetic thing that just happens."

"Yes, I think that's what it is. As I was saying about my dear mother..."

"And the phenomenon is also pretty common after the change of life. But, Marilyn, there are other possibilities you must hear about."

"Thank you for the information, Carol," Marilyn said, "That's all fascinating but now we'd better be going."

"You feel uncomfortable with this, don't you, Marilyn? Hold her tighter, Arnie, there's more that she needs to hear." The counselor took a deep breath and looked down at a set of notes. "While unusual, serious conditions might be at work. Tumors of the ovary and the adrenal glands, polycystic ovarian disease and Cushing's disease can all promote male pattern hair growth. Marilyn, these are remote possibilities. But they are possibilities, nonetheless. They cannot be ignored. Hence, I recommend – no, I insist on – two courses of action.

First, you must see a doctor for a physical examination and a few blood tests. You're probably wondering if I can do this for you, but, although I am a caring professional, I'm not certified to conduct these particular medical procedures. So you need to go to an M. D. Second, we need to take a proactive spiritual step. Since we have a healing God, we should have a healing service just in case there's a serious problem."

"A healing service?" the Klings said in tandem.

"Yes, just to be on the safe side, we should have a healing service. On Sunday, after Arnie's public confession, we will invite the church leaders to come forward and lay on hands while I, or the pastor if he so insists, anoints you with oil."

Arnie and Marilyn wagged their heads. "Carol," Marilyn said with a warbled self-pity, "we simply couldn't do what you're suggesting."

"Absolutely not," Arnie enjoined, "Marilyn is right. We simply couldn't do any of that."

"With the power of God you can, and you will. It will be a wonderful service that our church will never forget. It will be a marvelous time." She clapped her hands. "You will never feel so loved. Now you two scoot along and I will arrange everything with the pastor."

"But, Carol..."

"I'm sorry. Time is up. Besides I have a lot of work to do to prepare for Sunday."

She ushered them and their protests out the door.

She was made for this, Carol thought. Her prescribed therapeutic action steps were just what the Klings needed to bring about marital, spiritual and physical healing. When all of this was finished, she planned on writing an article about it for some Christian psychiatric journal.

She wished her ex-husband could see her now that she was a success. He had never believed in her. When he had left her....

TWENTY-SIX

....

LETTER BOMBS

When Mike returned to the church after a lunch appointment, he found a blue envelope taped to the door of his office. On it was written, "Reverend Michael Lewis." He opened it and read the following typed note:

Dear Pastor,

When Carol Harmon contacts you about our participating in a public church service, please inform her that we have chosen not to do so. In fact, we will not be attending Meanwhile Baptist Church any longer. We will not be part of a church that humiliates its members. Tell Carol that we no longer have any use for her services. We further desire that no one (including yourself) call or visit us. We just want to be left alone.

Sincerely Yours,
Arnold and Marilyn Kling

Slowly laying the note on the desk as if he was afraid it might break, Mike covered his face with his hands and squeezed out a long sigh between his palms. "What in the world?" he wondered out loud.

While he pondered his response, he noticed a blinking light on the answering machine. It was a phone message from Carol asking him to call her right away. You bet he was going to call her.

"Carol."

"Pastor Mike, how are you doing?"

"Currently, I'm not doing well." He went on to read the note. "Can you give me any idea where this is all coming from?"

"Hmmm. No, not really. I recently met with them and thought the appointment went really well."

"When did you meet with them?"

"This morning," she admitted. "But like I said, it went well. Super, in fact."

"What did you talk about? And what was this about their participation in some public service?"

"Mike, I'm not sure I like your tone of voice. And I don't have to answer your questions. Doing such might betray confidentiality."

"If you tried to get them active in a public church service, I have a right to know what is going on. Apparently something was discussed that made them so uncomfortable that they won't return to church."

"Now that's unfair. Nothing that I recommended would have led to their humiliation. I had a great plan that would have liberated them from their burdens and provided acceptance by the body." As Carol spoke her voice gained a growing confidence. "No, I'm certain that this is not my fault. Maybe you offended them in some way. You know how you can be. I hope you haven't ruined my therapy procedure for the Klings. I assure you that everything done and said in our sessions was all designed for their mental and spiritual improvement. I am a professional."

"Carol, taking a little class and reading a few books doesn't make someone a professional." He regretted his comment as soon as he said it. At least part of him did.

"Shame. Shame. Shame. Now you are attacking me."

"I'm sorry, but –"

"You are sorry. Right now you are a sorry excuse for a shepherd. I think we better discontinue this conversation until you are thinking more sensibly and speaking with more sensitivity." There was a click.

Well, that went well. He used both hands to mess up his hair and then called her back. "Carol, I am sorry that I offended you but we really need to talk."

She said nothing.

"You left a message on my machine saying you had something to tell me. Can we at least discuss that?"

"No, thank you, Pastor Lewis. I don't feel comfortable with this conversation at this time." And she hung up again.

"No," he said to a dial tone, "thank you."

He read the note again and decided to call the Klings. This was a hopeless situation. If he called them, he might get scolded for not following their request to leave them alone. But if he did nothing, they may just vanish into the night thinking that he didn't even care enough to pursue them.

"What?" the normally sweet Mrs. Kling said sharply.

"Hello Marilyn, this is Pastor Mike."

"I'm sorry, pastor, but I thought our letter made it clear that we no longer desire to have contact with you or anyone else from Meanwhile Baptist Church. Have a good day but please don't call back." And she hung up.

Why is everyone hanging up on me today? Mike slammed the receiver up and down a few times just to get the feel. "Well, what do you know, that is kind of fun," he said to no one.

He opened up his file cabinet and dropped the note into a file entitled "Letter Bombs." He had another file entitled "The Smile File" that was filled with encouraging letters. He wished that was the file he had opened today.

The Letter Bombs file held a half dozen letters. Most were unsigned. One chastised him for not always using the King James Version. It harangued him for being a neo-evangelical and asked if he was pushing for a one-world, new age church.

There were three, probably from the same person, complaining that Meanwhile Baptist Church was deserting the values of the historic church by using nontraditional music. He glanced through some of those letters and read choice quotes:

"Hymns are the marching music of the old-time religion. And if they are good enough for our fathers, they are good enough for me..."

"Contemporary Christian music is nothing more than secular rock and roll with a few Hallelujahs thrown in. Why do we borrow our music from the world rather than from heaven?"

"I was pleased that we only sang hymns last night. But unfortunately, the words were put up on a screen using an overhead projector. I felt like I was in a movie theater. If they aren't sung out of a hymnal, they don't count."

"When the guy doing special music pulled out a guitar, I almost walked out. I was afraid that he would start gyrating his hips like Elvis. I predict that pre-marital pregnancies will escalate in our church."

And then there was a poem:

> "Come, We That Love the Lord"
> and sing hymns about the Word.
> "O Come, All Ye Faithful"
> and cling to the traditional.
> "All Hail the Power of Jesus Name"
> Don't just play the latest church game.
> Celebrate the "Rock of Ages"
> Not rock and roll that rages...

The poem went on for three pages. He sympathized with the writer. He, too, had grown up with hymns and appreciated the role they had played in his spiritual formation. He still loved them. But he didn't want to confuse his dedication to God with a commitment to a cultural style of music. Nor did he appreciate a selfish personality that demanded one's musical likes be satisfied to the exclusion of the preferences of others. It was even worse when the selfishness was cloaked in a poorly reasoned spirituality.

Another letter complained the church wasn't friendly enough. Everyone just hung out with cliques. Maybe he as the pastor should preach a sermon series about snobbery.

And then, of course, there was a letter from Stan Glass. At least he signed his name. It suggested that his preaching could be sharpened by listening to preaching "giants." A tape was enclosed that had a sermon by Dr. E. B. "Bobby" Baddington. Bobby was a full-energy, high-volume preacher who started with stories that made you laugh and ended with stories that made you cry. Mike enjoyed some of those parts. But sandwiched in between was a message on prophecy that was built on inaccurate Bible study and wild imagination. In one case, Dr. Baddington counted the number of words in a verse and said that numerology suggested Christ would return in April.

Stan thought this kind of preaching was deep. *Deep?* In Mike's opinion Baddington would drown in a theological puddle. Stan's letter said, "Dr. Bobby goes below the surface level of passages to reveal truths that most miss." Mike thought Baddington revealed truths that didn't exist. He was tempted to return the tape to Stan with a note that said, "Since Dr. Bobby missed the date of Christ's return, what do you think of him now?"

He closed the file cabinet and thought again about the Klings. He decided to give them a little space and hope they would be more open for a contact after they had softened. Though their "clingy" ways could be irritating, he loved them and would miss them.

....

TWENTY-SEVEN

THERAPY WITH
DR. MITTEN

"Carol, taking a little class and reading a few books doesn't make someone a professional." *Those were the pastor's exact words.* No paraphrase. No spin. An exact quote.

Carol Harmon paced back and forth across her small living room. As she walked faster, the room grew smaller. Soon she felt so squeezed that she had to get out. She grabbed her coat and mittens from the closet and hurried out the front door.

"Tell Carol that we no longer have any use for her services." That's what the note had said—the note the pastor had read to her. And, as she rehearsed his narration in her mind, she thought he had read it with a smug tone of voice. Smug.

"Smug, smug, smug, smug, smug, smug." Her words matched her rapid steps down sidewalk. They stopped when her toe caught on a piece of cracked concrete and she stumbled. She turned around and stomped on the crack. "No use for my services?" she said out loud. Then she stomped again and continued her frenzied walk.

"You invest your valuable time—for free, no less—in the service of others and do you get gratitude? No, you get rejection." She didn't care if anyone saw her talking to herself. It wasn't healthy to stuff your feelings and hold them in. You need to let them out.

"With a heart of compassion and a spirit of sacrifice, I have offered my counseling gift repeatedly to people in this church and they have spurned me. Then, after the high and mighty reverend pastor can't do anything with the Klings, he refers them to me. I give them my heart, my time, my wisdom, my counsel and then what? They send a cruel letter, not to me, but to the pastor, saying that they have no use for me."

She could visualize the letter. Written in large caps. In red ink. Full of exclamation points. And then she imagined the pastor reading it over the phone to her. Veins were popping out on his forehead. His eyebrows were butted low over his beady eyes and his lips were snarled. Then, of course, he had to amplify the evil letter by reading it with a loud, condescending voice. Totally smug.

"Smug, smug, smug, smug, smug, smug, smug."

She halted at the Banfield Park, a small lot that had some playground equipment for the kids of the neighborhood. It had been a long time since she had been on any of those toys but the swing set called her over and she accepted the invitation. It took a while for her to catch the rhythm but when she did, she swung faster and higher than she had ever swung in her life. The cold wind whipped through her hair and stung her face, causing her eyes to tear up and her nose to run. She came to a stop and used a Kleenex from her coat pocket to blow her nose and dab at her eyes. But the tears continued. It wasn't just the wind; she was crying. With her elbows around the swing chains she hugged herself and allowed an escalation into loud, jerky sobs.

"No use for her services," She said robotically.

"I could use someone's services right now. I could use a good therapist. I could use a Counselor Carol."

She looked at her mitten and randomly thought that if she put some button eyes on it, it would look like a puppet. It looked back and said, "Yes, you could. Everyone could be helped by a little therapy—even you."

Carol looked around to see if anyone was watching. She didn't really mind if others saw her talking to herself but carrying on a conversation with your hand might be perceived as eccentric. Fortunately, there was no audience. And although she knew she was just talking with a hand puppet, she thought the role play might be therapeutic. So she asked, "Dr. Mitten, do you think you can help me?"

"Not directly, but I think I can help you help yourself. Tell me why you came to me today."

"I don't know where to start."

"Start anywhere. We can stitch the pieces together later. Just let your words flow. I'm listening."

His voice sounded so empathetic she felt a freedom, no, a compulsion, to share her feelings. "Doctor, I haven't had an easy life. I grew up an only child to older parents. It was often lonely."

"Awwww."

"But I loved them and I know they loved me."

"That was a gift."

"It was; it really was. But as great as they were, I think I grew up in my own little world. And then that world came to an end during my early twenties when they both died."

"Then you really felt alone?" Dr. Mitten asked.

"I did."

"That must have been so hard."

"It was." Tears came to her eyes and Dr. Mitten gently wiped them away.

"I was very vulnerable and I..."

There was a long silence but the doctor did nothing to hurry her. Carol looked around at the bare gray trees sparsely clothed with a few clumps of dead brown leaves. She got up from the swing and went over to a merry-go-round and sat. Her arm wrapped around a steel handle bar and Dr. Mitten was now eye level and very close.

"You were very vulnerable?"

"Yes, and I... I married the wrong man. He wasn't a Christian. We were so different. We didn't even have compatible personality types. We were just wrong for each other. He had a lot of problems and all my attempts to help him change just made him angry and distant. It was partly my fault; I fear that I wasn't very tactful."

"And?"

"And he left me."

Dr. Mitten patted her shoulder. "Oh, my sweet, sad child."

"I fought the divorce and begged for us to do marriage counseling, but he kept saying that it was too late and that he had had enough."

"Carol, outside of the loss of a child, I don't know if there is anything harder than an unwanted divorce -- and in some ways it is even more difficult because of the feelings of rejection that are piled on top of the grief."

"Exactly. Not many people understand that. Then there is also the shame and blame baggage. That's why I have kept my divorce secret from the church. I just tell them I have always been 'solo' to avoid the issue."

"Hmmmmm."

"I know. I know. A tad deceitful and guarded. Whatever. Anyway, to fast-forward everything, I moved here

to Meanwhile because the school district had a job opening for a crossing guard and then I started all over again.
I returned to church and got more serious about God. I
read the Bible and tons of self-help books and I remade
myself. Then I went to a Sunday School convention at
the Cobo Hall in Detroit and took a lay counseling
course that was revolutionary for me. Suddenly it felt
like my life had purpose again."

"You discovered your calling?"

"Yes, my calling. I believed that God had called me to
help people with problems -- people like my ex-husband.
But maybe I was wrong."

"Wrong?"

"It appears that I may have been dreadfully wrong. I
keep trying to help people and they just get mad at me. I
offer to counsel people in the church and they get
weirded out and then avoid me. And now, just when I
think I have really done a great job diagnosing the marriage problems of the Klings and providing a brilliant
therapeutic strategy plan, they get in a huff and leave the
church."

"They didn't just leave the church, they left *who*?"

"I'm not sure what you are asking."

"I think you do," said Dr. Mitten.

Carol sniffed and said, "They left me."

"Your parents left you through death. Your husband
left you through divorce. And now in the church, people

are leaving you through rejection. Is that a fair representation of your feelings?"

"Oh, doctor, I've never thought of that angle before. You are remarkable."

"No, Carol, you are the remarkable one. I'm just asking the right questions that are opening the doors to your own innate wisdom."

Almost feeling envious, Carol marveled at him at his counseling skills. He was, she had to admit, a much better counselor than herself. He drew answers out of her, while she, in her typical approach, tended to push her answers on to her clients. Perhaps he could be her mentor? But that would have to wait. Now she had to deal with her own issues.

"Well, that explains my feelings," Carol continued, "but I still question my calling. I am getting no affirmation from the people in the church or the pastor. And now that I finally get a chance to do some real counseling, it blows up."

"Carol, you are taking responsibility for the actions and attitudes that only the Klings should own."

"Meaning?"

"I mean this. If the Klings had chosen to follow your counsel, do you think it would have helped them?"

"I do. I definitely do."

"Then?"

"Dr. Mitten, I see where you are going. I can't blame myself for their refusal to follow good counsel. I am not a miracle worker. I can only point people in the right direction and it is up to them to decide to go that way or return to the paths that have always led to failure."

Dr. Mitten nodded. Carol thought that his little mitten lips had a small smile.

"But what about the pastor?"

"Maybe he has insight that you could listen to? Think about it. But maybe he is just young and insecure. Threatened by your greater counseling skills, possibly? Perhaps he has a chauvinistic bent and thinks you don't know what you are doing because you are a woman. And maybe he even has some dark spiritual problems and is being used as a tool of the devil."

Carol shuddered. "Doctor, I think you are on to something."

"Now be careful, Carol. I have no way of knowing what's in the pastor's heart; I'm just laying out some possible scenarios. Just give some thought to it."

"I definitely will." She pursed her lips and nodded slowly. "I definitely will. But that still presents the problem of the rest of the church. When you have a spiritual gift, I think it should be matched by the affirmation of God's people."

"Usually, Carol, but not always. I have heard many a story about missionaries who received no support from their home churches but went on to have excellent ministries. Even Jesus said that a prophet is without honor in his own country."

"True."

"And let me ask you this, how can people evaluate something they have never seen?"

"I'm following you. They have never seen me counseling so they have no confidence in me. If they could only see me in action."

"But?"

"But that's impossible because counseling is a private, confidential affair. So I am in a conundrum."

"Conundrum. I like that word, Carol. You have an excellent vocabulary."

Carol felt her face flush. It was flattering being complimented by an intelligent doctor.

"You are so sweet. I wish everyone –like the pastor, for example—was as gracious as yourself. But now back to the conundrum. How can I let people see me in action?"

"Carol, look at me. What do you see?"

"I see Dr. Mitten."

"What do you really see?"

Carol hung her head and sadly said, "I see my hand in a mitten."

"Don't be dejected. If I thought that you believed that I was real, I would really be worried about you. You have a firm sense of reality and that is absolutely wonderful. But, even though that is the case, has this role play still been valuable?"

"It has been invaluable."

"Is there any way that you could devise a means for other people to see you role playing a counseling situation? Then, perhaps, they would get a glimpse of your genius and come to you for counseling."

"I don't know. What do you have in mind?"

"That's not for me to tell you. That is for you to discover. Remember, I'm only here to help you help yourself. And now, my precious friend, I think our time is up." Dr. Mitten went into Carol's pocket.

Carol Harmon walked slowly back to her house at quite a different pace from the one that had brought her to the park. Her mind was full of brainstorms. How could she give the members of Meanwhile Baptist Church a demonstration of her counseling skills?

As she approached her home, she stumbled over the same sidewalk crack that had tripped her up earlier. "I am such a klutz," she said.

Muffled chuckles came from her pocket. "Yes, you are."

"Dr. Mitten, you hold your tongue."

"I don't have a tongue."

They both cracked up.

TWENTY-EIGHT

··

COUNSELING THE DUMMY

Just as Carol was drifting off to sleep that night, the idea came. A big idea. An *intuitive, inspirational insight.*

She'd been thinking about the public role play idea given to her by Dr. Mitten and wondered if she could do a simulation skit with someone. But who would be willing to do that with her? No one, that's who. Then she even thought about using Dr. Mitten but she knew he was a private person and would never agree. And even if he did, she feared that an act with a mitten might be perceived as odd by some—that's just the way some people are. But, she felt she was on the right track.

That's when she remembered the recent Harvestween Festival with teen-aged ventriloquist Gerald Roberts and his dummy, Herkemer Heathcliff Vanderbilt, the III. It wasn't necessarily a good memory. She hadn't been in the mood to indulge in the *frivolous funnies* that were filling the church with laughter. Instead she was studying her *Christian Counselor's Pocket Encyclopedia* and dreaming about the day when she would have a full-time practice. The laughter had interrupted her thoughts. *How irritating!* She looked around at everyone with the thought, *There, but for the grace of God, go I!* It was important to be patient and humble. Then she started listening and discovered that little guy was using demeaning humor and that the people were encouraging him. She had felt it necessary to reprimand them. Being a counselor is a heavy burden.

She almost left, but first she gave Herkey one of those "you're-out-of-line" looks. At that very moment, the mannequin winked at her—right at her. She felt a chill go through her. It wasn't an amorous wink; it was a knowing wink. *It was a message.* She looked at him intently, searching for meaning but found none—none until now.

The *intuitive, inspirational insight* had arrived.

* * *

That Sunday Red Monkmeier spared no enthusiasm when he, in the evening service, made a theatrical announcement. "Tonight, instead of special music, we have a giant surprise. This is a surprise so big that not even the pastor knows about it. Tonight, on this very stage, we are going to welcome a brand new guest to our church. His name is Jerubbabel and he comes to us with his friend, Carol Harmon."

Seated at the back of the platform, Mike grimaced. Anything Carol did made him nervous, but he couldn't imagine what she was going to do with some guy named Jerubbabel.

Carol stepped through a door from a side room off the stage. In her arms was an inexpensive, ventriloquist dummy. It was a "Jerry Mahoney" model she bought at Kmart.

Mike managed to stifle a groan.

"Ladies and gentlemen, I would like to introduce you to a new acquaintance."

"Hi," said the dummy with a deep, guttural voice, "my name is Jerubbabel." Carol's lips moved with every word, but they practically bounced when she said his name.

"Tell me, Jerubbabel, why have you come to talk to me today?"

"I came to talk to you about my problems."

"Why me, Jerubbabel?"

"Because, Miss Harmon, I understand you are a gifted counselor."

"That's quite the compliment, Jerubbabel. I accept it humbly not because there is something extraordinary about me, but only because the gift of which you speak was given to me by God. It's not something that comes naturally, it's a supernatural endowment from heaven itself."

"How true," the dummy said.

"This gift to me is actually a gift to others that is given through me. Recognizing the responsibility that I bear, I have attempted to hone this tool with additional training. I am now a certified counselor who longs to help people break free of their problems so that they can accelerate their spiritual and psychological progress."

In the pews, members of the congregation stole glances at one another, perplexed. *What?*

"Miss Harmon," Jerubbabel said with deep emotion, "that's what I want. I need to break free from my problems."

"Go with that," Carol responded empathetically. "And please just call me Counselor Carol."

She squared her shoulders toward Jerubbabel, leaned forward, and gave him complete eye contact. Mike guessed that she was displaying the physical listening skills she learned in her counseling class.

"Counselor Carol, I struggle with an inferiority complex."

"Jerubbabel, that's a common malady. Even I've wrestled with bouts of insecurity about my significance. I truly feel your pain."

"Thank you, I can tell you really care."

"Let's probe some root causes to your problem, Jerubbabel. When is your complex the most severe?"

"Well, I often feel low self-esteem when people call me a dummy."

Expecting this to be a humorous skit, the congregation was waiting for an opportunity to laugh. And with this line, they took it -- especially the kids. It was a mistake. Carol arrested the audience with a stare and then began a lecture.

"Jerubbabel has done a brave thing being transparent with his feelings. Laughing at him could cause a major setback."

Now it was the adults who laughed. They didn't believe Carol was serious.

Her face became red but it was the dummy that gave voice. "Stop it!" he yelled. Then turning to Carol, he said, "They're laughing at me again. They're not laughing with me, they're laughing at me."

"How does that make you feel?" She asked.

"It makes me feel bad. Bad and sad. It makes me feel like a nobody."

Carol turned to the audience and began to scold them. "Do you see what you have done? Do you? Due to your insensitivity, Jerubbabel feels like a bad, sad nobody. Is that how Christians are supposed to act?" She stared at them as though she expected an answer. But they took their chastisement with mute silence. Each was afraid that the slightest smile would sic Carol on them.

Mike, however, was struggling on the stage behind her. This absurd drama was causing an eruption of hilarity to well up within him. But he shut his eyes and managed to hold it in.

"Jerubbabel, you are not a sad, bad nobody; you are special... very, very special."

At that, Mike looked out at the audience and saw Beth Kurick shiver, stoop forward and look at the floor. Beth had told Mike about the night that Carol had used the "special" speech on her. Mike, too, had heard it repeatedly. But hearing it applied to a dummy had a different effect on him than it did on Beth. In bemusement, he began to shake. He folded his arms across his chest in an attempt to still his body and prayed for self-control. He even tried to sober himself by visualizing tragic events.

He thought he'd succeeded when Carol continued. "Jerubbabel, repeat after me, 'I am special.' Mike squeaked as tears swelled up around his eyes.

Then he made his big mistake. He looked at Sandy just as the dummy repeated, "I AM SPECIAL!" Sandy looked like she was ready to pop. Both hands were covering her mouth but her glance at Mike said it all. She broke his self-control and Mike busted out in laughter.

The audience took his example as permission and burst forth as well.

Carol looked like someone had just kicked her mother. She spun around and shouted, "Pastor, please!" But he couldn't have stopped if a gun was pointed at his head. He rocked back and forth choking on his chortles.

Then the dummy's head turned completely backwards toward him and shouted, "SHUT UP! SHUT UP! SHUT UP!"

This only caused him to laugh louder. Mike had now reached the point where he struggled to catch a breath. Hysteria snagged others as well. Bert Van Dyke fell off his pew and rolled onto the floor of a side aisle. The volume in the building kept growing.

Carol stood and shouted, "Stop it! What's wrong with you people?"

This only egged them on. So, in frustration, she flung her hands in the air. This resulted in Jerubbabel's dummy head flying out of his body, ricocheting off the organ and bouncing on the floor.

Carol jumped up and down. "Look what you've done. You've killed him. You've killed Jerubbabel!"

Then she picked him up, a piece in each hand, stalked down the center aisle, and out of the rear of the sanctuary. Stan Glass, one of the few people who had seen no humor in the night, followed her and gave empathetic support. Harold T. Broadmoor also surfaced with encouragement. "Carol, your material was weak tonight but I was impressed with your theatrical skills. I've got a part for you in the 'The Perfect Gift' big-time Christmas production. It's just the right role for you. You are going to be a star."

After the hullabaloo fizzled out, Mike struggled to preach. Five minutes into the sermon someone, thinking about the dummy skit, snickered and started a new wave of laughter. Mike settled them down and tried again. But when the pattern reoccurred, he gave a *Cliff's Notes* version of the message and closed the service early.

TWENTY-NINE

THE STING

W hen Carol Harmon attended the Wednesday night prayer meeting, people acted surprised to see her. That baffled her. Did they think she would leave the church or start playing hooky after her Sunday night public humiliation? *Not her!* According to her *Christian Counselor's Pocket Encyclopedia*, weak people practice "fight or flight" reactions to conflict. They either get in brawls or head for the hills. *Not her!* She would show her strength through perseverance.

When the pastor had called to apologize, she cut him off with the question, "Why don't submarines get crushed under an ocean's pressure?" That stumped him, so she explained, "They have pressure on the inside that's strong enough to withstand the pressure on the outside. Do you catch the analogy, pastor? I'm okay because of my inner strength." To make sure that he understood, she explained the principle with further illustrations about airplanes, balloons, fish, and space suits. Pastor Mike just listened. She wished he would tell her he was taking notes, but at least he was listening.

Two things really bothered Carol. She still couldn't understand what was funny about her public counseling session with Jerubbabel. Role-playing was a common teaching technique in academic circles. Were these people really so backward? The pastor certainly should know better. He was showing his dark side again.

She was also disappointed that the disruptions during the skit prevented the congregation from seeing her counseling skills. That meant she would have to work even harder in building her practice person by person. She would have to aggressively pursue every opportunity. Hopefully someone at the prayer meeting would need her services.

Mike looked around the room and counted eleven people—an average attendance for the midweek service. He once suggested the board replace it with small home groups. But they voted that motion down. They felt that the church would undergo spiritual decline if they lost their "hour of power." The Midweek Prayer Service was "the furnace," it was said, for all of the ministries of the church.

Mike tried to point out that the small groups would include prayer times and it was likely more people would participate, but the board members didn't buy it.

He didn't point out that few of them ever attended the very church prayer meeting they were vigorously defending.

Although the pastor thought small groups in homes might provide a more intimate setting for sharing prayer concerns, he was determined he would work hard at making the traditional midweek service the best it could be. He prepared a weekly Bible study and used creative models of group interaction to help the attendees develop transparency so they would pray about critical spiritual matters and develop more accountability.

Despite his efforts, the meeting remained pretty static. When he asked for sentence prayers he got sermon prayers. When he tried to get the people to pray thematically, like for example, for their neighbors, they would ignore him and pray the same prayers they had used the week before. While there were refreshing exceptions, the trend was to only pray about health concerns and "the missionaries on the foreign fields." It wasn't that these issues weren't important; it was just that Mike wished they could begin with intense worshipful adoration of God and then pray about other vital matters like spiritual temptations or their unsaved friends.

The big prayer item this week consisted of lifting up Lorraine Nagy's husband. That week, on a business trip to Tampa, he had received bee stings on the ankle. On the plane ride home the allergic reaction became so severe that he was now in the hospital. Since Byron Nagy showed no interest in spiritual things, there was also prayer that his physical plight might get him thinking about his need for God.

As Lorraine talked, Carol Harmon heard an inner voice declaring that Mr. Nagy needed counseling – *counseling by Carol*. Not only was she a skilled helper, she had also been stung by a bee once and would be able to empathetically relate. It was obvious to her that an appointment had just been set. Professional courtesy dictated, however, that she get a green light from Lorraine. So as soon as the prayer meeting ended, she pulled Lorraine aside to a quiet corner and said, "I sometimes stop by the hospital to visit with people. Even though I have never met Byron, do you think it would be okay if I paid him a visit?"

"Well," Lorraine said with hesitation in her voice, "I guess that would be fine. But please be careful not to pressure him on anything."

"You have no need to worry. I'm a professional counselor, you know."

She found Byron's name on a fourth floor hospital door and cheerfully breezed into the room. "Hi! I'm Carol."

"Hello, Carol, I'm..."

"I know who you are," she said, cutting in, "and I know about your affliction. Your wife told me all about it and suggested I pay a little visit."

"She did?" he responded dubiously.

"Oh, yes. You see, I'm a care specialist and she thought I might be of help."

"I already have a doctor."

"I'm sure that he's a good one. But he will only deal with the surface problem. I can help you delve into deeper difficulties. So relax and let's just chat a little, okay?"

"Well, I guess that'd be fine."

"I, too, have gone through your ordeal. It hurts, doesn't it?"

"Yes, it's quite uncomfortable."

"Is it red and swollen?"

He gave her an embarrassed smile. "Well, I'm not sure. Obviously I haven't looked at it."

"Well, I'm not squeamish. Pull back the sheets and let me take a look."

He blushed. "Let me understand something. Are you a doctor or a nurse?"

"No, I'm a certified counselor."

"In that case, I'd prefer to keep my sheets where they are."

"You don't need to be so private. Your little booboo is nothing to be shy about. I just want to get to the bottom of things and see how bad it is before I counsel you. Now let me have a little peek." With that she reached for the sheet.

"Stop it!" he said, clutching his covering. "I'm not going to give you a little peek and I don't need any counseling. So back off."

"That's no way to talk to someone who just wants to help. You are a special man. Very special. But I think you have a little problem that we should talk about."

"Forget it. Please leave."

"Oh no, that wouldn't be good. You wouldn't want to miss a free consult, would you?"

"Yes, I would. Leave now or I'll call a nurse."

"But --"

"Leave. Leave now."

Carol reached for her purse and coat. "Fine, I will go. But let me leave my card. Maybe when you are off mind-altering medications, I can be of more help."

"Get out of here! I mean it!"

As she scurried out of the room, she almost bumped into Lorraine Nagy, Pastor Mike, and a man in a wheelchair. "Hi Carol," Lorraine said pleasantly, "this is my husband, Byron."

"This is your husband? Who is that man in his room?"

"Oh, that's his roommate." Then, lowering her voice, Lorraine whispered, "*He's got hemorrhoids.*"

Carol staggered. Mike reached for her arm and said, "Carol, are you alright?"

"Sure, I'm fine. I just have to go. I'm in a hurry." With that she scooted down the hallway.

In her car Carol rewound her conversation in the hospital and replayed it over and over. Each time she cringed. Then she imagined the patient telling the story to the pastor and the Nagys. They were laughing. She could see them; oh, yes, she could see them. Laughing real hard; tears coming out of their eyes. How hateful! And the pastor was laughing the loudest—just like he had on Sunday night. How could he call himself a man of God? Here was clear evidence. *He was pure evil!*

While Carol fumed, Mike got the opportunity to start building a relationship with Byron. He hoped they would become good friends. He also hoped that he might also get the chance to eventually introduce Byron to his best Friend.

THIRTY

CLASHING WITH THE COUNSELOR

She startled him. When Mike returned to his office from his hospital call, he didn't expect to find Carol Harmon here, sitting in the chair by his desk.

"Carol?"

"Pastor, I need a minute of your time," she said curtly. "Please take a seat."

Carol had treated him coolly the last two times he had seen her -- at the midweek service and a little while ago at the hospital, but the look she wore now looked really cold. *Was that an icicle hanging from her nose?* He guessed that she was still upset about his laughing during her ventriloquist counseling session. He hoped that repairs could be made right now.

"Tell me, Carol, are you okay?"

"To be honest, pastor" she said, "this is a difficult day. I've been given a job by God that I really don't want to do." The look she gave him suggested he ought to feel sorry for her, but he already knew that he was going to feel sorry for himself.

"Oh?"

"Yes, Pastor Mike. Though this is difficult, it's necessary that I confront you with a deep concern. You see, I think I know what your problem is."

She paused and stared at him until he was forced to say, "Go on." It took effort to make those two words sound calm and natural.

"Well, this is hard for me to say, but pastor, I think you are a carnal, backslidden, spiritual sad sack."

It was a sucker punch that took the wind out of him. Mike looked at her for more but only got another frozen glare. Losing the staring contest, he looked at his hands for a while before he responded.

"Carol, that hurts. I enjoy the personal relationship that I have with Jesus Christ and try to walk closely with Him. I wonder why you would doubt that. Is there something in my life that leads you to believe I am struggling spiritually?"

"Pastor, I don't want to hurt you. I want to help you."

"Then please tell me why you would make such a comment."

"Pastor, I really don't want to go into that."

"Well, you have to."

"No, I don't."

"Yes, you do. You can't just walk in here, question my spirituality and then not give any explanation for why you feel that way. What did you call me? A spiritual sad sack?"

" A carnal, backslidden, spiritual sad sack."

"Yes, of course. I wouldn't want to leave any of that out. That kind of harsh description requires an explanation."

Carol speared him with a warning glance. "Pastor, listen to yourself. Do you hear how dark and defensive you are?" Her small dark eyes glanced away and then quickly back.

"It is true that I am frustrated." Mike said.

"Dark and defensive! In fact, there's a seething volcano of anger boiling within you! You have got to exercise a little self-control!" Carol pounded her sharp little fists on the table.

Mike couldn't resist looking down to see if there were dents. He bit his lip and tried to appreciate the irony but failed. Though he had only spoken with a soft voice, this woman had suddenly began shouting at him about a loss of control. He simply took a breath and allowed himself a small smile. It was probably not a good idea.

"I see that smirk," she said as she leaned toward him in a threatening way. "You have problems. Big problems! Emotional problems. Spiritual problems. Why, I wonder if you aren't even possessed!"

"Carol, here's what I wonder. What are you really so angry about?"

Carol went scarlet, the splotches on her face bursting like fireworks. "You!"

Never had a pronoun seemed so hostile.

Mike said nothing more. It would be futile.

Suddenly, like a human yo-yo, she softened, patted the top of his hand and said, "Pastor, I hope that you will think about what I have said and humble yourself in repentance. You are a special person. *Special!* You get these problems sorted out and you will have great potential."

He decided to make a further attempt to gain better understanding. "Carol, are you still angry about the Sunday night ventriloquist skit?"

"No. It's not just that. And it's not the hospital incident, either. It's far more than that."

"What hospital incident?"

"You know. Enough said. And besides, I said it was far more than that."

"I know of no hospital incident. I have no idea what your imagination has conjured up."

"Pastor Michael, don't turn this around and make it an attack on me. You know and I know you know."

"I don't know, Carol. But go on. Could you give me a few specifics about what there is in my life you think I should address?"

"Do you want an answer?"

"Yes."

"Do you really?"

"Yes, I really do."

"Then go to your prayer closet. The answer you seek is in the closet." And then, springing to her feet, she added, "Thank you for your time, pastor. I truly hope that I have been of help. That's why I'm here, you know. It's part of my ministry. Good bye."

"Good riddance," he whispered.

"What?" she said, spinning around and planting herself in the posture of a cage-fighter.

"Nothing. Nothing. Good bye."

After she left, Mike blew off his steam by taking a brisk walk around the block. Halfway through he was able to turn it into a prayer walk. It was then that he wondered if he might be the cause of any of this tension. He ended up at the parsonage. After describing his conversation with Carol, he asked Sandy if there were blind spots in himself that he wasn't seeing.

"If there are, honey, I'm blind to them, too. Don't let Carol get to you. She's just weird."

"But she's not alone. There seems to be a growing number of people antagonistic to me."

She hugged him. "Hopefully, they are a minority."

"How do we know that? Stan, Maxine, Carol, Betty... maybe the Klings? Maybe many, many more."

"But probably less. Let's stay positive and assume they're a minority. I don't think we should even count your maybes. And if there are people on the fence, they'll eventually fall your way. Give this church time. The more they know you, the more they'll love you. I do!"

"Oh, babe, I love you, too." They kissed.

"Well, I better go back to the office and try to get some work done." Glancing around, he said, "Did you see where I put my coat?"

"Do you want an answer?"

"I'd appreciate one."

"Really?"

"Really," he said, cocking his head.

"Then go to your closet. The answer you seek is in your closet!"

....

THIRTY-ONE

DUMB, DUMB, DUMB, DUMB

Carol struck again on Sunday. At the end of the service, Mike took his regular place at the back of the sanctuary to shake hands. Sandy was often with him but on this particular Sunday morning he was alone. Today the last person through the line was Brenda Strickland. Mike was impressed with the high-schooler; for her age, she really had her act together. Since she was last and no one else was close enough to hear, he used the occasion to ask her if she knew Whit Carson.

"Yes, I know him a little. I don't think anyone knows him real well. He transferred in about two years ago... or maybe it was a year and a half. Why do you ask?"

"Well, to be honest, he has chosen to be a mystery man. I would like to get to know him better and help him more but he is very guarded around me."

Brenda gave a nod, "Mystery man. That is a good description. You're not alone. A lot of us have spent time trying to figure him out. He's got all the looks and personality to be really popular if he wanted to be but instead he acts rather aloof -- but not in a prideful sort way. It just seems like he needs time to himself more than he needs with others. I've wondered if he's been hurt and is now being protective? Yup, he's the mystery man."

"Brenda, you are very perceptive. Could it be that he's just shy?"

"Oh goodness, no. He's got this air of security around him that can almost be intimidating. During most classes he doesn't interact much but then out of the blue he will suddenly take control of everything. Like, sometimes Whit gets in verbal contests with teachers -- usually at a time when one of them is acting a little arrogant or is picking on a student. And he always wins. Always." She laughed again. "We call him 'Quick Whit.' Maybe now, I will call him 'Quick Whit, the Mystery Man.'"

"It sounds like he's a mystery that you would like to solve?" He smiled mischievously at her and raised one eyebrow.

Brenda's face colored red and she slapped him lightly on his forearm. "Pastor Mike, you're teasing me. You're as bad as my dad. But to quickly change the subject, I'm really glad that he's coming to church and I've been praying for him."

"That's great, Brenda."

"And sometimes," she said with a comical whisper, "I even pray *for* him, if you get my drift. And don't you dare tell my dad I said that!"

She flipped her hair. "Gotta go. Bye." As she walked away, Mike looked at her with admiration. She was emotionally and spiritually mature beyond her years.

Suddenly behind him he heard a voice. "Matthew 5:28 – 'I tell you that anyone who looks at a woman lustfully has already committed adultery with her in his heart.'"

"Huh?" he said.

It was Carol. "Your thought life must be grungy. Eeew. It makes me want to go home and take a bath!" She shook her head at him and walked away.

He was caught flat-footed. Did Carol misinterpret the way he had looked at Brenda? When her implication fully registered, Carol was gone. Mike felt a surge of anger. She had really ticked him off this time. To hide his emotions, he ducked into his office where he paced back and forth and carried on an animated conversation with himself.

"*Matthew 5:28 – 'I tell you that anyone who looks at a woman lustfully has already committed adultery with her in his heart,'*" he said out loud, imitating her high pitched, precisely modulated speech.

"What is with this lady? Why does she insist on thinking the worst of me?"

"*Because you're possessed!*" He answered with her voice.

He was silenced by a knock on the door. When he opened it he was met by the perplexed stares of two of his deacons -- Kenny Frasier and Morris Ubody. Looking around the room, Kenny said, "Am I interrupting a conversation?"

"No, I'm alone. I was just, ah, ...well, never mind. This is embarrassing. I was just talking to myself. Needless to say, it wasn't a very bright discussion." He smiled. They didn't. "Come in, what's up?"

Kenny lifted one finger, to indicate he preferred to delay his answer. Turning slightly, he used a hand gesture to direct Morris to close the door.

Mike's gut tightened.

"Pastor, Carol Harmon told us something we need to talk to you about."

Mike felt like he had just taken a swig of cough syrup. Instant heat surged through him. He decided to make an attacking, defensive charge.

"I don't care what she told you. I am not lusting after women."

"What?" Kenny said, his eyes getting big.

"I'm not! If you think that I would ogle a young lady, you are quite mistaken! It was just an admiring look. That's all. *An admiring look*. It wasn't lust!"

Kenny and his shadow, Morris, looked like mannequins that had been placed in uncomfortable postures.

"Pastor," Kenny whispered, "we don't know anything about your admiring looks at girls; we just came to talk about Carol's suggestion that we start a counseling center at the church."

"Yes," Morris echoed in the same slow, soft voice, "we came here to say that we don't think our church has the money to do something like that. But Carol thinks we have a problem with the 'financial sphere of our faith.' We don't think so... But we were wondering what you thought?"

Mike's lips moved but nothing came out.

His awkwardness made them just as awkward. Mike grimaced and they looked at each other with matching shrugs. Morris finally said, "Well, ah..." and then turned to Kenny for help. Kenny jumped in with a voice that sped into third gear. "But we don't have to talk about this now. We can discuss it at our next board meeting."

"Absolutely. No need to talk about it now!" Morris concurred. "Pastor, we'll just deal with this at our next meeting." While he spoke, his hand fumbled behind him for the doorknob. Finding it, he pulled the door open. "Kenny and I need to be going now. We probably shouldn't have even stopped. We're in a hurry."

"Wait!" Mike said as the men scrambled for the exit. "Let me explain my comments about lusting."

Kenny said, "No need. Glad to hear you're not lusting."

"Didn't suspect you did." Morris said. "Never even thought about it, frankly. But, like Kenny, I'm glad that's not a problem. So bye now."

They were gone.

Dumb, dumb, dumb, dumb, dumb... Mike knocked on his forehead with his fist.

....

THIRTY-TWO

THE BIG SQUEEZE

After his experience that morning, Mike almost avoided going to the rear of the church after the evening service to do his post-sermon handshakes. Almost. Later Mike would think about the subject of "almosts." Most of life's experiences navigate around them. If Mike had followed his hesitation, he'd have missed "The Big Squeeze" and Sandy would have been deprived of a story that she would tell repeatedly through the years.

"Pastor Mike and Sandy, I would like to introduce you to my cousin. This is Bellevista Norsink." Mike tried to look at Dorothy Monkmeier's relative with a neutrality that ignored her overwhelming size. To call her a large woman would have been a gracious understatement. "Bellevista is visiting from Paw Paw. She came over to do some pre-Thanksgiving Christmas shopping with me this afternoon and then she decided to stay for our evening service."

Mike said, "It's good to meet you, Bellevista. I hope your shopping was successful and that you enjoyed our church service."

"I loved your service. Loved it." Without even glancing at Sandy, she took his outstretched hand and sandwiched it between her own. "And I must say this, Pastor Lewis, your message..." Her eyes became springs of water. "Your message really, really moved me. I needed it so much—"

Her voice cracked and her body began to quake. "I really needed—" She staggered with an outburst of sobs and Mike stepped closer to right her if she began to fall. She took this motion as evidence of support and threw her arms around him. Together, they shook.

Sandy's mouth dropped open. But for his arms sticking out, Mike would have totally disappeared. She heard his muffled voice saying, "There, there" and watched one of his hands attempting to pat her back. It only reached her side but he thought it should still have accomplished its purpose. After two pats, hugs are supposed to cease.

Bellevista misunderstood the signal and with a loud, whiney "Ooohhh," squeezed him tighter. Sandy realized she should be empathetic about the woman's emotional overflow but knowing her husband and the embarrassed discomfort he must be feeling, she couldn't help but be amused. A sudden vision of his knees buckling and the embracing twosome tumbling over brought her hand to her mouth.

Pat, pat went his hand -- again in vain. Bellevista began to rock him back and forth. Then, like a tag-team wrestler, Mike gestured for help from his spouse.

Tapping Bellevista on the shoulder, Sandy said, "Excuse me for cutting in, but may I have this dance?"

Her attempt to lighten the situation with humor earned chuckles from some of the smiling bystanders. Maxine Glass was an exception. She turned to Stan and said, "Did you hear that? She wants to dance."

Sandy tapped harder. "Bellevista?"

Dorothy stepped in. "Bellevista! Let go!" She grabbed the large finger of her cousin's left hand and pulled. The grip loosened and Mike broke free.

"Whoops, I got a little carried away, didn't I?" She reached a hand toward Mike but he backed away. "I'm sorry. I... I just got a little moved. I'm a feeler; I'm prone to spikes of emotionalism."

Mike finger-combed his hair and stepped behind Sandy. "Bellevista, maybe you would like to go somewhere and pray with Sandy?" He felt his wife reach back and dig her nails into his leg.

"Oh no, I'm fine. When I get moved I get a little expressive, that's all. I'm totally fine. Thanks for the good sermon. I like a message that moves me. I'm returning next month to see the Christmas program that Red and

Dorothy have created. Aren't the Musical Monkmeiers wonderful? Every single one of them are so musically talented. Will you be preaching then, too?"

"Just a short sermon. Sandy and I have parts in the program and a small devotional is tucked into what we will be doing."

"What a shame; I could listen to you for hours. But I'm sure the Christmas program will be exciting; that man with the beard and long white hair made it sound amazing. He sounded like a carnival barker. When he promoted it during the announcement time, I got goose bumps. Here, feel my arm, pastor, I think they are still here."

Mike's eyes widened. "Ah, I think I will pass. Sandy, do you want...?"

"No," Sandy broke in, "I've never felt real comfortable around goose bumps but thanks for the offer."

"Okay then." Bellavista shrugged. "Well, I better run. I've got to drive all the way home to Paw Paw. Bye bye." She wiggled her fingers at them.

Sandy said, "Bye bye to you." Mike just waved. Then he noticed Maxine Glass and Carol Harmon. As though choreographed, they were both shaking their heads with disgust.

On their walk back to the parsonage, Sandy said nothing. She just kept giggling. Mike felt like rubbing her face in the snow.

"I need a break," he said. "I'm glad Thanksgiving is this week. It should provide a needed diversion from church stuff. And then one month after that we'll be able to get out of here for a week of Christmas vacation. I've never needed one more."

"Honey, you're just a little discouraged from a draining day. Vacation may be helpful, but do you know what you really need?"

"What?"

Sandy said, "You just need a big hug!" Then she wisely ran. Unfortunately, she was slower than the snowball.

THIRTY-THREE

....

TURKEY DAY

On Tuesday evening, Stan Glass dropped in unannounced on Mike and Sandy. When he saw Mike's wranglers he raised an eyebrow but refrained from speaking of them. Instead he said, "Maxine and I want to give you a little holiday gift. On Thanksgiving we not only give thanks to God for His blessings but we also try to be used by God to be a blessing to others." From behind his back he pulled out a bag and presented it to them. With a big grin he said, "It's a Thanksgiving chicken."

After he left, Mike said, "Because Stan gets under my skin, I don't appreciate him enough. Today he gives us a chicken. In October, for Pastor Appreciation Month, he also gave me a gift."

"That book on preaching?"

"Yes, *Preaching With Revival Fire*. I know he gave it to me because he thinks I'm not enough of a pulpit-pounder, but even still, he went out of his way to give me the gift. And he's also generous with his time. No one in the church volunteers more than he does."

"Stainglass does have his good points. But a Thanksgiving chicken? I can't serve our guests chicken on Turkey Day." They had invited two couples, the Jacksons – old friends from college, and Byron and Lorraine Nagy. Ever since Mike visited Byron in the hospital they had enjoyed a growing friendship. And Lorraine and Sandy were meeting weekly to pray for Byron to come to know the Lord personally. There was a good chemistry between them all.

The Thanksgiving meal went off without a hitch. The food was great and the personalities of the three couples jelled wonderfully. After they were stuffed they waddled into the living room to watch the Detroit Lions play the Green Bay Packers on the large RCA in the corner.

"Hey, this is great," Byron said of the large, comfy room. "A bunch of guys come over to our house every Monday night to watch football and it gets really cramped in our puny TV room. It feels like one of those 'stuff the phone booth' contests."

"This was designed to be large enough for church groups. Would your friends have any interest in coming here for Monday Night Football?"

"Mike, I wasn't trying to fish for an invitation."

"I know that but I'm serious about my offer. I'd enjoy hosting a weekly football party. Games are more fun to watch with other fans."

"Well, I can ask them."

At half-time Whit Carson, who had lately begun dropping-in, came over. "I was afraid this house wouldn't have any Packer fans, so I decided to come over and be a positive role model."

"Whit," Sandy said with a smile, "I didn't know you were a cheese head."

"You bet. I was born in Oshkosh, Wisconsin and raised in Milwaukee. "

"Really?"

"Absolutely. Here look at the back of my neck." He spun around and pulled down his shirt collar.

Confused, Sandy lifted his long hair and looked at his skin. "I don't see anything. What should I be looking for?"

"A tag that says, 'Oshkosh ByGosh.' I've never seen it either but my dad said it was there -- that every kid born in Oshkosh gets one stitched on at the hospital."

"Oh, Whit, is he as much a teaser as you are?"

"He was... He doesn't do any teasing anymore..." Whit spoke softly and turned his head away to signal that the conversation was over.

As proof that their food was settling, someone suggested they play some touch football when the game on

TV was over. The idea was adopted enthusiastically and during commercial breaks, Byron made phone calls and invited some of his friends to join them.

After they gathered in the large lawn next to the church, they divided into teams. Each team was so competitively matched that the score was tied going into the final play. It pitted Mike against Whit. Whit was quick and had good hands but Mike had run track in high school and was still very fast. Charles Jackson, a gifted athlete who had played QB in high school, tossed the ball to Whit who bee-lined for the end zone. Mike, who had been guarding someone else, ran Whit down and made a superman dive toward him. But in anticipation, Whit dodged to the left and let the pastor fly past him. Touchdown and game. The victors got to be first in line for dessert.

....

EATING GOURMET

The Jacksons, having stayed with Mike and Sandy through the whole Thanksgiving weekend, insisted on taking the Lewises out to dinner following the Sunday morning church service. "And," Charles said, "I insist on picking the restaurant. Mike has no sense of class and I am in the mood for a fancy restaurant."

After their gourmet meal was over, they emptied their trays into the trash and walked out to the parking lot. "Mmm," Sandy said, "my McNuggets were spectacular. Charles, you spoiled us."

"That's my beloved husband," Danika laughed, "I affectionately call him Mr. Generosity."

"That's me, Mr. Generosity. And now I am so full after my exotic, expensive Big Mac that I would like to walk home for exercise. Mike, you with me? The fair ladies can take the chariot."

Mike relished the one-on-one time with his old friend. They'd roomed together during their last two years of college and spent innumerable hours in thoughtful dialogue, theological debate and sharing ministry dreams. Charles Jackson was a perceptive thinker and Mike had always leaned on his judgment.

During the last couple of years, their time together had dwindled in frequency. Charles was now a member of *InterVarsity Christian Fellowship*, working with students at the University of Michigan in Ann Arbor -- a position that possessed his heart and time. And Mike was equally consumed with pastoring. But whenever they got back together it felt like no time had passed; they relationally fell back in step as naturally as their strides currently matched each other on the sidewalk.

"So Charles, you got a snapshot of our church this morning; I would like to get your impressions. And please be honest."

"How honest?"

"Real honest."

"Okay, you asked for it. I thought the preacher was excellent despite the fact that he's as ugly as a stump."

"Seeing that you once described me as being as ugly as a toadstool, I'm happy to hear I am looking better. And thank you for the compliment on my preaching. Now, please go on with your critique."

"Everyone was really friendly; extremely friendly, in fact."

"Extremely friendly?"

"Absolutely, it was practically smothering. Are they that friendly to everyone or did our being the only black couple in the church make us a special novelty?"

Mike laughed; he knew Charles enough to know they weren't on dangerous ground. "Honestly, the answer is probably both. They are a very friendly people but they may have gone overboard to prove that they aren't prejudiced. This is a mostly white area and outside of a few Hispanics, we are a lily-white church. We have one African American family that floats around through all the churches in town and each congregation is trying to catch them."

"You should offer a signing bonus."

"Good idea. I will buy you a weekly Big Mac if you will join our church and commute from Ann Arbor each Sunday."

"I will certainly pray about that. Not."

"Let's get back to your evaluation of the church. I need an outside set of eyes."

"Well, like I said, everyone was very friendly..."

Seeing through his friend's evasiveness, Mike said, "Come on, Charles, I'm a big boy, I can handle a straight answer."

"Okay, then, here's the skinny. I think the church seems to have a lot of nice people but it surprises me that this is the church you chose. We used to sit around and talk about what a church should be and this church isn't it. Think about it, if you were just an ordinary church shopper and you were to visit Meanwhile Baptist Church—what a blasé name, by the way -- would you choose to come back?"

"Hey, for better or worse, that's the name of the town."

"Whatever, but the name 'Meanwhile' gives the impression that nothing ever happens here... Hmmm, never mind, maybe the name is appropriate. Anyway, let's get back to the question, would you choose to come back?"

"Probably. Why do you think I wouldn't?"

"Because it just doesn't seem like it's very culturally relevant. Everything seems a little fatigued -- the facility, the music, the programming. Wouldn't you like to have a church that a Byron Nagy and his buddies would feel comfortable attending? I always pictured you pastoring a cutting-edge, high-impact church. And while it's unfair to make a judgment after one visit, your church appears old-fashioned and worn out. I'm afraid you're spending all your energies covering the thing with patches. I wonder if it wouldn't be wiser to trade it in for a new model."

"It's funny that you should say that. My mentor, Dan Hall, tried to talk me out of coming here. He thought I should become a church planter."

"Why didn't you?" Charles asked.

"I seriously thought about it and almost did go in that direction; I still might someday. But then I read a book on church revitalization that challenged me. The author contended that about eighty percent of churches in America are plateaued or declining and that we need a new generation of committed, turn-around pastors."

"Wouldn't it just be easier to start churches from scratch?"

"Yes, it normally is. He admitted that it's easier to give birth than raise the dead but He also insisted that God is big enough to do either miracle. He even said that there are fewer men qualified to lead turn-arounds than plant churches; it requires a unique blend of skills, perseverance and strategies.

"And you are one of those men?"

"That's the question I'm struggling with. I used to think so but now I'm having second doubts -- very serious doubts. The problem is this: it normally takes about five years before one of these churches can start making the turn. What if I spend five years here before discovering that I'm not a good turn-around pastor? I have wasted five years of my life and the church is no better off."

Charles added, "That, and the patience level. Do you have the patience to guide the church through such a long process? And does the church have the patience? And do they even want to go through the process?"

"You are right on. Every church says it wants change but they usually don't mean it. They really want you to successfully change them back into the success model that their faulty memories recollect from the good old days. And when you start shifting a church's direction they can resent it. They feel like you are rejecting their collective personality and values. Plus, change often ruffles feathers and makes some people choose to leave, which, in turn, causes panic. Even if you have more coming in than going out, people believe the ship is sinking."

"Some must honestly want change."

"True, but even many of those people evaluate you by their visualized future rather than yours. For example, I would like to shift this church away from its peripheral activities and back to what a church's key responsibilities ought to be. I want us to become more serious about simply making more and better disciples. Others want me to create new razzle-dazzle programs and productions that are flashier than the other churches in town. By their standard of success, I would be graded as a failure in the leadership department."

"What do you have to work with? Do you have many strong leaders? Do you have people with contagious personalities that others are drawn to?"

"All of that is somewhat lacking. That's what I am trying to develop. When a church stalls out, there's a tendency for people who want to accomplish great things to migrate to other churches that seem to be more fruitful. So you lose the brightest and best of your change agents. Good people are still left but they are work horses not race horses. So no, we don't have too many strong leaders or what I like to call velcro people -- those that draw others toward themselves. Just the opposite, in fact. We have a lot of what Dan Hall calls 'quirky people.'"

Charles laughed. "I think I spotted some of them today at the church service. Tell me this, is there an evangelistic aggressiveness?"

"Not really, but everyone believes in evangelism. They believe there's a lost world out there that needs God but they seldom share that message with anyone personally. They do, however, support a lot of missionaries and engage themselves in several mercy ministries. So in that sense they believe we are an evangelistic church."

"Well, I am happy to hear they are missions minded and have ministries of mercies. They can be a bridge to evangelism."

"They can be if you actually use them to cross the bridge. Our people are very caring. Many of them volunteer at a soup kitchen. If there is a house fire in town, our church will be there with food, meals and money. Twice a year we have a massive 'Serve Day' where we go all over town doing service projects. The list goes on and on. All of these are wonderful acts of 'niceness' and each could be used, as you say, as a bridge to evangelism. But few ever cross that bridge and share their faith. The word at the heart of evangelism is 'evangel' and it means to be a messenger of good news. If we don't actually get around to telling people how to come to God, we are not actually doing evangelism."

"Good sermon, pastor," Charles said with a smile.

"Sorry about that. It's just frustrating. Most Christians believe in evangelism but don't believe in themselves or God's ability to use them. I do have this one woman in the church, Lucille Swensen, who's giving it her best. She's the reason Whit Carson is coming to church. And I'm also trying to help our deacons adopt a strategy for helping our church become more outreach oriented; I'll bring that up at our meeting this Tuesday night."

"That's good. Do you have a target audience out there? A picture of the kind of people you are best positioned as a church to reach?"

"That's a good question. I just want to reach anyone and everyone. What is your 'picture' of the people most likely to come our way?"

"Hmm, let me look into my crystal ball." Charles held an imaginary globe in front of his face and shook it. "I see a frumpy, gray-haired couple coming your way. They have just moved to Meanwhile after living in another small town where they attended another small quirky Baptist Church."

"Isn't it time for you to go back to Ann Arbor?"

"What? You've got something against the elderly?"

"Absolutely not, our church is full of them."

"And that's why they are the easiest for you to get. But, if you want to turn this church around, I expect that you will need a wider variety of people -- maybe even a few of those 'colored people,' which is how one of your members described 'my kind' this morning."

"The more the better. Our lack of racial diversity is one thing that I truly dislike."

"Maybe I'll consider your offer of a weekly Big Mac. I will pray about it. Won't fast and pray. Just pray. I will pray while I am saying grace at my favorite posh, golden-arched restaurant."

They walked a few more minutes in silence before Charles broke the silence. "Mike, as one of the greatest jocks you have ever been around, do you think it's okay if I use a sports analogy?"

"Of course, O Great One, let me hear it."

"In order for a team to be successful, it normally needs three things: a good coach, talented players and a strategic play book. I think, regardless of your self-doubts, this church has a good coach. But your team lacks talent and is reluctant to run any of your plays. How can you win with that combination?"

"Charles, what is winning? Isn't it glorifying God by taking people wherever they are and stair-stepping them to spiritual maturity and productivity? If people are so precious to God that He died for them, He certainly will never give up on them. And think about it, Jesus took a ragtag group of disciples and transformed the world through them. I'm praying that the Lord will do the same thing here in Meanwhile."

"Good answer. And you can count on it, I will be praying with you."

*   *   *

Charles and Dankia Jackson left that afternoon so Mike and Sandy were free to mingle with the congregation after the evening service. Sandy was forced to think quickly when Stan approached her and asked how she had enjoyed their Thanksgiving chicken.

"Stan, here's the thing. We had several people over for Thanksgiving, so unfortunately your nice chicken wasn't big enough to feed everyone. Instead we ate a turkey." Stan's jaw dropped. "But we're really looking forward to the chicken. Why don't you and Maxine come over for dinner next Sunday and enjoy it with us. Do you think you could do that?"

"Well, thank you. That would be very nice..."

*　　*　　*

Four days after Thanksgiving day, Byron Nagy and some of his buddies came to Mike's place for Monday Night Football. It was a good time -- full of chips, noise and rowdiness, and for the rest of the season a growing bunch of football fanatics made weekly treks to a church parsonage. "Who could have predicted this?" one of them joked, "football at the preacher's pad. We ought to call our group the 'Holy Huddle.'" And they did.

THIRTY-FIVE

THE SIGN

Thursday evening hosted a deacon's meeting. There was perfect attendance -- Pastor Mike, Stan Glass, Tim Glass (Stan's nephew), Morris Ubody, Kenny Frasier, and Bud Swensen. The guys liked to meet but Mike agonized over their lack of productivity. Tonight he came with a step-by-step plan to help make the church more effective in outreach. It was the same proposal he'd brought to the last meeting, but it had been preempted by a discussion as to whether the church should be using communion bread, crackers or wafers. This time he hoped they could avoid distracting themes.

He started by sharing his philosophy of ministry as it related to church-wide, corporate evangelism. That was as far as he got. Morris's raised hand halted him.

"Isn't that circular thinking? I heard that phrase from my barber this morning and liked it. *Circular thinking.* It has a ring to it and I think it may apply here."

Mike was perplexed. "In what way, Morris?"

"Oh, I'm not sure I can pin that down, but it's thinking that just sort of goes around in circles."

Kenny chimed in. "I once had a cousin that walked in circles. Second cousin really. All started, I'm told, with an infection in his ear. Threw off his balance big time. He would cock his head to the left and go round and round. It must have turned into a habit because even after the infection was gone he kept doing those three-sixties."

Mike interrupted him, knowing that Kenny was about to launch into one of his famous long-winded recollections. "That's a fascinating story, Kenny, but can we get back to what I was saying?"

"It is fascinating. He used to wear out one shoe before the other – the left one, of course. Then he'd have to buy a new pair of shoes – even though his right shoe was still perfectly good."

"That's too bad. Now then, where was I?"

Kenny ignored Mike and moved on with his story. "It was bad. Carl – that's the name of my cousin. Er..., second cousin, that is. Carl was real thrifty so he couldn't bear to throw out those perfectly good right shoes."

Mike shook his head and looked at the ceiling.

"After a while he had several of them cluttering up the floor of his closet. This used to upset his wife, my second cousin-in-law. She could be a complainer anyway and with those useless shoes in her closet, she would really let him have it."

Kenny's story had hooked Morris. Nodding empathetically, he asked, "What happened next?" Mike wanted to shout, "Don't encourage him."

"Well, Carl couldn't bear to throw out those perfectly good shoes but he also couldn't bear listening to his wife harping about them. So what does he do? He starts wearing right shoes on both his feet. It was agonizing to watch. He'd have this painful expression on his face and he would walk in circles with those two right shoes. I hate to say it, but he looked just like a duck. Apparently his wife refused to watch him because she made him go outside. You can still see round paths in their front yard."

"Sad, sad, sad..." Morris muttered.

"Sure was," Kenny continued, "but it gets worse --."

Stan must have shared Mike's exasperation because he suddenly threw his hands in the air and said, "Here we go again!"

Morris snapped his fingers. "That's it! Here we go again! Kenny's story is a perfect example of what I was trying to say. Pastor, you wanted a definition of circular thinking and Kenny's story illustrates it, because, of course, it goes round and round in circles. Do you understand now?"

"Morris, I already knew what circular thinking was. But could you please tell me what I was saying that appeared to be circular in nature?

"Frankly, Pastor, I'm afraid I don't remember what you were saying. Could you please repeat it for me? That is, after Kenny finishes his story about Carl?"

Fortunately, that wouldn't happen. After a quick knock on the door, Harold Broadmoor bustled in and became the next obstacle to Mike sharing his outreach proposal.

"Good evening, gents. Hope you don't mind Harold T. Broadmoor popping in with a small item of business – an opportunity the church won't want to miss. Do you think you can squeeze me into your agenda?"

Harold was a big, neckless, soft lump of a man. His posture matched his clothing – saggy and tired looking. The shirt wasn't made that could stay tucked into his trousers. Even his trademark suits, one brown and the other white, didn't spiff him up much. He resembled a crumpled bag. But he had a charismatic radiance; the long white hair and beard that circled his red face drew attention and his eyes and voice were always animated. He was a man that overflowed with ideas and he shared them with a flourish.

Stan, the acting chairman, warned Harold that they were busy with a lot of important business. But the rest of the board gave him a warm welcome. "Come and sit down," Morris said, "we weren't talking about anything important anyway. Sit by me, there's room over here between me and Kenny."

Harold was one of those men who sat with his legs spread as far apart as possible. Horizontally, he required a good three feet. Morris and Kenny continued to move their chairs until he was no longer jabbing them with his knees.

He bent down and began to untie the laces of his cordovan shoes. "Hate these shoes." The posture squeezed his large stomach and he grunted. "They make my feet hurt. Mother says they keep me awake in church. Ha! My wife's a stitch."

Mike smiled; he couldn't imagine the quiet woman making jokes.

Harold loosened the laces, then sat up straight again and winked at Pastor Mike. "If everyone wore shoes like these, nobody would sleep during your sermons. I'll bet you'd like that, huh, preacher?"

"They've got to be better than my cousin's shoes," Kenny said. "Harold, have I ever told you about my second cousin Carl?"

Mike was relieved when Stan said, "Kenny, we don't have time for that story again. Harold has the floor now."

When he finally got settled, Harold began his presentation. "Gentlemen, you are deacons and I am not. Never have been. Got no experience. None. So I'm not going to give you any advice on how to deac.

"What I am is an entrepreneur... a salesman ... a PR man... a marketer. And in my field, I'm the expert. I say this not to build myself up but simply to establish that I have experience to back up what I'm going to say. I'm here with a golden opportunity for the church – one that will allow it to broaden its exposure and impact."

He rubbed his hands together and said, "Do I have your interest?"

What he had, Mike thought, was their skepticism. Harold wasn't esteemed as an expert, just an average pitchman that bounced around town selling for Sears, Bob's Tire World, The Furniture Barn and various other stores.

"You can have the greatest product in the world but if nobody knows about it, then you'll never make a sale. Or let me put it in religious language. If you keep your light under a basket it will never shine so people can see it. Surely that analogy resonates with outstanding spiritual leaders like you?"

"The point?" Stan asked.

"I'm getting there. Don't spoil the suspense, Deacon Stan. The point is this. You have a fine little church here but it's hidden away on a side street with little visibility. You have violated the first three rules of marketing: location, location, location."

"Aren't those all the same?" Kenny asked.

"That's what I was thinking," Morris added.

"Yes, they are. And in the case of Meanwhile Baptist Church, you've broken all three. You have a bad location, bad location, bad location. You Baptists may know the Bible but you don't know squat about positioning yourself for success."

"Did you say, 'you Baptists'?" Bud asked, "Aren't you one of us?"

And Morris whispered, "He also said 'squat.' You don't say those kind of words in church."

"Well," Harold responded to Bud, ignoring Morris, "as you know, I'm not a member, just a faithful attender – well, at least part of the year I am. During the summer, I run the root beer stand and miss many Sundays. But I'm loyal to the church and want to help it any way I can. And today I'm here to offer you a solution to your visibility problem. I have a marketing plan that will point new people to your church."

He swiveled his trunk, looked at each man and smiled. "The solution is a sign. Not just any sign... a big sign with yellow flashing lights." He leaned forward and gestured with both hands. "Due to my network relationship with Bob's Tire World, they've offered me a great deal. Since they're getting a new stationary sign, they've offered me their old portable sign—one with wheels—for only seventy-five buckaroos.

"So here's the plan. The church buys the sign and you can put it up in my front yard. As you know, I'm just three blocks down the road but my house on the corner is also situated on Main Street next to the 'Costal church. Main Street, is of course *the* main street in our fair town. We'll use catchy messages to grab the attention of motorists and point them toward the church. In no time at all our parking lot will be packed, our pews filled, and our offering plates overflowing."

He leaned back and waited for their applause. Since he only got silence, he went on. "We can also use it to promote special events like the 'Perfect Gift' Christmas production. As you may know, I'm not only one of the stars but am also the publicity chairman; that's why I'm giving all the promotional spiels during the Sunday morning announcement times. And although I'll unleash a special guerilla marketing plan to pack this church on Christmas Sunday, I think the sign will also help."

Other than the nods of Kenny and Morris, there was still no response. "Say something. Don't just stare at me like a herd of cows. Is this a boardroom or a pasture?" Harold laughed at his own joke and poked Morris. "Boardroom or pasture? Ha! Where do I come up with this stuff?"

"Now, now, Harold, 'stuff' that resembles insults isn't appropriate," Stan said. "We just need some process time."

"Deacon Stan, don't be so sensitive. I'm just playing with you. You need process time? Let me give you even more to process. The 'Costal church is your closest competition. They have a good location and they also have a sign. Unless you boys step up to the line, they're going to leave you Baptists in the dust. Remember Halloween? Despite all the coolness of our Harvestween festival, they still trounced us. With our new sign I think we can beat them at Christmas. Our sign will be bigger than theirs and it'll have those attention-getting, yellow, flashing lights. And besides, I'm more creative than the 'Costals. My sign slogans will be better."

"You know something, Harold," Mike said softly, "I'm not sure the good people over at the Apostolic Temple want to be called 'Costals."

"Preacher, you got a soft spot for the holy rollers? Maybe you're an undercover bapticostal." He laughed and again elbowed Morris in the ribs. "Bapticostal! Get it? Hah! Call them what you want, they have a sign on Main Street and you don't."

Morris, still rubbing his side, said, "Harold, I'm not sure I buy your logic. I think that you're using circular thinking."

"Morris," Harold grinned, "what do you know about logic? You wouldn't know logic if it bit you on the nose."

"Would too."

"You're dreamin', buddy boy. Your thoughts bounce around like a one-legged frog. Now, let's get back to the issue at hand. What do you say, gents, you gonna buy the sign or what?"

"Well, maybe we could form a committee to look at this more seriously," Stan suggested.

"Committee? You're toying with me, now, aren't ya? If we're going to capitalize on this for the Christmas production, we need to act now. Kenny and Morris, you are doing a great job building the stage and props. Pastor, I understand that you and your pretty missus will have central parts. Stan, your narrating skills will be wonderful. All the other singers and actors, both kids and adults, have been practicing. And my part, which I am keeping secret, is going to be a show-stopper. I'm telling you, this is going to be a killer production, but it will all go to waste if we don't get people to come. And this dandy sign will help. So we need to make a decision now. Do you think you boys can do that?"

"Harold," Stan said, "if impulsiveness is such a priority, we can make a decision tonight. If you wouldn't mind stepping out for a couple minutes, we'll deliberate and let you know what we think is wise."

When he left, it was decided to pass on the sign. Stan thought that using marketing was reliance upon the world's methods rather than a dependence on the Spirit.

Bud was afraid of the embarrassing messages Harold might put up; he was already bothered by the 'over-the-top' nature of Harold's announcements on Sunday mornings. Morris was still in a huff about the attack on his logic but he was still somewhat favorable. "It would be nice to get a lot of people here." Kenny thought that maybe they could go forward if Harold allowed Pastor Mike to pick out the words -- a suggestion that hung in the air with no one championing it, including Pastor Mike. Tim just shrugged and said, "I'm apprehensive but I don't really care; you guys decide." Stan called for the vote and it failed. They then called Harold back in.

Stan spoke. "I'm sorry, Harold, but we've chosen not to purchase the sign. We're grateful for your good intentions but our finances are tight and we have to practice careful stewardship. Hopefully, you'll be okay with that."

"Just a sec," Harold said, with one finger in the air. He turned away, removed his handkerchief, blew his nose thoroughly, one nostril at a time, loud, and put the hanky back in his hip pocket. "Now then," he said, returning to Stan and the subject, "I'm fine with it. Mother and I will just buy the sign ourselves. We'll use it to market our products and maybe we'll even put up church stuff some. I just wanted to give you an exclusive."

After Harold left, Bud said, "I'm worried about this. Harold Broadmoor is a loose cannon and I'm afraid of what he might put on that sign of his."

Stan waved down Bud's concern. "My office is close to Harold's home. I'll keep an eye on his sign and if anything gets out of hand I'll put him in his place. We probably shouldn't even have let him speak tonight. What he needs is a firm hand and I believe that I have the leadership authority to provide it."

The next week the sign was up. Harold kept himself busy changing the messages:

- "Tires -- $20. TV -- $50. Salvation – FREE! Visit Meanwhile Bapt Church."
- "Need some play time? Come to the Xmas Drama at Meanwhile Bapt Church and see me."
- "Church Christmas Play. 12/22. Shepherds, Angels and Dancing Girls. (2 out of 3 ain't bad!)"

THIRTY-SIX

···

AGAPE LOVE

The service that next Sunday was charged with energy. The music was inspiring and Mike preached a message that seemed to hit the bull's eye. Most of the audience was right there with him. It was as though he could see the words being grasped and held to their hearts.

During the invitation, Mike received a real surprise. Of all the people that could have possibly come forward, he would have never anticipated Carol Harmon. But there she came—right during the first stanza of *Just As I Am.* She marched up with a strong, deliberate gait, swinging her large, purple bag as she walked. Cautious, Mike met her at the front, told her that he was glad she had come forward and then said he was going to beckon a woman counselor to pray with her.

Carol demurred. "The reason I came forward is because God convicted me about my harsh feelings toward you. I need a few minutes to apologize and explain what God is teaching me."

Back in Mike's study she continued. "During your message, the Lord showed me that I haven't been practicing unconditional love for you."

"I don't remember making any mention about unconditional love."

"No, it wasn't anything you said. While you were preaching, I was studying *The Christian Counselor's Pocket Encyclopedia* and I came across a chapter on *agape* love. You know what *agape* love is, don't you?

She waited for his nod and then continued, "Good. Well, I've read the chapter many times before but this time I suddenly realized I wasn't directing that kind of love toward you. And Pastor Mike, I'm truly sorry. I repent with shame that I've been trying to love you with a reciprocal kind of love that needs to be earned by proper behavior. I was withholding my love until I felt that you gave me what I deserved and wanted. I was looking for sensitivity from you, but that didn't happen. I was looking for you to respect and greater utilize my giftedness, but that didn't happen. I was looking for you to preach the kind of sermons that would bring catharsis to my soul, but that didn't happen. I was looking for you to have pure thoughts, but then, of course, that didn't happen."

"Carol," Mike broke in, "I need to –"

"Pastor, please! Let me finish. As I was saying, I was waiting for all those things before I would love you. They didn't happen so my love didn't happen. When you didn't come through, I developed some bitterness towards you. I even questioned your faith and suggested you were possessed. Wasn't I naughty? Of course, I didn't really believe that, but I was overcome with spite. I now recognize that I should love you with a deeper kind of love, with God's kind of love, with *agape* love. So as of today I'm going to love you the right way. As an act of my will I'm going to choose to love you with a love that is based on my 'loveability' rather than your 'loveableness.' Even if you continue to be a letdown, I will still love you. It's true that I may not always like you, but that's okay, I'll love you. Isn't that wonderful? Isn't it special?"

"Umm, there are some parts of what you have said that are special. But, ah –"

"That's enough, pastor. You don't need to say anything more. That's because I love you regardless of what you say or do. I just love you so much. Now then, I think this matter is settled so I will scoot along. You just stay here and bask for a while in the warmth of my agape love."

She stood to her feet. "Oh, yes, and before I go I must give you a progress report about Whitfield Carson. I had an impromptu session with him last Wednesday night, and another personality revealed itself. You'll never guess who it was?"

"No, I'm sure that I won't."

"Lassie. Lassie, the famous collie."

Mike couldn't suppress a smile. "Tell me, Carol, what did the dog say?"

"I'm not sure, but I think he was trying to tell me that the barn was on fire."

"Oh, Carol—"

She clucked her tongue. "I don't want to hear it, pastor, you're just going to splatter me with skepticism again." She put her fingers in her ears and said, "I love you. I love you. I love you. It's my choice. I love you." When she was exiting, she was still mumbling the words, "I love you."

Mike leaned back in his chair and stared at the door. He was still looking at it when it opened part way and Kenny's head poked around it. "Can we come in?"

"Sure, Kenny." As Mike expected, Morris was following him.

"We just wanted to tell you that everything is progressing well on the staging that we are building for the Christmas production."

"You are going to be amazed when you see it." Morris agreed with a nod. "Amazed. It's going to have three different levels. Pretty big stuff for our little church."

Just then a folded slip of paper came sliding under the door.

"What's this?" Morris said as he picked it up and unfolded it. His eyes grew large. "Oh my goodness. It says, '*I love you. I love you. I love you with the deepest kind of love. I really do.*'"

Mike felt a bomb explode in his head. How was he going to explain this?

Kenny was looking over Morris' shoulder. "Does it say who it's from?"

"No, it just says, '*I love you. I love you. I love you with the deepest kind of love. I really do.*'"

Mike was waiting with dread for them to turn toward him with quizzical, distrustful eyes. But then Kenny did the unexpected. He asked, "Morris, who do you think would give you a love note?"

"I don't have a clue." Morris wore a startled look like a man who had accidentally walked into a crowded women's restroom. "But I know I'm not going into the hallway by myself. Come with me." They moved cautiously out the door, looked both ways, and then closed it behind them.

It took Mike a moment to catch his breath; it would have been difficult to explain the note if they had known it was from Carol to him. Then he stood, shook it off, and headed for home.

....

THIRTY-SEVEN

SOMEONE'S IN THE KITCHEN
WITH MARGARET

fter the Wednesday night prayer meeting, people were lingering to talk. Some were in the auditorium looking at the construction going into the set for the Christmas program; others were milling around the lobby and hallways. None of them anticipated that they were about to become witnesses to a physical assault nor that they would so enjoy watching it.

From the church kitchen, a fog-horned voice bellowed, "Yes, I think I do know what my problem is. MY PROBLEM IS THAT I HAVE NO PATIENCE WITH BUSYBODIES LIKE YOU!"

Carol Harmon had chosen to counsel the wrong person. Old Margaret McElroy fit no one's stereotype of a senior citizen. She was an energetic, two-hundred-pound bundle of candor. Her humor made her a favorite around the church, but she was also known to take on those who rubbed her wrong; in this case -- Carol.

"I refuse to star in one of your psychodramas. You've been running around this church trying to fix people when all the while you're the loose nut. You're trying to take slivers out of our eyes while you've got a two-by-four sticking out of yours. And my problem is that I'm not nice enough to put up with it!"

Old Margaret's booming voice was followed by silence... throughout the kitchen and beyond. Even those in the hallways stopped to listen.

"Margaret," Carol said, "do you think we could conduct our counseling session without shouting?"

This was an impossible request. Margaret didn't own an inside voice.

"I'm not shouting. I just have a stout voice, and THIS IS NOT A COUNSELING SESSION!"

Across the hall and down two doors was the pastor's office where Mike was. As he heard the commotion, he wondered whether he should intervene. He suddenly made up his mind. He got to his feet, walked quickly to the door... and closed it. Almost. He left a crack so he could eavesdrop.

Back in the kitchen, the tumult had turned into a staring contest. It was Carol's turn to respond but she struggled with what to say. She was stung by Margaret's attack and almost played the sympathy card with tears.

But then she remembered that as a skilled helper she needed to transcend her emotions and act for the good of her client.

"Margaret..."

"*Yes, Carol?*"

"Margaret, I sense you are angry."

"Carol, I'm amazed at your insight. Are you a psychic psychiatrist?"

Silence again. Time for a new tactic.

"Margaret..."

"*Yes, Carol.*"

"Margaret, it's obvious that I have made a big mistake and I would like to apologize."

"To me alone or should we get half the church in here to get the apologies that they deserve."

"Margaret, please. I'm talking to you. I realize I shouldn't have approached you at a time when you may not be receptive. I'm truly sorry about that. When you are more teachable and when you get to the point where your problems cause you enough pain, come to me. It's my ministry. I'm here for you." She punctuated her sentence with a condescending smile.

She shouldn't have.

"Missy, I'LL SHOW YOU SOMETHING ABOUT PAIN." The older woman grabbed a long wooden spoon from the counter and started after Carol. Her quarry raced around the other side of the island counter and shrieked, "Margaret, stop! This just proves you're being defensive and in need of therapy."

"Need? You're a spoiled brat in need of a spanking! And I am the one who has the privilege to give it."

"Margaret, violence is not the answer!"

"Spare the rod, spoil the child!" Suddenly, Margaret scooted around the island with an amazing burst of speed. All Carol could do was run. So around and around they went.

"Stop it!" But Margaret didn't. Her short, heavyset frame had a blocky strength that belied her age. With fluid movements characterized by the strong swipes of her stubby arms, she pursued her prey with the tenacity of a pit bull.

"I said, 'stop it,' you old bag. This isn't funny! You're acting like a psychotic."

"Dearie, everyone thinks I'm psychotic, except for my friends that live deep inside the earth."

"Real funny. Ha ha ha. Now back off. You touch me and I'll have you arrested for assault."

"I'll just plead CONTEMPORARY INSANITY!" Old Margaret picked up even more speed.

"Help me! Someone please help me!"

Then in a panicked escape attempt, Carol raced toward the open kitchen door. Seven feet. Six. Five. Four. Three. Two. One. Almost there! But just as she leaped into the hallway, she felt the sting of the wooden spoon on her posterior.

"Ouch!" she yelled. Looking around, she saw that she had an audience. At least fifteen people gaped at her with open mouths. Their presence caused both women to freeze.

Suddenly, someone started clapping. This caused the whole group to spontaneously erupt into laughter and applause.

Old Margaret McElroy grinned, thrust her hands in the air, danced a tiptoed pirouette and took a bow. This added hoots and more clapping.

"You people are evil! Evil! Evil!" Carol was spinning in her own little circle, pointing her finger at the crowd. "You're way beyond dysfunctional. You're pure evil!"

She made a pathway through the group by roughly shoving Red Monkmeier out of the way. She was headed for the exit when she saw the pastor's office. Without hesitation or knock, Carol barged through and plowed into Mike where he had been observing the scene through the door's cracked opening.

She stared at him so fiercely that he braced himself for a slap. But then her grit collapsed and she sank into a chair. Her eyes snapped shut and she folded up, clamping her hands around her knees. Then she began to rock, hard and fast.

Mike leaned over and touched her shoulder. Bird bones beneath cotton. "Do you want to talk about what you're feeling, Carol?"

She trembled and hugged herself tighter. A tear rolled down her cheek. Mike got a tissue box and placed it in front of her. Ignoring it, she stood abruptly and began to pace the office, holding her temples, the tears still coming.

When she spoke, her voice shook with sobs. "Why don't people like me? I'm just trying to help..."

"Oh, Carol..." Like the hallway crowd, Mike had enjoyed watching Old Margaret's pursuit of Carol. But now her shattered appearance moved him to pity.

"Carol, if you have the time, I'd love it if we could just talk a while..." And for the first time, they actually communicated.

THIRTY-EIGHT

....

IMAGINE THIS...

Five guys gathered in the Lewis's living room. The two couches—one green; the other, yellow—were rearranged so each got a good view at the wood-boxed RCA console television that swiveled from side to side on the floor. It was the second get together of the "Holy Huddle" Tonight's Monday night feature was a close battle between the Dolphins and the Patriots.

It had been a fun evening. Mike provided a variety of soft drink selections and everyone brought snacks to share. The noise level continued to grow as the joking and jousting had become competitive. There were fans for each team so they began to make pretzel bets with each other. Fun stuff, but the tone was about to change.

A commercial ended and the room grew quieter as Patriot's field goal kicker John Smith, the only Englishman in the NFL, loosened up his leg on the sideline. Mike pictured himself in Smith's spiked cleats, wearing the number #1 white jersey and shouldering such a big moment. He could almost feel the adrenaline rush that Smith must be experiencing as he now trotted onto the field. The pastor's visualization was suddenly side-tracked as analyst Frank Gifford's voice spoke gravely about something completely unrelated to football. Then Howard Cosell's distinct narration replaced Gifford's. He doused the game's excitement with the most serious announcement ever shared on their broadcast.

"Yes, we have to say it. Remember this is just a football game, no matter who wins or loses. An unspeakable tragedy confirmed to us by ABC News in New York City: John Lennon, outside of his apartment building on the West Side of New York City..."

At the sound of Lennon's name, everyone in the room froze and listened intently as Cossell continued to give the details about how Lennon had been shot twice in the back and rushed to Roosevelt Hospital, only to die on the way. Howard finished by saying. "Hard to go back to the game after that news flash, which, in duty bound, we have to take."

A bag of chips tipped over and several hit the floor. No one noticed but Deac, who eagerly wolfed them down. DeacDaDog loved the Holy Huddle and the crumbs they dropped.

Mike, feeling the gravity in the room, walked to the set and pushed the button beside the channel knobs. With the exception of a white dot that lingered in the center of the screen, everything else turned black. They needed a moment to process what they had just heard. The Beatles were one of the most popular music groups of all time—certainly the biggest rock band. As Cossell predicted, it was *hard* to get back to the game so they reminisced old Beatles memories, recollecting how old they were when the band was on Ed Sullivan, their disappointment over the group's dissolution and what their favorite hits and albums were.

"Here's the song I'm thinking about now," Byron Nagy said, "*Imagine.*" He broke into song. "Imagine there's no heaven...," They all joined in and finished the chorus.

"What do you guys think?" Byron said, "Is John Lennon imagining there is no heaven or hell now? Does he still think 'it is easy if you try'?"

Darren looked at Mike and said, "Heaven and hell. That's your department, isn't it preacher?"

"Well, it is a subject we can't ignore. The choices we make in this life determine where we will be in the next. What do guys think, is there a literal heaven and hell?"

Different men shared their opinions until Darren again directed the question back to Mike. "So what do you believe?"

"It makes no difference what I believe. Jesus believed it and talked about our eternal existence a lot. And that is the main reason he came to earth—to make it possible for us to live forever with him in heaven."

"That's only for the true believers, though. Am I right? Everyone else ends up like a marshmallow on a stick over an eternal campfire."

"Darren," Mike said, "Jesus doesn't want anyone to go to experience that. He loves you, man. He proved it by dying on the cross for you and now He offers you and everyone else an eternal relationship with Him. Those who accept that invitation and receive Jesus Christ as their Savior and Lord will enjoy eternal life with Him in heaven, but those who chose to have nothing to do with Him will have that choice sealed forever as they live eternally outside of God's presence."

"Hell?" Byron asked.

"Yes, hell," Whit replied softly.

"Oh, hell," Ed broke in with a laugh, "It's getting too heavy in here for me. Let's get the game back on. And, ah, sorry about the profanity, preacher."

"No sweat. And I am sorry if I came on so strong; this is obviously a subject I'm obsessed about. Let me turn on the set." He pushed the power button and returned to his seat.

Miami won the game 16 to 13 but Mike's mind wasn't on the game. He hoped he hadn't been too pushy with his heaven-and-hell spiel, but silence would have been a worse alternative. People need to hear the good news about Jesus; their destiny depends on it.

More attention-breaking news broke on Tuesday morning. This time, however, the story was light and local. "Hey, Sandy, look at this newspaper article. It is talking about the Meanwhile Angel." They were eating oatmeal at the kitchen table and the *Meanwhile Press* was spread open besides Mike's plate.

"The what?"

"The Meanwhile Angel. Last night before Howard Cosell's announcement about Lennon's death, the guys were talking about angel sightings in town. I thought they were just pulling my leg but this article says that people have seen this big, white angel on top of buildings around town.

"So funny. Do you think it's a hoax?"

"Well, obviously."

"Are you telling me, Pastor, that you don't believe in angels? Here you are always talking about the spiritual realm and yet when one little angel pops up in town you suddenly become a skeptic?"

"You caught me."

"What I was asking is, do you think that this is just a rumor? Or is someone dressing up like an angel as a joke?

"Sandy, I'm guessing it's a practical joker. Maybe we should dress up in black clothes and go out tonight with flashlights on an angel hunt."

"If I catch one, can I keep it?"

"Honey, this house already has an angel – you."

"Awww."

THIRTY-NINE

....

U. F. A.

It was 7:30 p.m. on Wednesday and the midweek prayer meeting that should have begun a half hour earlier was being side-tracked by discussions of the angel sightings. Several had reported that they knew someone who knew someone who had actually seen him -- whoever "he" was. The angel had shown up on the roofs of various restaurants around town – making some wonder if it was a hungry angel. It glowed with brilliance and had large fluffy wings.

With laughter everyone repeated the stories that they had heard around town. The frivolity stopped when Stan Glass spoke. Using his deepest, most somber voice, he cautioned everyone not to dismiss the angel too lightly. "I think" Stan Glass said, "there is the possibility that the Meanwhile Angel is actually a UFA."

"Tell me, Stan," Pastor Mike asked, "just what is a UFA?"

"Well, as you all know, for several years now there have been numerous UFO sightings. The government has, for its own nefarious reasons, chosen to cover up their existence with ridiculous claims that people are actually seeing things like weather balloons and swamp gas. Anyone who would swallow that is gullible or stupid. So then, what are these Unidentified Flying Objects? Many believe they are little green men from outer space who have come down to earth to check us out before a future invasion. More silliness. No, there is only one reasonable explanation. UFO's are UFA's. They are..." Stan held everyone in suspense with a long pause. "Unidentified Flying Angels. UFA's. Biblical scholars like Dr. Bobby Baddington speculate that that we are in the last times. During these days there will be a renewal of signs and wonders and with them will be visitations by angelic beings. Maybe, just maybe, the Meanwhile Angel is real."

Stan leaned back in his chair and folded his arms across his chest. No one spoke, they just let their heads rotate toward Pastor Mike. What would Pastor Mike say to this?

"That's an interesting theory," Mike said. "I would have to say there are many other Biblical scholars that might challenge it. And even though I don't buy it, let's not get into that debate tonight. I suspect that before too many days we will find out who or what this Meanwhile Angel is."

"Soon," Stan said, "we will all know. Isaiah says that in that day, 'the eyes of the blind will be opened and the ears of the deaf will be unstopped.' I just choose to walk around with my eyes open now."

A big scoop came on Friday morning. The newspaper printed photographs of the angel on top of McDonalds, the Waffle House, the movie theater and Mike's favorite morning haunt, Donut Nibbles. The pictures had been mailed anonymously to the newspaper but various eye-witness accounts confirmed that this was the angel they had seen. The identity of the messenger was still, how-ever, a mystery. The letters to the editor's section was filled with angel comments. Some were angry, blaming this farce on teenagers. Others relished the humor with which some prankster had blessed the town. And then there were a few who believed the angel sightings were real. One man, allegedly a little drunk, even claimed that he had seen a whole host of angels above the McDon-alds restaurant and that he had also observed a large tear dripping miraculously from one eye of the big Ronald McDonald statue.

That night Meanwhile, a town most Michiganders had never heard of, became famous in West Michigan. Channel four, a television station in Grand Rapids, made it a news item on their 5:00 evening news hour. Their story, and the pictures they showed, provided a small bonanza for the town. By the next day tourists with cameras began to drive into town. The merchants made the most of it; restaurants advertised Meanwhile Angel's Food Cake and the light posts along Main Street were decorated with angel wings. There was a pleasant festival feeling everywhere.

During the church service on Sunday morning Harold T. Broadmoor gave another promotional pitch to the congregation on how they just "had" to invite their friends and neighbors to "The Perfect Gift" big-time Christmas production. "And," he shouted, "tell them to come early because if they don't they may not get a seat. I guarantee this place is going to be packed. Packed, I tell you. Packed. Some of you look a little skeptical but you shouldn't be because I am giving you the iron-clad, Harold T. Broadmoor guarantee. P-A-C-K-E-D. Packed."

After the announcement, it was time for the sermon. Pastor Mike decided to work this week's news stories into his message. For his introduction he played *Imagine*. As a Beatles' fan, he had the cassette in his collection. He figured that some would like this but others would give him flack—which, of no surprise to him, he later received from Stan Glass.

284

"Imagine there is no heaven? No hell?" Mike let the questions hang out there during a long pause. "John Lennon is no longer doing any imagining; he is experiencing the reality of what God has already revealed in the Bible. Let's turn there now..."

Midway through the message, he read a passage from Revelations that mentioned angels. With a playful smile, Mike asked, "Do you think these angels in this last book of the Bible resemble our Meanwhile Angel?" In response to laughter, he said, "On my part, I don't think so."

After he had preached for twenty-five minutes, Mike returned to the Lennon illustration for his conclusion. "What was John Lennon trying to say through the song? In his words, 'It's not a new message: *Give Peace a Chance* —we're not being unreasonable. Just saying, give it a chance. With *Imagine* we're asking, can you imagine a world without countries or religions? It's the same message over and over. And it's positive.'" Now, no one can argue with this quest for peace. But on another occasion Lennon admitted that *Imagine* was an 'anti-religious, anti-nationalistic, anti-conventional song, but because it's sugar-coated, it's accepted.' He felt that religions just divide us—and I think he's often right. But what he never discovered was that Jesus wants to unite us. Through Him, we can have peace with God and peace with others. Ephesians 2:14 states that 'He is our peace' and that He has broken down the 'dividing wall of hostility' that keeps us apart.

"At the request of John's widow, Yoko Ono, today people are going to be gathering in Central Park to corporately spend ten minutes in silent prayer in remembrance of John Lennon. The police are expecting a couple hundred thousand people to show up. New York is a little too far away for us to attend but there is still a way for us to participate. I am asking you to pray for all the family, friends and fans that are experiencing grief today. And pray that they will find their peace in the person of Jesus Christ. If you want to imagine something, imagine this: imagine that in the future you are in heaven talking to someone who is there partially as a result of your prayers and witness."

When Mike ended his sermon, Red Monkmeier stepped forward. It was his practice to have the church sing one final song at the end of each service. But this was another of those times when he threw in a little surprise.

"When I was told a little earlier this week about the topic of this sermon, I felt led to do something special. So I have reworded the song *Imagine* and created some new lyrics that I think are more biblical. I would like to sing it for you right now." And then Red, using the familiar Beatles tune, sang,

Imagine there's a heaven
It's easy if you try
The Lord above us
To meet us in the sky
Imagine all the Christians living forever...
You may say I'm a believer
But I'm not the only one
I hope someday you'll join us
And put your faith in the Son

When he finished, his sons, Mathew, Mark, Luke and Bob suddenly stood up from where they had been hiding in the choir loft for the entire service. Each wore wigs that looked like the original Beatle haircuts. And they sang,

He loves you, yea, yea, yea
He loves you, yea, yea, yea
He loves you yea, yea, yea, yea....

FORTY

....

HALLWAY CONVERSATIONS

The evening service ended and Carol Harmon hurried out to the vestibule with the goal of leaving the church without talking to anyone. But then, hearing a loud holler behind her, she stiffened in fear. The big, gruff voice could belong to no one other then Old Margaret McElroy—a woman that Carol envisioned as a modern reincarnation of Tugboat Annie or Ma Kettle, only scarier.

"CAROL! You stop right there; I've got something for you."

Warily, Carol turned slowly around and Old Margaret thrust a large Tupperware container into her hands.

"What's this?" Carol said with caution. She held it way out in front of her as if it were a time bomb.

"This, dear, is a carrot cake. You'll like it. It's a special recipe."

"This is for me?"

"Well, sure. Enjoy."

"Well, thank you, but... why? I didn't think you liked me."

"Don't be silly, girl, I love you."

"But Margaret, you struck me."

The older woman cackled. "Yes, that was fun. But I didn't just do it for the entertainment; I also did it because I love you. Do you know the verse that says, whom the Lord loves, He disciplines? I do the same thing. You were misbehaving so I gave you a spanking. And now that I saw you this morning without your goofy, little psychiatrist bag, I'm giving you a carrot cake as a reward. I'm using the carrot and stick approach to set you straight."

It was the first time in two years that Counselor Carol had gone anywhere without her purple, embroidered "ready-for-anything" caregiver's satchel and she felt incomplete without it. But she had determined that she would give her counseling practice a rest and begin focusing on her own problems more. She was surprised that Old Margaret could deduce so much by the mere absence of the bag.

Margaret gave Carol a shoulder squeeze and a kiss on the cheek. "Baby girl, Old Margaret loves you." When Carol began to lightly tremble, the squeeze turned into a mama bear hug.

* * *

"Harold, I'm concerned about the lack of publicity for the Christmas production." Red Monkmeier shook his head. "You keep telling everyone that the church is going to be packed but I don't think we're doing enough publicity. I know you are making announcements during the church services and putting messages on the flashing sign in front of your house, but what about advertisements in the newspaper and the Penny Shopper? Or maybe posters in the library and the Wishy-Washy Laundromat?"

Harold laughed. "Red, don't you be fretting. Harold T. Broadmoor has everything under control. Marketing is my specialty and I have a plan in place."

Red's voice rose as he whined, "What is this plan? The production is coming quick and people have been working hard, the practices have been going well and everyone's learning their songs and speaking parts. The outfits are almost done and Kenny and Morris are making good progress on the stage. In fact, everything is coming along except for publicity. It would be a shame if there's a poor audience turnout."

Harold grabbed Red by both shoulders and stared deep into his eyes. "Look at me, Red, look at me. Now who do you see?"

"Harold, I just see you."

"Just? Red, open your eyes wider. You are looking at marketing genius Harold T. Broadmoor. No brag, just fact. Now you have to stop being a quivering, pansy-pantsed, worry-wart. I have a stealth plan in action right now and it's going great. I decided to bypass all the traditional, small-thinking, advertising techniques and put my efforts into guerrilla marketing. You wait and see, I am going to put Meanwhile Baptist Church on the map. And the Christmas production is going to be packed. And that's spelled P-A-C-K-E-D. Packed."

"Can you let me in on this secret plan?"

"Well, Red, seeing I know you so well, my answer is 'of course not,' but I will reveal something else. Mother has finished my outfit for the play and it is extraordinary. That woman of mine never ceases to amaze me with her talents."

*   *   *

Brenda Strickland was leaning up against a wall with her bangs hanging over one eye. "I know this may sound funny but I really miss the Klings. I've grown up in this church with them always here and the atmosphere feels emptier without them around. I wish they would come back to church."

"Me, too," Whit replied. "Me, too. I hope my little joke with her tearing off my sleeve didn't upset them."

"Are you kidding?" Brenda looked up at Whit with a big smile. "They love you. They were so proud when you wore that ugly shirt and tie at church. I'm disappointed you didn't wear it to school."

"Don't dare me, Brenda, I just might."

"Knowing you, I wouldn't be surprised. Oh, please do; and tell me when you do so I can bring my camera."

"Back to the Clingers..."

"The Clingers?" Brenda said, interrupting Whit.

"That's the behind-the-back nickname that someone I know gave them."

Brenda laughed. "It sure fits. How funny."

"Anyway, I wonder what it would take to get them back in church?"

* * *

Over by the library, Stan Glass was speaking animatedly with his wife Maxine and Betty Sweeting. "If the Meanwhile Angel turns out to be real, the pastor will be sorry he laughed about him in the morning message. Did you know that he'd never ever heard about UFA's before I educated him?"

Stan was building up steam and Maxine touched his arm to warn him to lower his voice. He gave her a cold stare. She returned it with even more ice and he wisely turned down his volume. "I don't think we should be quiet about this. First of all, our young preacher makes silly statements about the angel and then he has the audacity to eulogize John Lennon and say he likes Beatles music. That is a terrible example for our young people. I'm going to bring this up at the next deacon meeting."

Betty Sweeting nodded vigorously and said, "You should. You definitely should. And you need to also deal with Red Monkmeier. I thought I would die when he and his sons sang that Beatles song. We're lucky a bolt of lightning didn't flash down from the heavens and destroy the church. And you never know what he's going to do when he writes a new song; sometimes it's ear-bursting, rock-and-roll and other times it's country southern gospel. Next week it might be opera. I shudder to think about it."

*　　*　　*

Morris and Kenny were in the auditorium studying their work-in-progress set that they were creating for the Christmas play. They just finished the third level of the stage that afternoon. It was eight feet above the baptismal tank and built strong enough to hold a three-hundred pound man—their estimate for what Harold Broadmoor weighed.

"I can't wait to see Harold T. standing up there," Morris said. "I hope the stage is sturdy enough to hold him."

Kenny replied, "I'm not worried about the third level. We've built it with plenty of support. I am a little worried about the second level, however. It's hinged pretty well to the back wall but we only have two-by-fours holding up the front end. And they aren't anchored too secure."

"It'll be fine. We'll only have some light props on it. On the right side there will be the artificial Christmas tree and the wrapped Christmas presents, which, they tell me, will be empty. And on the other side is the manger and the cross. And since we made the cross out of Styrofoam, that is pretty light."

"Morris, I'm just saying."

"It'll be fine, I tell you. If we nail it down it could damage the carpet. And don't forget we're going to have to take all this stuff down after Christmas. For goodness sake, we aren't building a permanent addition. "

"Which is too bad. This is the coolest thing we've ever made for any production this church has ever put on. You can say what you want to about Harold, he has really got everyone in the church all revved up over this Christmas Play. I just hope visitors come. Every year we do one of these shows and supposedly the throngs are going to show up and then I look around and just see us and ours."

"Now, Kenny, you shouldn't talk that way. Harold T says this year is going to be different. After all, he's got his monkey plan started."

"It's a guerrilla plan, you big nut, not a monkey plan. He calls it guerrilla marketing. And it's got me rather nervous; I'm afraid the only thing it's going to do is make monkeys out of all of us."

"So it's both a gorilla plan *and* a monkey plan."

"Whatever, Morris."

"So who's the big nut now? Hmmmm?"

"You are."

"No, you are."

"No, you are."

....

FORTY-ONE

HARK!

"Hello, is this Pastor Mike Lewis of the Meanwhile Baptist Church?"

"Yes, this is Mike."

"Pastor Lewis, this is Cal Newell. I am a reporter for the *Meanwhile Press*. Would you have a few minutes to answer a few questions?"

Mike snuggled the phone closer to his ear. "Concerning?"

"What we have been calling the Meanwhile Angel. Surely you have been hearing about the angel sightings around town?"

"Sure, everyone in town has been talking about them, but I don't know anything more about them then I have read in your newspaper."

"Well, see, here's a new development that no one else knows about. We recently received a new photograph of the angel. Like the others, it was sent anonymously to our office. And this one is a picture of the angel stand-ing next to the steeple on top of your church building."

Mike coughed a chuckle. "You're kidding me. How did he get way up there?"

Cal laughed too. "Well, angels do have wings, don't they?"

"Surely you don't believe..."

"No, of course not; just joking. But I do need to ask you the same question and another one. Do you know how he could have got on your facility? And more im-portantly, might you know who he is?"

"Cal, I am totally clueless about both of your ques-tions. Tell me, has he appeared on other churches?"

"Not that we know of yet. I thought that a pastor like yourself might have a few insights on angels that we here at the office might have missed."

"I'm sorry. I know a little about angels in the Bible but I never took any seminary classes on Michigan an-gels."

"You have more knowledge than we do and, for that reason, the editor asked me to ask you if you would do a favor for us. Would you have the time to write a short piece on what the Bible says about angels? Maybe, due to the season, you could give special attention to the Christmas angels? Today being Tuesday, we would need it by Thursday."

Mike thought for a moment. It would provide a public forum for talking about a spiritual topic with the whole community. "Yes, I could do that. I am curious about something, though. Is this really that newsworthy? It seems like you are giving a lot of press to someone who is most likely just a practical joker."

"Between you and me, pastor, we are having the same debate down here at the paper. The die-hard journalists among us hate this stuff. But the editor and the ad salesman loves it. For a sleepy community like ours, a story like this grabs attention. So we are milking it for all its worth. Tomorrow, we will carry the picture of the angel on top of your church. Do you have any quotes you want included in the story?"

"Ah, let's see. Okay, here's one: 'Apparently, Meanwhile Baptist Church is an angelic place to visit.'"

"I will put that in. You should know, however, that it is not original. The manager of the Waffle House said the same thing about his restaurant."

On Wednesday morning Mike heard laughter in the auditorium from his office. He knew it would be the Monkmeiers. Red and his family were coming to the church quite often these days to prepare for the Christmas production. It was neat to see such a dedicated family. And since the kids were being home-schooled, they had the flexibility to work on projects together.

They all had parts in the musical and behind the scenes they also worked on props and costumes.

The pastor walked to the darkened lobby and looked into the sanctuary where he could see Red carrying things around the lighted stage. Mike could hear Dorothy and the children whooping it up with shouts and laughter, but he couldn't see them. Where were they? Oddly, he also seemed to hear... splashing? Then everything came into focus. He saw their bright red heads bobbing around the waters of the baptismal tank.

They had filled up the baptismal tank and turned it into a hot tub. The back of the auditorium was dark so he slipped his way into the last row and stood on a pew to get a better view. They were wearing swimming suits and playing with beach toys.

Should he do something? And if so, what? As a protestant he certainly didn't believe that this was holy water. So it wasn't as though anything was being defiled. And yet, the baptismal tank was set aside for a holy purpose.

The debate in his mind went back and forth.

There certainly wasn't anything wrong with fun in church and the kids and teens played a lot of games in their rooms so... But some members still wrongly treated the 'sanctuary' as the 'Holy of holies' and would be upset if they knew about this. This could be a divisive issue... But the Monkmeiers gave so much time to the church that they should be allowed some perks and even Mike and Sandy had come over with toy dart guns one Friday night and had a cheap date playing war in the darkened church. What was the difference?

Suddenly in his mind he heard the comic voice of Schultz, a zany character on the old TV comedy, *Hogan's Heroes.* "I see nothing. I know nothing."

Mike decided that was the way he was going to play it, too. So he crept out of the auditorium pretending to himself that he had never even been there.

*   *   *

On Friday evening Mike and Sandy took a long walk with DeacDaDog. The sun was just going down and they examined the roofs of every building with the hope that they would get to see the Meanwhile Angel. He wasn't on the roof of Donut Bites or McDonalds... and Ronald seemed to be extra happy; he wasn't crying tonight.

"Aw, shucks," Sandy said, "I really wanted to see the angel."

But it was a nice night and Mike and Sandy enjoyed the small ice cream cones that they purchased at McDonalds. Deac opted for a box of McDonaldland cookies -- which were periodically thrown to him all the way home. As they walked onto the porch of their parsonage they heard the phone ringing inside. Since the door, like usual, wasn't locked, Mike was able to rush in and catch it in time.

"Yes, it is... Really, officer, you caught him?"

The word 'officer' caught Sandy's full attention and she crowded in, trying to hear the other side of the conversation.

"One of ours? Are you sure? ...Okay, yes I can do that... I will come down right away."

Mike put the phone down and rolled his eyes. "The police captured the Meanwhile Angel—or maybe I should say that he turned himself in. And guess what?"

"He attends our church?"

"Yes, he attends our church."

"Mike, don't keep me in suspense. Who is it?"

"They didn't say and I didn't ask. But I am pretty sure that we both know who it is. Who is the prankster in our church?"

Sandy hesitated and then slapped her forehead. "Whit. Oh no. He's really done it this time. Do you think he is in a lot of trouble?"

"I don't know but I will soon find out. They want me down there."

"I'm going! I told you that I wanted to see the angel."

They got into their VW Bug and drove the three blocks to the police station. When they got out, there were bright flashes. Although their eyesight was now tattooed with white dots, they were still able to make out a man holding a camera.

"Pastor Lewis?"

"Yes?"

"I am Cal Newell, *Meanwhile Press* reporter. We spoke the other day? And then you sent in the baptism article - - which was excellent by the way."

"Ah, yes, of course, and, thank you. How did you get here so soon? Did the police call you too?"

"No, we received a call from the Meanwhile Angel himself telling us to send a reporter down here because he was going to turn himself in at exactly 8:00 p.m. So I got here early and waited for him to show up. Then at precisely eight, I heard a loud voice shout, 'Hark!' I looked up on the roof by their sign and there he was, a big chubby angel dressed in a white tuxedo, large feathery wings and a white beard."

Sandy turned to Mike and said, "Whit doesn't have a white beard."

"No, and he isn't chubby."

Sandy clapped her hands. "It's not Whit. It's Harold T. Broadmoor, the master of marketing."

The reporter broke in. "Wait, let me write this down. His name is Harold T. Broadmoor?"

"We don't know that for sure," Mike said, "we're just speculating."

"Well, if that's true, it explains a lot." Cal smiled big and chuckled. "After he shouted 'hark,' he went on to sing the Christmas Carole, 'Hark, the Herald Angels Sing.' But he sang it, 'Hark, the Harold Angel Sings' and then shouted, 'And that is spelled H-A-R-O-L-D.'"

Sandy laughed and gave Mike a shove. "That is something that Harold would do. He is a funny man."

"Let me finish my story," the reporter said. "He sang the song while I was busy taking pictures. Then he rang a little bell, an obvious take from the film *A Wonderful Life,* and climbed down that ladder over there. He told me that he was turning himself in and I asked if I could interview him first. 'No,' he said, but that he would give me an exclusive after he was bailed out. So I agreed, but I did ask him one more question. I asked him why he did it and do you know what he said?"

"What?" Mike and Sandy said together.

"The angel told me that he was providing publicity for a Christmas play that will be happening soon at Meanwhile Baptist Church. So, I need to ask you one more time... Pastor, are you sure that you knew nothing about any of this?"

"I assure you. Absolutely nothing. And I think that Harold, if that is, indeed, who it is, will back me up when he gives you his exclusive interview."

Soon Mike and Sandy were sitting at a table in a small room talking to Officer Robert Pierson. He was a tall man with broad shoulders, dark hair and a mustache. Under the right circumstances Mike was sure that he could be threatening but with them he was gentle, soft spoken and very winsome. The officer confirmed that Harold was definitely the so-called Meanwhile Angel. He went over the history of all that had transpired and talked about some of the potential charges. "But," he said, "I have talked to the chief and he and I agree that we would prefer not to press any charges. Mr. Broadmoor had no malicious intent and he brought no harm to any individuals or property. I have talked to all the business people involved and no one wants to charge him with trespassing. Apparently, his stunts just brought them a heck of a lot of publicity and extra customers. That leaves you and us. He was on our roofs. Do you want him charged?

"No, sir, I don't."

"We don't either. He has gotten real popular in town and we would get a lot of flak for being killjoys. From the editorials I've read in the newspaper, your angel in the cell down the hall caused a mini business boom around here. That being said, we still have a problem. If we don't do anything, I'm afraid that we will encourage teenagers and nuts all over town to create their own little costumes and start popping up all over. Copycats. So here is what the chief and I are suggesting. I would like to you to go with me to Mr. Broadmoor's cell. There I am going to give a loud, threatening speech about the trouble he will be in if he ever does something like this again. Then I am going to let him loose under the condition that he be under your unofficial custody, pastor. I will also ask him to do thirty hours of community service under your supervision. Now, none of this is according to Hoyle, legally; it is all being based on backroom handshakes. But if he agrees, I get him out of my hair. I am spared lots of paperwork and potentially getting roasted by public opinion and you get a slave for thirty hours of whatever you want him to do. What do you think of this proposition? Are you up for it?

Before Mike could speak, Sandy asked, "He is under our custody? Does that mean he has to live in our house?"

"No," said Officer Pierson with a laugh, "that would be cruel and unusual punishment for you and you haven't done anything wrong. No, just keep tabs on him. Think of yourselves as his parole officers. Sound okay?"

With apprehension Mike agreed. He wondered if anyone could really keep Harold on a leash.

"Good, then come with me and we will go see Mr. Broadmoor. Let me warn you, I'm going to do the stereotypical bad cop act. It is my job to scare the devil out of him and it is your job to get God into him."

Harold seemed contrite and submissive in the cell, but once he walked out the front door of the station, he thrust his fist into the air and shouted, "I love it when a plan comes together. Now I am going to leave you two and do an interview with this gentleman over here. The resulting article will be better than a hundred billboards all around town—and it is totally free. The *Perfect Gift* big-time Christmas production is going to be packed. And that is spelled p-a-c-k-e-d."

"Harold," Mike said, "I don't condone anything you've done and tomorrow I am going to schedule an emergency meeting with the deacons to determine whether you should even be in the Christmas play. I'm going to recommend that you are not."

Reporter Cal had just joined them and asked, "What part was Harold going to play?"

"I'm the angel, of course," Harold said with aplomb.

Cal looked inquisitively at the pastor.

"I know what you are thinking," Mike said. "I should have figured out that Harold was the Meanwhile angel— since he is going to be one in the play. And maybe I should have, but my part is somewhat apart from all the others so I haven't even been to a practice yet. I didn't even know that he was an angel in the play. And because of this stunt, I doubt that he will be."

"Now, Pastor Lewis, I urge you to reconsider about his absence from the play," the reporter said, looking intently into Mike's eyes. "I think the people in Meanwhile would like to see Harold up there. They've heard so much about him; everyone will want to see him in person."

"Exactamungo," Harold said.

"Well, that will be up to my deacons, but I know what my recommendation will be. Now. Sandy and I are going home so we will leave you to your interview—an interview, by the way, I wish you wouldn't conduct."

"Oh, I have to do the interview and I would also like to interview you, too."

"No, thank you. I prefer to pass."

The deacons were able to gather at nine the next morning. Due to the late notice only Kenny Frasier, Morris Ubody and Stan Glass were able to make it. Stan was furious and quickly seconded Pastor Mike's recommendation that Harold be prohibited from being in the Christmas production. But then something totally unexpected happened; Kenny and Morris voted against the motion and it failed. This confounded Stan and Mike. Kenny and Morris were followers; they had never been known to buck their leaders before. Stan spent ten minutes giving them a bombastic sermon on why Harold should not only be restricted from the play but also placed under church discipline but Kenny and Morris never responded back nor gave any reasons for their vote. They slumped in their chairs, looked at the floor or the ceiling and did a little hem-hawing, but they wouldn't change their vote.

Later Mike recounted the decision to Sandy and she was surprised... but also delighted. She, like the reporter, wanted to see the Meanwhile angel on their stage. Then she asked Mike a question. "Do you think Harold had any accomplices?"

"I don't think so. We know that he didn't at the police station. He has a truck and a ladder so he could do it all by himself."

"Who took the pictures?"

"Cal, the newspaperman."

"No, Mike, he was only at the police station. One or more people had to be with Harold on the other occasions. It would have been difficult for him to take pictures of himself."

"Sherlock, you are absolutely right. Unless he has some fancy photographic equipment -- which I think I would know about -- he had to have had outside help. I doubt that he would involve his frail wife, he's way too protective of her."

"Whit maybe?"

"Perhaps, but I doubt it. I haven't seen the two of them hobnobbing. The pieces are all falling together here. I am guessing that his accomplices just may have been... Kenny Frasier and Morris Ubody. Those stinkers!"

FORTY-TWO

....

A SURPRISE CALL.
A SURPRISE VISIT.

Mike hoped this angel mess would just fizzle out. Nope. And it was Will Statler's fault. Will Statler was, along with James Craig, one of the most popular meteorologists in West Michigan. Most people were familiar with his trademark moustache that bridged a big, friendly smile. Mike often tuned in to get his weather reports on channel four -- the same television station that had already done a segment on the Meanwhile Angel. Statler was a professing Christian who occasionally taught seminars on Biblical creationism. Mike had been to one of those and although they didn't get acquainted personally, he had been a big fan of the celebrity ever since. But on Friday morning, just two days before the Christmas production, Will Statler called him at the church to inform him that the station would like to send a news team, consisting of Statler and a camera man, to the church on Sunday morning to get a clip of the "Harold Angel" in action at their Christmas program.

Mike's emotion wasn't excitement; it was shock.

"Are you sure that you are Will Statler? This isn't a prank call, is it?"

"No, this is the real me. You can call the station and reach me for confirmation if you desire."

"But, Mr. Statler, you do the weather. Why would you want to do this?"

"WZZM sometimes uses me for human interest stories and, for whatever reason, this story about your angel has stirred up a lot of interest."

"I'm not sure this would be worth your time; we are a small church in a small town doing a small, simple Christmas play."

Will said, "I'm sure you're being modest but let us be the judge of that. We will come down, do some pre-interviews with you and Harold Broadmoor and then get some clips of him in the play. If we don't think they are valuable enough to put on the air, we just won't use them."

"Well, that's your call; I won't tell you 'no,' although I admit that I'm still hesitant. But, if you are going to be here, would you mind doing a greeting to our church at the beginning of the service? Maybe you could do a short testimony, as well?" The pastor went on to tell how he had seen Will's creation presentation at a previous church and how much he'd enjoyed him. Will Statler was happy to oblige but he also said that his greeting would have to be on the side; they wouldn't use it on the air.

When the call was over, Mike hurried to the parsonage to tell Sandy that "the circus is coming to town!"

*   *   *

After lunch Mike decided he was going to make a very important home visit. Arnold and Marilyn Kling may have left the church but they still clung to Mike's heart. He felt their absence and thought it was tragic they were gone. He'd tried to give them the space that they had requested but now he decided that he was going to ignore their request to stay away; it was time to ambush them with a surprise intervention.

He drove to their home with anticipation of further rejection. This dread made it hard for him to even get out of his car, walk up the sidewalk, and ring the doorbell. He suspected that one of them was going to open the door, see him and scowl. Ugh. Fortunately, the reception was just the opposite.

"Pastor Mike! How wonderful it is to see you." Marilyn said ecstatically. "Arnold, come quick; Pastor Mike is here."

Arnold hurried out and soon Mike was being smothered by the old Clinger full-court- press attention that he had once disliked. At the moment he loved it. They avalanched him with hugs, squeezes, tugs, pulls, and a blizzard of words—all delivered at very close range.

The three of them were sitting on the couch, with Mike in the middle. Over coffee, they talked and talked, and then... talked more. For an hour, Mike learned about Counselor Carol's 'therapeutic' plan to bring them to the front of a church for a combination public confession and healing service—something they thought Mike was in on. The visualization of that kept them from returning to church.

"But someone changed our mind last evening," Marilyn said with a smile.

"Who?" Mike said.

"Don't tell him, Marilyn," Arnie broke in, "let me show him." Arnie stood, went into their bedroom and returned with a package. "Pastor, can you guess what is in here?"

"No, Arnie, I don't have a clue."

"Then let me show you." He pulled out a plastic-wrapped shirt and tie. "Ever seen this before?"

"Ah, I don't think so... wait." The shirt did look familiar. Green-and-red stripes. Where had he seen that before? Suddenly it hit him. "That's the shirt and tie you gave Whit Carson. Did he return it to you?"

"No, he still has his shirt and tie. He found this at the same sales rack where we bought his. He brought this by and gave it to me as a gift."

Marilyn took over. "Whitfield said that he and everyone else at the church wanted us to come back. Then he gave Arnie that shirt and tie and suggested that they both wear their matching outfits on Christmas Sunday. It was so precious. Obviously, we couldn't say 'no' so we agreed."

"And Pastor Mike, after that we have been so excited about coming back. That's why we were so thrilled to see you. Did Whit send you?"

"No, I haven't spoken to Whit this week."

"Then," Marilyn said, "God sent you."

"Yes," Arnie repeated, "God sent you."

"And what about Whit?" Mike asked, "Did God send him, too?"

"Oh definitely," they both agreed. "Definitely."

Marilyn used Mike's sleeve to pull him close. She softly said, "God has his hand on that young man."

Mike went on to tell them that Will Statler was going to come to the Christmas program and film a news clip. The Clingers both bounced on the davenport with excitement, and due to their attachment to his arms, took him along for the ride. They assured him that they were going to call everyone with the news.

As Mike left the house he couldn't resist the urge to ask one more question. "I've noticed that you two are still in your robes and pajamas. Do you always sleep in so late?"

"No, Silly," Marilyn gave him a goodbye hug. "Arnie and I are still getting over the flu."

FORTY-THREE

....

THE FINAL REHEARSAL

Red Monkmeier was the writer, producer and musical director of the annual Christmas program. Convinced it was a masterpiece, he'd insisted that it be "aired primetime" – during the Christmas Sunday Worship Service. That would be tomorrow. But this morning he gathered all the participants together for their final rehearsal. Harold Broadmoor, his right hand man, stood beside him.

"Today we are going to review everything and do a final run through. This will be a snap because the program is simple in design. It's purposely planned that way. Simplicity leads to clarity." Red looked around at the cast members and parents who had gathered in the church auditorium. "Let me repeat that. Simplicity leads to clarity. And clarity results in a clear message – the Christmas message. And that's what it's all about. Amen?"

"Amen, amen," Harold echoed.

"Simplicity does not mean insignificant. Make no mistake about that. This may be the largest, most moving production this church has ever seen. Everyone with me?"

"Listen to the man, people," Harold shouted. "This is going to be huge. H.U.G.E."

Red smiled at his companion and then addressed the group, "Let's make it real easy. Think three."

Beside him, Harold raised one hand with three fingers.

Red nodded. "That's right. Three. The drama has three acts, which will be done on the three stage levels."

Harold raised his other hand; three more fingers waved in the air. Subtract a finger from each hand and it would have looked like an imitation of Richard Nixon.

Red continued, "The three acts are the caroling, the Christmas story and a mini Christmas message. Now then, please look up at our stage area. Level one, located on our regular platform looks like an ordinary living room, doesn't it? Does anyone recognize whose living room it is? The furniture should look familiar. Anyone? Yes, William?"

"Is it the pastor's?"

"Exactly, my boy. We have transferred their living room to our stage. And that is where our production will begin. Mrs. Lewis will be knitting in her living room when all of you kids come caroling. That's where you children will sing the Christmas songs you have been practicing – including the special number I have personally written for this production. With you will be Carol Harmon. She will be your adult leader. So, and catch this because it is pretty funny, you will be *caroling with Carol.*"

The kids looked at Red with blank expressions.

"Caroling with Carol? Doesn't that sound funny? Oh, never mind. Sandy, you'll invite them in and then call for Pastor Mike to join you. Pastor Mike, you... hey, where's Pastor Mike?"

"Back here." Mike was standing in the back holding a shovel and wearing a coat. Due to a heavy snow, he had been helping Kenny and Morris shovel the sidewalks around the church.

"Kids, look at the pastor. He's going to be dressed quite differently tomorrow. He'll be wearing pajamas— right here in church."

The children finally laughed.

"It's okay to laugh now but tomorrow you can't. That would spoil the moment. Remember now—no laughing. In our dramatic scene, we will come caroling in the evening and discover that Pastor Lewis is already prepared for bed. Pastors go to bed early, you know. Mrs. Lewis will still be in her clothes because it wouldn't be proper for us to see a woman in a robe. Now that makes sense to everyone, doesn't it?"

"My dad sleeps in his underpants."

"William, pastors don't sleep in their underpants and it's a good thing. That would really mess up our program." Red's laughter drowned out the other chuckles.

"I guess I could never be a pastor," Harold said.

"We aren't going there," Red said. "Anyway, the pastor will come in and volunteer to read the Christmas story to everyone. That's the proper thing to do with carolers. It's a tradition that pastors follow. He'll start reading Luke chapter two when suddenly the lights will fade. Pastor Lewis will get quiet and all of you must freeze in place. No moving." Several of the children became statues. "Yes, that's it."

"The spotlight will then light up the right side of level two. Can you see where Kenny and Morris have constructed it in the choir loft? Look back at Kenny and Morris and give them a hand."

While everyone clapped, Harold hooted and whistled. That got Solomon Bing to whistle also. He shifted into the tune *For He's a Jolly Good Fellow*.

Red cut him off. "We have several people to thank for their donation of time, lumber and indoor/outdoor carpet. And most of all we need to thank Harold here. I was just going to put all the action on the stage but Harold insisted that we make this real big. He drew up the design on paper and then recruited the workers."

More clapping and a bow from Harold.

"Back to level two. On one side you can see the Christmas tree surrounded by decorated Christmas presents. They will, as Pastor Mike will share at the end in his sermonette, illustrate temporary, earthly gifts."

"We were going to put Santa up there but one of the deacons vetoed that." Harold looked over at the play's narrator, Stan Glass.

Defending himself, Stan said, "Everyone knows that Santa is a metaphor for Satan. Surely you have noticed that the letters in their names, although arranged differently, are identical. Satan? Santa? Both dress in red? Hmmmm?"

People gasped. Children turned in shock to stare wide-eyed at their parents. Harold, someone who already looked like Santa Claus anyway, laughingly said, "Ho, ho, ho, that is ho-larious!"

Red shouted over the conversation buzz that had ignited in the pews. "Let's not talk about that now. We have a production to prepare for. Refocus on the second level stage. On one side are the Christmas tree and presents but the other side has a cross and a manger with the Christ child. We have put a bow on the manger to symbolize that it contains Jesus – the perfect gift. The pastor is going to contrast the two different kinds of trees, an evergreen and a dead cross, and the two different kinds of presents, temporary and eternal. Isn't this powerful?"

"Tell them about the third level," Harold said.

"Ah, yes, the third level—the crow's nest built over the baptismal tank. It's covered with cotton to represent clouds. That is where the angel will be. There should be several angels but that platform is only big enough for one—especially when the angel is a very big angel." He pointed his thumb at Harold and everyone laughed. "For a long time, we kept his part a secret; but now that he has appeared around town as the Meanwhile angel, I think everyone knows his role."

"That's me—the biggest angel in these parts. Now, because of my many sightings around town, I have become famous all over Michigan. And I did all of that to promote 'The Perfect Gift' Christmas production. Tomorrow people are going to come from all over to see me standing up there in the clouds dressed in my wings and white tux."

"That is, if you aren't in jail," Red said with a laugh.

"You can't keep an angel in jail. I've proven that."

"Yeah, you're just lucky Pastor Mike and Sandy sweet-talked the police and got you out of there." Red looked at Sandy in the first pew and said, "Frankly, I think it was your charms that got this jail bird free."

Sandy smiled and gave him a playful wink.

"So then, those are the three stage levels. Now for the three acts. First, the carolers led by Carol, will come down the center aisle dressed in their winter coats and singing the songs we have practiced. Second, they come to the parsonage we've reenacted on the first level and Sandy invites them in. Pastor Mike joins them and he reads the Christmas story. As he does, the carolers, who are now seated on the floor, freeze and the lights go out. As he continues to read, using the desk light, the spotlights highlight the angel..."

"Fear not!" broke in Harold, "For I bring you glad tidings of great joy."

"Later, Harold. After our summary, we will practice the play and you can all do your parts. Now, where was I? Oh yes, while the pastor reads the Luke two narrative, the spotlights will shine first on the angel up there, then the shepherds over there by the piano and finally on the manger scene. That brings us to the third act. When the story is finished, Pastor Mike stands up and moves to the front of the stage and addresses the audience with his short sermon on *The Perfect Gift*. Besides the light on him, the spots will be on the entire second level with the two trees and the two kinds of gifts. When he finishes, the carolers will stand up, gather around him and again sing the signature song that I wrote, also called *The Perfect Gift*.

And that, my friends, is the whole enchilada. In a moment, we will all take our places and run through this one more time. Then we can go home and relax until tomorrow. Just pray and relax. This is going to be a piece of cake."

"Enchilada and cake," Harold said. "Quite the meal."

"A simple meal," Red said. "Delicious, nutritious but simple. And don't forget, everyone, simplicity leads to clarity. And clarity results in a clear message. Now, everyone move to your spots."

It was all quite simple, Mike thought, but he had a sense of deep foreboding. There really was no reason for anything to go wrong, but if history was a predictor, it would. Last year's Christmas production had been an embarrassment and he feared a repetition; only this year there might be a lot more people to witness it—and a television camera. He was still shivering from what he figured was his time outside snow shoveling, but, along with the shivers, he felt a shudder quiver through him.

FORTY-FOUR

....

TWAS THE NIGHT BEFORE CHRISTMAS SUNDAY

That night Mike woke with the flu—apparently a Christmas present from the Clingers. Its volcanic symptoms sent him repeatedly to the bathroom. Due to dizziness, each trip was a zig-zaggy, staggered journey that required him to reach out to dressers and walls to keep his balance. A fever roasted his thoughts and they came out dark and burnt. A bad dream pursued him from slumber into consciousness and, though now awake, he still felt entrapped within a nightmare.

"Why now?" he mumbled to Sandy, "The most important Sunday of the year and I'm sicker than a dog."

"Awww, I feel so terrible for you. Here, let me get something for you."

Sandy returned quickly and put a wet washcloth on his forehead. It cooled him a bit, but he wished its moisture would soak through the surface and soothe his anxiety. He worried about the next day and allowed his dread to taunt him with premature humiliation.

"It's ironic; I keep encouraging people to invite friends to church and now that it looks like we might have a lot of guests, I almost wish they would stay home. People are going to show up expecting a spectacular production and instead witness a hokey little program put on by hack amateurs wearing bathrobes and towels on their heads. They will be dressed just like they did at the Harvestween festival. We will be laughed at by people all over town—or maybe, due to the television coverage, all over the state."

"Mike, it's going to be wonderful. You're just tired and sick and that's making you melancholy. Relax and go back to sleep."

"It's going to be awful. I hope the Lord returns before tomorrow morning."

"Baby, that would be super but even if He doesn't, He's going to be there tomorrow and I'm sure He will enjoy it." Her words came out slurred and groggy; she fought to stay awake to comfort her husband. "Do you want me to pray for you?"

No, he didn't want her to pray for him. He didn't feel like getting spiritual and positive; he had a lot more griping he wanted to indulge in. "Sure," he lied, "that would be nice."

"Dear Heavenly Father..." She paused and then slowly pushed out more of her prayer, "please heal Mike's body and... ah, calm his anxieties... and, ah... please help... tomorrow to, ah...."

Thinking he was going to hear something meaningful, he waited for more.

Her breathing got heavy and she emitted a small snore.

"'Could you not watch with me one hour?'" Mike said, quoting the words Christ said to His sleeping disciples in the Garden of Gethsemane the night before He was crucified.

"Well, maybe this is for the best; now you won't be interrupting my dark diatribe with your sunny Sandy routine. As I was saying," he said to no one other than himself, "I predict tomorrow will be a disaster. We will have to listen to Stainglass do the narration with his high-toned, monotoned, megaphoned, listen-to-my-deeply-spiritual voice. Then Harold will be up on his perch in his white tux waving his angel wings and trying to get all the attention. I hope he doesn't start singing 'Hark the Harold Angel Sings' again. And Counselor Carol will probably stop the production to scold the kids for something. And, of course, Red and all the little Reds will step in front of the rest of the cast and sing extra loud. Wouldn't surprise me if they don't add a dance number. This will be their chance to go pro and start a

'Musical Monkmeiers' concert tour. Say, Sandy, speaking about the Monkmeiers, did they ever empty the water out of the baptismal tank after they were using as a swimming pool?"

Sandy slept on. She looked so peaceful he almost woke her up.

"And don't forget Whit. You know he's going to use this occasion to pull off one of his monster pranks. He's gone too long without doing anything mischievous; he's got to be saving up for something big. I hope it's nothing terrible. Maybe it'll just be something sweet and innocent like nailing Harold the angel with a snowball. Yes, that would be okay. Or, even better, Stainglass."

For the first time since he got sick, he smiled; his evil little thoughts brought some pleasure. But another weaving dash to the can doused his brief respite of merriment and the dark storm clouds again blanketed his mind. Now he thought back about the people—his mentor, Dan Hall, his buddy, Charles Jackson, the visitors, Mr. and Mrs. *Snodgrass*, and others—who all thought that Meanwhile Baptist Church was overly populated with quirky, peculiar people. He normally fought those accusations but tonight his angry critical spirit agreed wholeheartedly. Of course, he thought, he was the worst of the lot. What had he accomplished since being here?

Why, Lord? What is the point of all this? I always thought you wanted to do something great. But this church is filled with a bunch of losers being pastored by a bigger loser who is clueless on how to turn things around. Mike immediately felt guilty for using his spontaneous prayer to disparage the church people but he felt no remorse for slamming himself. *And now it is Christmas Sunday, and on top of everything else, I am feeling pathetic--inside and out. Why, Lord?*

It was almost a rhetorical question; Mike expected no answer. But then a verse came to his mind. "My grace is sufficient for you. My strength will be displayed through your weakness."

Mike was startled. Where did that ray of hope come from? A word from the Lord, maybe?

Really, Lord?

Mike visualized Jesus with a smile and a nod.

Thank you, Lord Jesus. Please tell me more."

He prayed that the Lord would cleanse him from wrong thoughts and give him a heavenly perspective. Then he waited and listened.

Another scripture came, this time from First Corinthians. Mike didn't remember it word for word but he did recall that the first chapter said that God did not call many who were wise, powerful or of noble birth; instead He even picked those considered low and foolish to show His glory.

Mike meditated further and slowly a sense of peace soothed him and allowed him to drift into a restful sleep. When morning came, he felt better. For a while in the night, he thought that his part in the drama would have to be written out. But now he decided—wrongly, he would later discover—that he was up for his role.

FORTY-FIVE

······································

GOT JESUS?

The big day had arrived and from the window of his office, Pastor Mike could see that the parking lot was already filled. Kenny was using the plow on the front of his Chevy truck to clear snow from the church lawn and Morris followed up by waving vehicles into the newly created spots. Mike could also see the nativity scene by the front of the church and the members of the adult choir who surrounded it, singing carols for those entering the building.

Due to his illness, Sandy had quarantined him here and told him he could only leave when the program began. Suddenly the door flew open and she burst in with a whoop. "Oh baby, you should see it out there. It's just like Harold T. 'What an Incredible Marketer' Broadmoor predicted; the place is p-a-c-k-e-d, packed. Everybody and their distant relatives are out there. They're having to set up folding chairs in the aisles and in the foyer. This is so much fun."

331

"Is Will Statler here?"

"Yes, and he is so nice. He told me to tell you that he's sorry that you're sick and that he won't be able to interview you. So sad."

"I didn't want to be interviewed anyway."

"You're a big party pooper. Who wouldn't want to be on television? You should see the size of the camera. They came down in this big news van and everything. Right now they are interviewing our resident angel, and let me tell you, Harold is really hamming it up."

"Of course."

"And guess what? Byron Nagy is here. Lorraine is just beaming to have him in church."

Mike clapped his hands together. "That's great."

"And Bud and Lucille's neighbor came. Do you remember what her name is?"

"Gloria something."

"Yes, that's right – Gloria Mead. Oh, and here's something else I was supposed to tell you. Red told you to relax and stay back here until it's your part in the play. He'll take over the beginning part of the service and do all the preliminary stuff like the opening hymns, the offering and the introduction of Mr. Statler and everything. So you aren't supposed to worry. You just need to stand by the back side door of the auditorium and wait for your turn. When you hear me call for you, it's time for you to come out in your pajamas. Hey, how come you aren't in your pajamas now?

"I am... under my clothes. I feel stupid standing around in pjs."

"Okay, hun, see you later then. I should be out there talking to people and getting ready."

After the service started and the hallway by the office emptied, Mike stripped down to his pajamas, went to the auditorium's back door and opened it a crack just in time to see Will Statler finish speaking. The crowd clapped loud and as he descended from the stage, he gave them a wave and one of his trademark smiles. Then the lights slowly faded and everyone grew quiet.

"Ladies and Gentlemen," narrator Stan Glass sounded like a circus announcer, "Meanwhile Baptist Church is happy to present..." The organ played a drumbeat before Stan stretched out the last three words, "theeeeeee Perfect Gift!"

Old Margaret shouted out, "Yeehaah!" and Solomon Blink gave a shrill whistle.

A spotlight hit the two center doors leading into the sanctuary as Carol Harmon and ten children, all dressed in winter coats, scarves, gloves and stocking caps entered. There was William, Kim, Kristy, Johan, Kerry, Sophia and, of course, Mathew, Mark, Luke and Bob. They were singing, "I'm Dreaming of a White Christmas."

Carol dressed much like them except she was only wearing one mitten—which, it appeared to Mike, was singing along.

The floor was covered with shredded paper made to look like snow. William gave the first line with gusto. "Do you know what I like about a white Christmas?"

"No," said the rest of the children, "what?"

"This!" he shouted. Then he reached down and grabbed two white Styrofoam balls from the floor and threw them into the audience. Several children shouted, "Snowball fight" and they all started throwing snowballs at the people in pews." There were peals of laughter.

"That's enough, children," Carol Harmon said loudly, "we are on our way to the pastor's house to do some Christmas caroling and we don't want to be late."

Kristy, a born actress, gave a big dimple-faced smile and said, "But wait, Miss Harmon, do you know what I like best about a white Christmas?"

"No, Kristy, what?"

"The snow covers up all the dirt and makes everything clean. It reminds me of the Bible verse that teaches us that we are as white as snow when God forgives our sins."

"You are exactly right, Kristy, and that is why Jesus was born into this world. He came to save us from our sins by dying on the cross for us. Those who accept Him as their Savior are born again spiritually and receive the gift of eternal life."

"That's the perfect gift," all the children said in unison.

"And that," Matthew said," reminds me of a song that my father, Mr. Red Monkmeier, wrote. I think you all know it. Let's sing it together as we head to the pastor's house." As they continued down the aisle toward the platform, they sang,

Merry, Merry Christmas from all of us to you.
Merry, Merry Christmas, may Jesus Christ bless you.
He gave you life for this present earth,
But to get to Heaven you need a second birth.
So celebrate His birthday and your birthday, too,
And always remember His perfect gift to you.

So far, so good, Mike thought. At this point he didn't care if the production wasn't anything flashy -- few small church Christmas programs are. If things went smooth, he would be satisfied.

On stage, Sandy was sitting on her green couch with Deacon on the floor by her feet. She was "knitting"—something she never did in real life—when she heard the singing. As the youngsters came up the steps of the platform, Sandy stood, opened an imaginary door, listened to them sing some more familiar choruses and said, "Hi, boys and girls, I love your singing. Thank you so much for coming to carol for us. Please come in while I call for the pastor." She turned to the door where Mike was waiting and shouted, "Honey, come here, we have a wonderful surprise."

Mike took two steps when his head begin to swim and he staggered to keep his footing. *Oh no, it's back!* Afraid that he was going to fall, he returned to the wall to catch his equilibrium.

"Honey," Sandy shouted again in vain and when no honey appeared, a titter went through the crowd. "Let me go check on him," she said to the kids, "sometimes when he is reading the Bible, he—."

"Falls asleep!" William interjected. "That's what happens to me when I read the Bible." That got a laugh.

"I was going to say that he gets so engrossed that he tunes everything out, but if you kids can keep a secret, I'll admit that William is right. Sometimes he does fall asleep. But let me go check on him."

She went down the back stairs of the stage into the darkness where she found Mike bent over, propped up against the wall. "Baby," she whispered, "Are you okay?"

"I'm not. Sick. Dizzy. But I have to go on. Brace me as we go up the stairs and be prepared to read the Christmas story and give the devotional."

"Michael, I can read the story but I'm not giving a devotional. I can't think on my feet like you can; I wouldn't know what to say. But let's get you up there and maybe you will feel better." She gripped him by the arm and moved him toward the stairs much like a man would steer a drunk out of a bar.

They got to the top of the platform and Mike said, "Okay, let go, I'm going solo." He leaned for a moment against a two-by-four that was propping up this end of the second level of the stage and then launched himself forward into the part of the stage that was lighted. "Hi gang! It is wonderful to see you!"

Before he could react, Kim and Kristy and the other members of their official "hug club" ran to him, and, like they did each Sunday when they saw him, gave him hugs. William held back and said, "I don't do hugs."

And because of that, Mike thought, *you may be the only one not sick tomorrow.*

Sandy quickly intervened. "Kids, please sit down on either the furniture or the floor. My hubby and I will sit over here and read the Christmas story to you out of Luke two."

Mike began to sit when he felt the sudden stomach churning that had warned him all last night to dash to the bathroom. "Be right back," he said, hurrying out of the room. As soon as he was out of the lights he began to run—which he did for four steps. That is when he ran into the two-by-four that he had been leaning against just a few minutes before. His head struck first and he bounced back clutching it in pain. It was such a collision he not only saw stars, he saw planets. But he charged forward again. Making it to the bathroom was a mission he was devoted to.

He didn't make it, however. He did make it to the drinking fountain and, although that was better than most alternatives, it was still nasty. He went to his office and used some tissues to clean himself up. There he looked up on a poster on his wall that quoted Philippians 4:13. He read it aloud as a prayer; "I can do all things through Christ which strengtheneth me."

While he was gone, Sandy slowly read the second chapter of Luke. When she reached the part where Mary placed her firstborn into the manger, she paused as the spotlight focused on the manger on the second level stage above them. As she read verse eight, the spotlight swung over to the back of the first level stage where there were shepherds and fake sheep. And then the moment came that most of the crowd were eagerly anticipating. She read, "An angel of the Lord appeared to them and the glory of the Lord shone around them and they were terrified." That's when the spot hit Harold T. Broadmoor in his perch high above the baptismal tank. In his white tux, white wings and white beard he really glowed and the crowd clapped.

Harold shouted out, "Fear not." He yelled it so loud he scared many of the people in the church. Then he went on to say, "for, behold, I bring you good tidings of great joy, which shall be to all people. For unto you is born this day in the city of David a Saviour, which is Christ the Lord. And this shall be a sign unto you; Ye shall find the babe wrapped in swaddling clothes, lying in a manger."

After his part, Sandy took over again and finished just as Mike stepped back into the darkness of the back shoulder of the auditorium. "And that is the end of the Christmas story," Sandy said loudly. Mike figured the volume was for his benefit; she was signaling him to let him know that he was needed immediately. "Isn't Luke two wonderful? Maybe if the pastor isn't back soon, I will read it again. Would you like that?"

"Again?" William asked.

"I'm coming," Mike yelled from his spot in the dark. Again he ran. And again he ran into the same two-by-four. This time he knocked it over and although the second stage was attached to the wall, it tipped forward with a lurch and all the Christmas gifts began to fall off to the stage below where the children were.

"Presents from heaven!" William shouted and ran to catch one in the air. Not to be outdone, all the rest of the children followed his example. Deacon added to the chaos by barking loudly and playfully chasing after some of the kids. The audience began to laugh loudly.

That was all brought to a halt by Old Margaret. With the bellow of a bull moose, she shouted, "GET JESUS!" All attention was then focused to the other side of the second stage where the cross and manger were placed. Fortunately, they were nailed to the floor but baby Jesus was teetering on the edge of the tipped manger.

The baby wobbled a little more and, with a collective gasp from the audience, fell. And that was when Counselor Carol discarded her recent reputation as a goat and became a star. Those who witnessed her action that day claimed they had never seen a greater play in any NFL football game. She ran across the stage, jumped up in the air unto the couch, bounced high off its cushions and flew, like Superwoman, through the air. With arms outstretched she caught the doll with one hand and then fell from view behind the sofa.

Up she stood, holding the baby high with one arm, and shouted, "I got Jesus."

There was a thunderous applause and then the crowd, spurred on by Old Margaret who was waving them to their feet, gave her a standing ovation. Carol, caught up in the moment, began to dance in a circle with the Christ child still lifted above, and repeated the line, "I got Jesus, I got Jesus, I got Jesus."

Mike knew this was the time to improvise so he stepped into the spotlight and clapped along with the crowd. No longer feeling as ill, he was energized and looking forward to taking this unexpected drama to a new level. When the clapping died down, he motioned the people to sit down and then turned to the children and said, "Kids, please pick up your presents and bring them back to the living room. And Carol, please take this chair and continue to hold on to baby Jesus."

When they had all repositioned themselves, he said, "On the count of three, I want each of you children to open your gifts. One. Two. Three!"

They tore off the wrapping, opened the boxes and then began to complain, "They're empty."

"Yes," Mike said, "they are all empty. You did what most of us do in this life, you ran after the brightly colored gifts that look good on the outside but are really empty. Oh, they may hold temporary treasures but eventually they will rust, break or fade away from importance. In the end, you will have left what's in your boxes -- nothing. Emptiness.

"But Carol over here," he paused and made his way to behind her chair where he gently placed his hands on her shoulders. "Carol Harmon made the greatest choice. She decided to 'Get Jesus.'" Turning to the audience, he pointed at Old Margaret and said, "Margaret, that was excellent advice you gave -- Get Jesus!"

"You betcha," she shouted back. "Get Jesus. You hear me everyone?" She yelled even louder, "GET JESUS!"

"I am sure everyone in town can hear you, Margaret," Mike said. "And I hope they will listen to you. When people get Jesus, they get the perfect gift. John 3:16, a verse that may be the most quoted verse in Scripture, says 'For God so loved the world that He gave His one and only Son that whosoever believes in Him will not perish but have eternal life.'"

Mike walked to the front of the stage and, in a soft conversational voice, said, "Jesus Christ was given by God the Father to us, and those who choose to receive this gift also receive eternal life. Do you know what that is? It is an everlasting, never-ending relationship with Jesus Christ Himself. You will enjoy His presence in this life and then will live with Him forever in heaven after you die. That, my friends is *the perfect gift*. If you have yet to receive this gift, let me tell you how you can do that right now with a simple prayer of faith..."

Mike finished his message and most of the cast joined him at the front of the platform where they ended the production by singing the theme song, "The Perfect Gift" one more time.

When a final wave of clapping died down, narrator Stan Glass again used his stain-glassed voice to say, "Thank you for coming, everyone. Can we give special appreciation to director Red Monkmeier?" Red stepped out and gave a bow. "And let's also thank Pastor Mike Lewis and his wife, Sandy." Mike gave a nod and Sandy waved. "And those kids, weren't they great?" The volume picked up more as the children bowed and William turned his bow into a somersault. "And before I say the next name, let me remind you that it is normally not proper to run and jump in church but today one person showed us an exception to that rule. Let's give it up for Carol Harmon." The audience added cheers to their clapping. Carol lifted baby Jesus aloft one more time and shouted, "I Got Jesus. You can get Him too."

Stan said, "The shepherds deserve some attention, don't they?" There was only polite applause. "And finally, let's show appreciation to that man standing directly above me." Stan looked up from where he had positioned himself just in front of the baptismal tank, "Harold 'the Meanwhile Angel' Broadmoor." This time the clapping was almost drowned out by laughter.

Harold gave an exaggerated bow and when he came up he lost his balance. There was a railing on the front side of his perch but not on the back side so while he pin-wheeled his arms trying to right himself, he looked behind him with apparent fear.

"Watch it!" Old Margaret yelled.

But the warning did no good—he went over backwards. Maybe the large feathered wings created an illusion but he appeared to be doing a graceful back dive. Down he went head-first and landed in the baptismal tank with a giant splash. A tsunami doused Stan but he held on to his microphone and said, "Angel down. Angel down. We have a fallen angel. Let's hope he's alright."

The people were all standing -- trying to see if Harold was injured. There was quiet murmuring but mostly there was a tense silence as people waited to see what had happened to Harold. But he stayed submerged.

"Pray, people!" Stan shouted into the microphone as he scrambled closer to the edge of the tank. "I'm going to try and save him."

And that's when Harold burst out of the water with his arms stretched upward and his fingers pointed straight like an Olympic gymnast finishing a routine. In the front row, Whit Carson, sitting next to a similarly dressed Arnie Kling, hurriedly scribbled a big "10" on a piece of paper, turned around, stood on the pew and displayed it to the crowd.

Harold grabbed Stan's microphone and shouted, "Don't you folks just love a big finish? Come back soon!" Then he grabbed Stan's arm and pulled him into the tank. "Come on in, the water's fine."

Pandemonium broke loose. While little Bob Monkmeier played *Silent Night* on his trumpet, people spoke animatedly with each other about the amazing play they had just witnessed.

....

FORTY-SIX

DESSERTS

The "Perfect Gift" Christmas production was over but the festivities continued. In the fellowship hall there was a Christmas Pie Potluck and although Mike could hear the hubbub of happy voices coming from that direction, he had been reluctantly confined to his office by Sandy. Now that he was feeling a little better, he was antsy and wanted to be enjoying the fellowship and desserts.

When he heard voices in the hallway outside his door, he got snoopy. So he went to the door and listened to the conversation.

"Kid," he heard Harold T. Broadmoor say, "we make a great team. You keep feeding me your good ideas and we will keep having a ball."

"Mr. Broadmoor, can you keep your voice down? You promised to keep my part in all of this a secret."

That was Whit Carson's voice.

"Look around you, boy," Harold said, "Do you see anyone in earshot? And as to our secret, Harold T. Broadmoor has kept his lips sealed. But I don't know why you want to keep this mum. Your idea of me appearing around town as an angel was genius. Did you see how many people showed up today due to our covert publicity campaign? You deserve the credit for that."

"No way, I just gave you the idea, but you executed the plan. You stand in the spotlight; I prefer to be in the shadows."

"But son—" Harold bellowed.

"Shhhh," Whit said, interrupting Harold. "Please hold it down, someone could be listening."

"Who? Where?"

"Did you ever think that the pastor might be in his office?"

"Young Whit, you're just paranoid; he's not in there."

"Yes, he is," Mike said from his side of the door.

"Well," Harold said in a softer voice, "I doubt if he heard anything,"

"Yes, he did," Mike said as he opened the door and joined them. "So you two have been partners in crime, huh?"

"Well, partners in something I suppose. But never mind all that. Merry Christmas, pastor. Now I better hustle along. Mother is waiting for me in the fellowship hall. And Whit, you better come with me before all the pie is gone."

"Run off, you coward," Mike said with a laugh.

"Well I'm also remembering that you have the flu," Harold said back with his own laugh. "Unclean," he yelled. "Unclean!"

Whit turned to Mike and stepped up close. "Pastor Mike, I know I often pull a lot of pranks but I want to tell you something right now I am totally serious about. I want to not only wish you a Merry Christmas but also tell you how grateful I am to you. Knowing you for the last couple of months has helped me get closer to God and sort through some things in my life. I have a long way to go, but I think I'm now heading in the right direction. So, thank you; thank you very much."

Mike choked up and for a moment he just smiled at Whit. Then he reached out and put a hand on the teen's shoulder. "That means a lot, Whit. And getting to know you has been a great privilege for me. After the holidays, I hope we can spend more time together. Maybe you will even open up and tell me more about yourself and stop being such a mystery man?" "Well... maybe. Who knows what the future holds?" Whitfield flashed a sly smile, turned and walked away.

A few minutes later Sandy came bustling in. "Okay, my sicko hubby, I've got lots of good news and a note. What do you want first?"

"News."

"Okay, well first of all, everyone—except for Stan Glass who's mad about getting pulled into the baptismal tank—is saying they loved the play. Most people don't even know about all the accidents that caused your improvisations. They think it was all planned—even Counselor Carol making that diving catch of baby Jesus. And speaking of Carol, she is suddenly real popular. There's a gang of people around her right now and she is still holding the doll with that one hand in a mitten."

Mike smiled. "Well, what do you know?"

"And," Sandy said, "it gets better. After the program Lucille got to lead her neighbor, Gloria, to the Lord."

"That is awesome! Give me more details."

"When it was over, Lucille asked Gloria if she liked the Perfect Gift—meaning the program. Gloria said the gift sounded wonderful but she didn't think she had ever received it herself. So Lucille told her that the best time was right now. They went to a side room and Lucille took a tract out of her purse and used it to explain the plan of salvation. Gloria prayed right then to accept Jesus Christ as her Lord and Savior."

"How phenomenal! That makes this Christmas very special."

"There's more. Byron Nagy told me to tell you that he got a real kick out of the program and that he is going to spend this Christmas season thinking more seriously about spiritual things. Mike, I really think he's getting close. Lorraine was just beaming when he was talking to me."

"When he gets saved, I'm going to do cartwheels."

"And God is going to throw a party in heaven," Sandy said. "And finally, here's your note. It's from Will Statler."

"Would you read it for me?"

"I'd love to. It says, 'Pastor Lewis, I am sorry that we didn't get to meet personally but I had a wonderful time at your church and really enjoyed the program. We got several good video clips so you can expect to see Meanwhile Baptist Church on the air soon. Have a very Merry Christmas! May God bless you richly!' It's signed, 'Will Statler.'" Sandy clapped her hands and exclaimed, "Isn't that cool?"

"It's very nice but I don't think I want us on the air. I'll bet they just show the Meanwhile Angel doing a high dive into the pool."

"I sure hope so; I would like to watch that over and over."

"I'm sure you would. Well, let's go pack the car and take off on our Christmas vacation. But first, I just want to glance in the fellowship hall and see what I'm missing."

"But Mike, you have to promise to just glance and not go in."

"I promise."

Mike kept his promise. He stopped at the entrance and looked in. People, holding dessert-laden red or green plastic plates, were enjoying conversations. The sound of happiness was high volume. At the center of the room were tables filled with pies of every variety – apple, blueberry, cherry, pecan, chocolate, lemon meringue and more. The selection was as diverse as the people who brought them.

"I love our potlucks," Mike said to Sandy.

"And I love our church," she returned.

Mike hugged her. "Me, too."

And then came the booming voice of Old Margaret. "Look," she yelled, while pointing at them with a spatula, "there's Mike and Sandy."

The room grew quiet while everyone turned to stare. And then clapping began and grew into loud applause.

Mike felt his face grow hot. He slowly looked across the room, giving a smile and eye contact to as many as possible. Then, raising a hand to quiet them, he shouted, "Merry Christmas everyone and a Happy New Year."

It suddenly hit him that he really meant it—he was looking forward to a new year with the Potluck People.

ABOUT THE AUTHOR

Ron Sheveland, like many of the characters he writes about, is a tad quirky—okay, more than a tad. His offbeat sense of humor and story-telling skills have often entertained friends and audiences. He is an avid church man—so, lest you think he is ridiculing the peculiarities of typical churches, you would be wrong. He just thinks it's healthy to "laugh at ourselves."

Ron was nurtured in a godly home that modeled love and service for the Lord Jesus Christ. He accepted Jesus Christ as his Savior as a child and later, at a bible camp, surrendered his life to full time Christian service. As a teenager, he was already active speaking at camps, churches, and vacation Bible schools. At age eighteen, when he entered Cornerstone University, he became a youth director at Dalton Baptist Church in Muskegon, Michigan. In the years since he has pastored churches in Michigan, Colorado and California. And for ten years he was the director of an association of churches called the Michigan Baptist General Conference.

Currently, Dr. Sheveland is the director of I-Training (www.i-training.info), a ministry that allows him to train church leaders around the world through international teaching trips and internet resourcing. He also serves the church as a published author, church consultant, preacher and conference speaker. He is a graduate of Cornerstone University (B.A.) and Denver Seminary (M. Div. & D. Min.).

Jesus Christ is the joy of his life. In Ron's words, "It is my passion to know God better and share that knowledge with others." Family is his next priority. Jodi and Ron treasure their relationship and work hard at keeping it fresh. They are partners in all their life endeavors – including ministry. They have been blessed with two children: Luke and Jessica.

You can visit Ron at www.potluckpeople.com or befriend him on Facebook.

The sequel to *The Potluck People* is coming soon. Sign the guest list at www.potluckpeople.com and you will be notified when it is released.

SOME OTHER BOOKS BY RON SHEVELAND

Discover Your Personal Mission explains a Biblical process that will help you discover your particular ministry niche. God has a wonderful adventure waiting for you; don't miss it! The Creator has designed and equipped you to be fruitful and fulfilled in a unique mission He has hand-picked just for you.

The Perfect Gift is a ten-chapter book co-written by Ron Sheveland and Robert Laidlaw. It gives head-and-heart reasons for why you will want to accept God's gift of eternal life and includes a simple description on how to do so.

Returning Home—An Old Testament Christmas Story describes the drama and message of the book of Ruth and details its connection with the Christmas story. In the sweep of redemptive history, Ruth paves the way for the coming Christ child and contains a number of picturesque types of the Savior. Just as the book of Ruth prepared the way for the coming Christmas story, it can also prepare you for Christmas. You will learn how to overcome your hurts or burdens and experience a "Merry" Christmas. Dr. Ron Sheveland combined his skills as a novelist and professor to write an inspirational book that blends vivid story-telling with biblical accuracy.

Baptism & Communion—Appreciating God's Artistry. Baptism and the Lord's Supper are two stunning pictures painted by the Master Artist. Due to disagreements within the Christian Church as to the nature of these symbols, we sometimes allow the debate to sidetrack us from gazing at their enormous beauty. BAPTISM & COMMUNION is a short book that clearly explains the Biblical issues, but then goes on to explore many of the facets of God's artistry displayed whenever a baptism or communion service takes place.

~ ~ ~ ~ ~ ~ ~ ~

**Dear reader, if you enjoyed this book,
please consider posting a review of it.
Thank you!**

Made in the USA
Monee, IL
28 October 2021

80787259R00203